THE

László Krasznahorkai

THE WORLD
GOES ON

Translated from the Hungarian
by John Batki, Ottilie Mulzet, and George Szirtes

A NEW DIRECTIONS BOOK

Manufactured in the United States of America
First published hardcover as a New Directions Book in 2017
and as New Directions Paperbook 1593 in 2024 (ISBN 978-0-8112-3751-2)
Design by Erik Rieselbach

Library of Congress Cataloging-in-Publication Data
Names: Krasznahorkai, László, author. | Batki, John, translator. |
Mulzet, Ottilie, translator. | Szirtes, George, 1948– translator.
Title: The world goes on / László Krasznahorkai ; translated by John Batki ;
with additional translations by Ottilie Mulzet and George Szirtes.
Description: New York : New Directions Publishing Corporation, 2017.
Identifiers: LCCN 2017014033 | ISBN 9780811224192 (alk. paper)
Subjects: LCSH: Krasznahorkai, László—Translations into English.
Classification: LCC PH3281.K8866 A2 2017 | DDC 894/.51134—dc23
LC record available at https://lccn.loc.gov/2017014033

10 9 8 7 6 5 4 3 2 1

New Directions Books are published for James Laughlin
by New Directions Publishing Corporation
80 Eighth Avenue, New York 10011

CONTENTS

HE

HE

I. SPEAKS

WANDERING-STANDING

I have to leave this place, because this is not where anyone can be, or where it would be worthwhile to remain, because this is the place—with its intolerable, cold, sad, bleak, and deadly weight—from where I must escape, to take my suitcase, before everything else the suitcase, two suitcases will be precisely enough, to stuff everything into two suitcases, then click the lock shut so I can dash to the shoemakers, and resoling—I have resoled, and resoled again, boots are needed, a good pair of boots—in any event one good pair of boots and two suitcases are enough, and with these things we can set off already, inasmuch as we can determine—because this is the first step—exactly where we are right now; well, so a kind of ability is required, practical knowledge is required so we can decide where we are exactly—not just some kind of sense of direction, or some mysterious thing residing in the depths of the heart—so that in relation to this knowledge, we can then choose the right direction; we need a sense, as if we were grasping some particular sort of orientation device in our hands, a device to help us state: at this point in time, we are here and here in this point in space, located, as it happens, at an intersection that is particularly intolerable, cold, sad, bleak, and deadly, an intersection from which one must leave, because this is not where a person can be, or can remain, a person—in this swampy, disconcertingly dark point in space—can't do anything else besides say: leave, and leave right now, leave at once without even thinking about it, and don't look back, just follow the route determined

5

in advance, with one's gaze fixed firmly ahead, one's gaze fixed, of course, on the right direction, the choice of which doesn't seem so agonizingly difficult, unless, of course, it becomes clear that this practical knowledge, this particular sense—as it manages to identify the coordinates of the points extending through sadness and mortality—suddenly states: under "ordinary circumstances" what normally happens is that we say that from here, we have to go in this or that direction, in other words, we say this direction is the right direction, or the complete opposite direction is the correct direction: but there are certain instances, so-called "unordinary circumstances," when this sense, this practical knowledge, justifiably highly valued, announces that the direction we have chosen is good, it tells us: go right ahead, that'll be it, this way, fine—and that same sense also simultaneously tells us that the opposite direction is good too, well, and that's when the state known as wandering-standing sets in, because here is this person, with two heavy suitcases in his hands and a pair of excellently resoled boots, and he can go to the right, and he wouldn't be making a mistake, and he can go to the left, and in that he certainly wouldn't be making any kind of mistake either, so that both of these directions, diametrically opposed to each other, are judged as perfectly fine by this practical sense within us, and there is every good reason for this, because that practical knowledge, indicating two diametrically opposed directions, operates by now within a framework adjudicated by desire, namely that "go to the right" is just as good as "go to the left," because both of these directions, in terms of our desires, point to the most distant place, the place farthest away from here; the point to be reached in any given direction, then, is no longer decided by practical knowledge, sense, or ability, but by desire, and desire alone—the yearning of a person not only to be transported to the greatest distance from his present position, but to the place of greatest promise, where he may be tranquil, for surely that is the main thing, tranquility, this is what this person seeks in the desired distance, some tranquility from the unspeakably oppressive, painful, insane disquiet that seizes him whenever he happens to think of his current situation, when he happens to think of his starting point, that infinitely foreign land where he is now, and from where he must leave, because everything here is intolerable, cold, sad, bleak, and deadly, but from where, in the very first moment, he can hardly bear to move from the shock when he realizes—and he really is consternated—as he realizes that his hands and feet are essentially bound fast, namely it's because of his faultless practical sense that his hands and feet are bound fast, because that practical sense points in two opposite directions simultaneously, telling him: just leave already, that's the right way, but how can anyone leave in two opposite directions at once, that is the question, and so the question remains, he stands as if he were anchored here like a ramshackle boat, he stands hunched beneath the weight of the heavy suitcases, he stands, he doesn't move, and like that, standing, he motionlessly starts off into the untamed world, in a direction—it doesn't matter which, it could be any direction—and he doesn't budge even an inch, already he has gone very far, and his wanderings in the untamed world have begun, because while in reality he is motionless, his hunched form, almost like a statue, engraves itself into an inability to be left behind here; he appears on every route: he is seen in the north by day, he is known in America and he is known in Asia, he's recognized in Europe and he's recognized in Africa, he traverses the mountains, and he traverses the river valleys, he goes and he goes and he doesn't leave off wandering for even a single night, he rests only now and then for one hour, but even then he sleeps like an animal, like a soldier, he doesn't ask anything, and he doesn't stare after anyone for a long time; people inquire of him: so what are you doing, you crazy person, where are you going with that obsessed look in your eyes? sit down and have a rest, close your eyes and stay here for the night; but this person doesn't sit down and he doesn't rest, he doesn't close his eyes, he doesn't stay there for the night, because he doesn't stay for long, because he says—if he says anything at all—he must be on his way, and it's obviously a waste of time to ask him where to, he will never betray to anyone where he is headed on this forced march, because he himself doesn't even know what he possibly knew at one point earlier, when, still standing with these two heavy suitcases in his hands, he set off for the untamed world; he set off, but his journey, as a matter of fact, wasn't a journey, along the way it couldn't even have been a journey, he seemed instead like a kind of pitiful phantom of whom no one was afraid, no one tried to frighten children with him, his name wasn't murmured in the temples so that he would steer clear of the cities, so if he turned up here or there everyone just brushed him off: oh, it's him again, because he turned up again and again in America and in Asia, he turned up again and again in Europe and Africa, and people began to get the impression that he really was just circling around, circling all around the globe like the second hand of a watch, and if in the beginning there was something noteworthy about his presence here or there, as there might even be in the aspect of a pitiful phantom, when he turned up for the second time, or the third time, or the fourth time, they just waved him off, and really, nobody was interested, so that there were fewer and fewer occasions when people tried to ask him something or offer him a place to stay, fewer and fewer occasions when food was placed in front of him, just as with the passage of time no one was really happy to have him in the house, because who knows—they noted amongst themselves—what's really going on here, although it was obvious that they had just lost interest already, they had definitively lost interest, because he, unlike the hand of a watch, didn't indicate anything, he didn't signify anything, and what bothered the world most—if anything at all could be said to bother this world—it was first and foremost that this person was worthless, he just went and he had no value in the world at all, so that the time came when he moved about in this world and in point of fact nobody noticed him, he disappeared, on a material level he practically evaporated, as far as the world was concerned he became nothing; namely: they forgot about him, which of course doesn't mean he was absent from reality, because he remained there as well, as he went indefatigably between America and Asia, Africa and Europe, it's just that the connection between him and the world was broken, and he became, in this manner, forgotten, invisible, and with this he remained once and for all completely solitary, and from that point on he began to notice, at the individual stations of his wandering, that there were other figures, exact replicas of himself: from time to time he found himself face-to-face with such figures exactly replicating him, as if he were looking into a mirror; at first he was startled and quickly left that city or that region, but then from time to time he already would forget the glance of these strange figures and begin to examine them, he began to seek the differences between his own physiognomy and theirs, and as time went on and fate brought him together ever more with these exact replicas, it became ever more clear that their suitcases were the same, the hunched back was the same, everything, how they held themselves beneath the weight, how they dragged themselves onward along this or that road, everything was the same, namely it wasn't just a likeness, but an exact replica, and the boots were the same too, with the exact same expert resoling, he noticed that too as he entered once into some larger hall to drink some water, the resoling on their boots was just as good as his, and the blood in his veins ran cold, he saw that the entire hall was completely filled with people who were exactly the same as him, he quickly drank up and hurriedly left that city and that land, and from then on he didn't even set foot in any place where he hypothesized, or felt, that he might encounter such wanderers; from that point on accordingly he began to avoid them, so he remained definitively alone, and his wanderings lost their own fanatic contingency; but he went on indefatigably, and then an entire new phase of his wanderings commenced, because he was convinced that it was only through his decision to confine himself to a labyrinth that he could avoid, inasmuch as possible, all of these exact replicas, so that it was only from this point on that those dreams began, that is to say that he slept in completely accidental places, and at completely accidental hours, briefly and lightly, and during some of these infrequent periods of brief and light sleep, he began to dream as never before: namely he dreamt the exact same dream, in hairsbreadth detail, over and over again, he dreamt that his wanderings had come to an end—and he now sees before him some kind of huge clock, or wheel, or some kind of rotating workshop, after waking he is never able to identify it with certainty, and in any event he is in front of something like this, or some sort of grouping of these things—he steps into the clock, or the wheel, or the workshop, he stands in the middle, and in that unspeakable fatigue in which he has spent his entire life, he crumples onto the ground as if he'd been shot, he topples over like a tower collapsing into itself, falling onto his side, he lies down so that he can finally sleep like an animal exhausted onto death, and the dream continually repeats itself, whenever he turns his head down in some corner, or gets some kind of bunk to lie down on, he sees that dream, with hairsbreadth accuracy, again and again—he, though, should have seen something completely different, if he had raised his glance, if he had just once—in the course of his wanderings seemingly lasting hundreds and hundreds of years—just raised his head, eternally hanging down, just once, he should have seen that he was still standing there, with two suitcases in his hands, the expertly resoled boots on his feet, and there he is rooted to that shoe-sized piece of earth upon which he stands, so that there is no hope whatsoever anymore that he can possibly move from there, for he must stand there until the end of time, his hands and feet bound in two simultaneously correct directions, he must stand there until the very end of time, because that place is his home, that place is exactly where he was born, and that is where he will have to die one day, there at home, where everything is cold and sad.

ON VELOCITY

I want to leave the Earth behind, so I dash past the bridge over the stream by the meadow, past the reindeer-feeding trough in the dark of the forest, turning at Monowitz at the corner of Schuhkammer and Kleiderkammer, into the street, in my desire to move faster than the Earth in whatever direction this thought has taken me, for everything has converged to such a point of departure, leaving everything behind, leaving behind the Earth, and I set off, rushing instinctively, doing the right thing by rushing, because it isn't East or South or North I am heading or in some other direction in relation to these, but West, which is right, if only because the Earth spins from left to right, that is to say from a Western to an Eastern direction, that is right, that's how things are, that's how it felt right, was right, from the first half-fraction of the instant in which I started, since everything moves most definitely from West to East: the building, the morning kitchen, the table with its cup, the cup with its steaming emerald-colored tea and the scent spiraling upward, and all the blades of grass in the meadow that are pearled with morning dew, and the empty reindeer-feeder in the dark of the forest, all of these—each and every one—moves according to its nature from West to East, that's to say toward me, I who wanted to move faster than the Earth, and rushed through the door over the meadow and the dark of the forest, and had to move precisely in a Western direction, while everything else, the whole of creation, the whole lot, each billionth of a billionth component of this overwhelmingly vast world, was continuously spinning at unimaginable speed from West to East; or rather I, who wanted to move faster, therefore fixed my own speed in the opposite, wholly unexpected, direction, one beyond the realm of physics, that's to say having chosen to do so with evidently instinctive freedom, I had therefore to run counter to it, counter to this terrifying world and everything in it that comprises the street corner, the meadow and forest, or rather, no, as I painfully realized in the second half of the instant, no alas, of course not in that direction, opposing its movement being precisely the worst choice, my instincts had led me to turn in precisely the wrong direction at the corner, over the field, and past the dark of the forest, when I should have chosen to move in the same direction, from West to East as Earth did in its, O! Entirety, and so, in the blink of an eye, I immediately turned around on my axis wondering how my instincts could have led me to move so firmly in the direction opposite the Earth's movement since, if I did this now, its speed would be the same as mine, its and mine the same, they would have a positive relation to each other, combining with each other to greater effect, would, in effect, be doing the same thing, the Earth turning from West to East, I moving from West to East, the majestic immovability of the starting point presumably an absolute value, although it would be practically impossible to see how the smaller part belonged to the Greater Whole, and how the Greater Movement would allow space for this little counter-movement, the one independent of the other, the two linked only in one way, in that the Greater Movement, permitting this small counter-direction to function within it, and what a short circuit that would be, I concluded, as I was already turning, but then why was I thinking this, instinctively thinking, moreover, since if we are talking about one single relationship, then that could be no other than that of one thing comprehending the other, so that one contained the other, so that one was part of the other, its subservient part, its subsidiary, its little brother or its little sister, carried by the Greater, whichever way it moved, and the Earth was quite certainly, and indeed correctly, moving in the one direction it could move, that is from West to East, and I was a part of it, inside it, I who had desired to be faster than the Earth to whose movement mine was demonstrably related in the most strictly logical way, since the velocity—that is to say of the Earth—contained my velocity, my sprinting, the fact being, one way or the other, that whatever else the Earth did, its velocity certainly comprised mine, after all, whatever Grand Perspective was employed it didn't matter whether I ran counter to its direction of movement—that is to say registering as a minus quantity—or in the same direction, that is constituting a plus, it was just that, to me personally, it was a matter of supreme importance since what I precisely wanted was to move faster than the Earth, in other words it was the plus, the positive value, I needed, that's to say what mattered was to have the Little Independent Micro-totality moving as part of the Great Free Macro-totality—the fact is I was simply running within the Great Inwardness of the Laws of Physics, but this time in absolutely the right direction, that is to say from West to East, according with the movement of the Earth, since it is precisely in this fashion, in precisely this manner, of course, I'd have to run in order to be faster than the Earth, running with it so to speak, from a western direction to an eastern direction, and—suddenly the thought hit me like a bolt of lightning—I was already faster, since my velocity now comprehended that of the Earth, that is to say it included it without my having to do much more than move a muscle, and this way, by running over the Earth's surface from West to East, I had made the task so much simpler, I could breathe ever more easily, since the air was fresh out here, I was enjoying the night or the dawn of freedom, or something between the two, I was locked into that interval between night and dawn, feeling perfectly calm, because thinking that I now chose the correct direction, I was moving faster than the Earth, since *the Earth is thought,* as I thought right at the beginning, and now I wanted to move faster than thought, to leave it behind, and that had suddenly become my aim, so that was what I did when I turned at Monowitz on the corner of Schuhkammer and Kleiderkammer, across the meadow with its pearly grass, past the bridge over the stream, beyond the dark of the forest, passing the empty reindeer-feeding trough, so it was right that I should have set out in the wrong direction at first, on instinct, and then corrected myself and on a dime turned and moved in the right direction, from West to East, a small micro-totality within the Greater Macro-totality, in which case I had only to add my speed to its speed, which I did, running as fast as I could, my feet pounding on under the enormous sky that was changing from night to dawn, and there was nothing in my head but the sense that everything was as it should be, that I was simply contributing my share of velocity to the Earth's, my velocity to its velocity, when suddenly a new thought struck me that, fine, this was all very well, but how *did* my speed relate to that of the Earth, how much faster was I, and was that an interesting question in the first place? that is to say I broached the question of how much faster was I than the Earth? and no, it's not interesting, I said to myself, my feet pounding all the while, since all that was interesting was that I should move faster than thought, that is to say, I should outrun the Earth, but then the little brother within me started making calculations in my head, arguing that there, on the one hand, there was the Earth's velocity, that majestically challenging, vast, eternal *per secundum,* and there, on the other, were my best efforts at running at whatever *per secundum* the occasion offered, and then, it seemed to me, any relative value would do for me to run ahead of the Earth, that I needn't run particularly fast since it would make very little difference if I did slow down a bit, so I immediately slowed, and it was clear as clear could be that there were innumerable ways of being faster than Earth, it being enough for me to continue in a West to East direction, and enough simply just to run, putting aside the magnetic drag of the various latitudes that would cumulatively increase, and there was an infinite number of velocities to choose from, infinite values were therefore available for my own running-speed and what is more, I thought, further decreasing my velocity all the while, the fact is it would be enough if ... if I moved at all, just put one foot in front of the other, the essential thing being to move in a West to East direction, enough simply not to stay still, since there were billions on billions of possible velocities, in which case I was free, entirely free—or so I observed as my steps instinctively slowed—perfectly free to choose just how fast I moved since any movement in the right direction would result in moving faster than the Earth and therefore faster than thought, since the Earth is itself thought, and that was the way I was thinking, even before I started the whole process a little while ago, that was the way I was thinking when I dashed past the bridge over the stream by the meadow, past the reindeer-feeding trough in the dark of the forest, and turned at Monowitz at the corner of Schuhkammer and Kleiderkammer. Providing I made no mistakes, I told myself, providing I kept going in the right direction, providing I simply moved, just carried on walking through the fresh dawn air, I would achieve what I had set out to do, and be faster than the Earth—it was just the darkness of the forest that would recede into the distance, just the meadow, the street tcorner, just the scent of that emerald-colored mist vanishing into time forever, into infinity, beyond recall.

HE WANTS TO FORGET

We are in the midst of a cynical self-reckoning as the not-too-illustrious children of a not-too-illustrious epoch that will consider itself truly fulfilled only when every individual writhing in it—after languishing in one of the deepest shadows of human history—will finally attain the sad and temporarily self-evident goal: oblivion. This age wants to forget it has gambled away everything on its own, without outside help, and that it can't blame alien powers, or fate, or some remote baleful influence; we did this ourselves: we have made away with gods and with ideals. We want to forget, for we cannot even muster the dignity to accept our bitter defeat: for infernal smoke and infernal alcohol have gnawed away whatever character we had, in fact smoke and cheap spirits are all that remains of the erstwhile metaphysical traveler's yearning for angelic realms—the noxious smoke left by longing, and the nauseating spirits left over from the maddening potion of fanatical obsession.

No, history has not ended, and nothing has ended; we can no longer delude ourselves by thinking that anything has ended with us. We merely continue something, maintaining it somehow; something continues, something survives.

We still produce works of art, but no longer even talk about how, it is that far from uplifting. We take as our premise all that until now denoted the nature of *la condition humaine,* and dutifully, in fact without a clue, obeying strict discipline, but in fact foundering in a slough of

17

despond, we sink back once more into the muddy waters of the imaginable totality of human existence. We no longer even make the mistake of the wild young ones, by claiming that our judgment is the last judgment or declaring that this is where the road ends. We cannot claim that, since nothing makes sense anymore, for us works of art no longer contain narrative or time, nor can we claim that others might ever be able to find a way toward making sense of things. We declare that it has proved useless to disregard our disillusionment and set out toward some nobler goal, toward some higher power, our attempts keep failing ignominiously. In vain would we talk about nature, nature doesn't want this; it is no use to talk about the divine, the divine doesn't want this, and anyway, no matter how much we want to, we are unable to talk about anything *other than ourselves,* because we are only capable of talking about history, about the human condition, about that never-changing quality whose essence carries such titillating relevance only for us; otherwise, from the viewpoint of that "divine otherwise," this essence of ours is, actually, possibly of no consequence whatsoever, for ever and aye.

HOW LOVELY

How lovely it would be, a world that we could end by organizing a series of lectures—anywhere in this departing world—and give it the general subtitle, "Lecture Series on Area Theory," where one after another, as in a circus arena, lecturers from all parts of the world would talk about "area theory": a physicist, followed by an art historian, a poet, a geographer, a biologist, a musicologist, an architect, a philosopher, an anarchist, a mathematician, an astronomer, and so on, and where in front of a permanent, never varying audience, that physicist, that art historian, that poet, that geographer, that biologist, that musicologist, that architect, that philosopher, that anarchist, that mathematician, that astronomer, and so on, would relate his thoughts about area from his own respective point of view, keeping in mind the overall title for the lecture series, "There Is No Area," pointing out the peculiar relation between this title and the subject, so that the artist or the scientist would speak about this, approaching it from his respective perspective of poetry, music, mathematics, architecture, fine art, geography, biology, the language of poetics and physics, philosophy, anarchy, telling us what he thinks, and what he recommends we should think about area—and all this under the aegis of a summary statement denying that this subject, area, *exists at all.* The contradiction, however, is only apparent; this lecture series could just as well bear (bitterly) the title "All Is Area" as objectively as its actual title "There Is No Area." For the lecturers would speak about the significance—for them and for us—of a being from whose *point of view,* when looking at the universe, area does exist; they would lecture about the importance of the question, namely: can the undeniably limited nature of the human viewpoint possibly lead us to the weighty, if unprovable assertion—and according to another viewpoint besides the human it is conceivable—that there is no area, that this is how matters stand, yet, nevertheless, for us, regardless of where we look, we see ruined and intact *nothing but area,* area upon area everywhere; given that we have reached a point where, trapped in the bewitchingly confined space of the human viewpoint, as we near the incidental termination of an excruciating spiritual journey, we must arrive at the conclusion: beyond this bewitching confinement we in fact insist on nothing else, nothing else, not even on existence of any kind, we no longer insist even on existence, only on the promise that for once in some area, amidst the most profound beauty and decay, we may glimpse something, anything that *refers to us.*

AT THE LATEST, IN TURIN

Well over a hundred years ago, in 1889, on a day like today in Turin, Friedrich Nietzsche steps out of the gate of the house at number 6, Via Carlo Alberto, perhaps to go for a walk, possibly to pick up his mail at the post office. Not far away, or by then all too far away from him, a hackney cab driver is having a difficult time with his—as they say—intractable horse. When after some goading the horse still refuses to budge, the driver—Giuseppe? Carlo? Ettore?—loses patience and starts to beat the animal with his whip. Nietzsche arrives at the crowd that has presumably gathered, and with this the cruel performance of the cab driver, doubtless frothing at the mouth with rage by now, ends; for the gentleman of gigantic stature with the bushy mustache—to the barely disguised amusement of the bystanders—unexpectedly leaps in front of the driver and sobbing, flings his arms around the horse's neck. Eventually Nietzsche's landlord takes him home, where for two days he lies motionless and mute on a sofa, until he utters the obligatory last words (*"Mutter, ich bin dumm"*), after which he lives on, a harmless madman, for ten more years, in the care of his mother and sister. We do not know what happened to the horse.

This story of highly doubtful authenticity—nonetheless granted credibility via the natural arbitrariness expected in such cases—serving as a model of the drama of the intellect casts an especially keen light upon the endgame of the spirit. The demonic star of living philosophy, the dazzling opponent of so-called "universal human truths," the inimitable champion, the nearly breathless naysayer to pity, forgiveness, goodness, and compassion—hugging the neck of a *beaten* horse? To resort to an unforgivably vulgar but inevitable turn of phrase: why not hug the cab driver's neck?

With all respect to Doctor Mobius, for whom this was a simple case of the onset of *paralysis progressiva* caused by syphilis, what we late heirs witness here is the flash of recognizing a tragic error: after a lengthy and tormenting struggle, Nietzsche's very being said nay to a chain of thought in his own philosophy that was to be particularly infernal in its consequences. According to Thomas Mann the error was that "this gentle prophet of a life of untrammeled passion considered life and morality to be antagonists. The truth is," Mann adds, "that they belong together. Ethics is the mainstay of life and the moral man is a true citizen of life's realm." Mann's claim—the absoluteness of this noble declaration—is so beautiful, that it is tempting to take some time and sail away with it, yet we resist, our ship is steered by Nietzsche in Turin, and this calls for not only different waters but a different set of nerves, one might even say, to seize a handy turn of phrase, nerves made of steel cable. And we shall need them indeed, since to our shock and dismay, we will arrive at the same harbor where Thomas Mann's dictum leads; we shall need these nerves of steel because even though the harbor is the same, our feelings there will be quite different from what Mann promises.

Nietzsche's drama in Turin suggests that living in accordance with the spirit of moral law is no rank of honor, for I cannot choose its opposite. I may live my life *in defiance of* it, but this does not mean I am free of its mysterious and truly unnamable power that binds me to it with indissoluble ties. For if that is what I do, live in defiance of it, I can certainly find my way within a societal existence evolved by humankind and therefore not unsurprisingly pitiful, a life in which—as Nietzsche stated—"living and being unjust are one and the same," but I cannot find my way out of the insoluble dilemma that time and again situates me in the midst of a longing to discover the meaning of my existence. For just as I am part of this human world, I am also part of what, for some unknown reason, I keep calling a greater whole, a greater whole that has—to use an expression with a tip of the hat to the categorical Kant—planted within me this and precisely this imperative: along with the melancholy empowerment of freedom is the freedom to break the law.

By now we are gliding among the buoys that mark the harbor, navigating somewhat blindly, for the lighthouse keepers are asleep and cannot guide our maneuvers—and so we drop our anchor into a murk that instantly swallows up our question about whether this greater whole reflects the higher meaning of the law. And so here we wait, knowing nothing, and we merely look on while, from a thousand directions, our fellow humans are slowly nearing us; we send no messages, only look on, and maintain a silence full of compassion. We believe that this compassion inside us is appropriate as such, and that it would be appropriate, too, in those who are approaching, even if it is not so today, it will be so tomorrow ... or in ten ... or in thirty years.

At the latest, in Turin.

THE WORLD GOES ON

I t had been fairly securely bound but then it got loose, and all we know about this is that the same thing unleashed it that had secured it before, and that is all, it would be the height of folly to state, to represent, to categorically designate the power, that is to say specifically this unleashing of power, that immeasurably vast, baffling system that is truly immeasurable, truly baffling, in other words: the for us forever incomprehensible workings of the ineluctable modality of chance, in which we have sought and found laws, yet in fact over the heroic centuries of the past we have never got to know it, just as we can be certain that we shall not get to know it in times to come, for all we have ever been able, are able, and will ever be able to know are the consequences of ineluctable chance, those terrifying moments when the whip cracks, it cracks and comes down on our backs just as the whip cracks over this fortuitous universe we call the world, and unleashes what had been securely bound, that is when—namely now—it is once again unleashed upon the world, the thing that we humans forever and repeatedly insist on calling the new, the unprecedented, even though it surely cannot be called new or unprecedented, after all it has been here ever since the creation of the world, or to put it more accurately, it arrived simultaneously with us, or still more accurately, by way of us, and always like this, so that we were and are only able to recognize its arrival after the fact, retrospectively; it is already here by the time we realize that it has arrived again, always finding us unprepared, even though we ought to be aware that it is coming, that it is secured only temporarily, we ought to hear its chains scraping, loosening, the hiss of knots coming undone in the until then tight cordage, deep down inside us we ought to KNOW that it is about to break loose, and that is how it should have been this time too, we should have known that this is how it would be, that it was bound to come, but we only awoke to the realization, if we awoke at all, that it was here already, and that we were in trouble, we ascertained that we were helpless, by which we only meant that we always were so, for we are forever helpless—when it is here—helpless and defenseless, and to think about this precisely during the first hours after the attack proved so uncomfortable that instead we began to worry about finding out what had happened, how it had happened, who they were and why they did it, to worry about the collapse of the Twin Towers and the caving in of the Pentagon, how this had happened, how they collapsed and caved in, and who the perpetrators were, and how they did it, whereas what we first of all should have been, and by now certainly must be, worrying about and realizing at long last: what has actually happened cannot be comprehended, which by the way is no wonder, since the arrival of the one, of what had till now been fairly well contained but had now somehow broken loose, without exception always signals that we have entered a new era, it signals the end of the old, and the beginning of the new, and nobody had "consulted us" about this, no, we hadn't even noticed when all this had been happening, the words "turning point" and "dawn of a new era" were hardly out of our mouths when precisely this critical, time-bound nature of a turning point and a dawn was rendered ludicrous as we realized that all of a sudden we were living in a new world, had entered a radically new era, and we understood none of it, because everything we had was obsolete, including our conditioned reflexes, our attempts to understand the nature of a process, how "all of this" had "consequently" proceeded from there to here, everything was as obsolete as our conviction to rely on experience, on sober rationality, to lean on them as we investigated causes and evidence that this had truly happened to us, the nonexistent or for us inaccessible causes and evidence, now that we found ourselves indeed in a brand-new era, in other words here we stand, every last one of us as of old, blinking and peering around in the same old way, our aggressiveness betraying old uncertainties, a fatuous aggressiveness at a time when we haven't even begun to be afraid yet, still insisting on the lie, that no, no way was this a radical change in our world, no way was this the end of one world epoch and the beginning of a new, every last one of us obsolete, myself possibly one of the most obsolete of all, now feeling a long-absent sense of community with others, very obsolete, indeed speechless in the deepest possible sense of the word, because on September 11 I flashed on the fact, like a twinge of physical pain, that, good god, my language, the one I could use to speak out now, was so old, so godforsaken ancient, the way I strung it out, quibbling, twisting and turning, pushing and pulling it to move ahead, pestering it, advancing by stringing one ancient word after another, how useless, how helpless and crude this language is, this language of mine, and how splendid it had been formerly, how dazzling and supple and apt and deeply moving, but by now it has utterly lost all of its meaning, power, spaciousness, and precision, all gone, and then for days I pondered this, would I ever be able, would I ever be capable of suddenly learning some other language without which it would be completely hopeless; I knew at once, watching the flaming, tumbling Towers, and then envisioning them again and again, and I knew that without a brand-new language it was impossible to understand this brand-new era in which, along with everyone else, I suddenly found myself; I brooded and pondered, tormented myself for days on end, after which I had to admit that no, I had no chance of suddenly learning a new language, I was, along with the others, too much a prisoner of the old, and there was no recourse, I concluded, but to abandon all hope of ever understanding what was going on down here, so I sat in profound gloom, staring out the window, as again and again those giant Twin Towers kept falling and falling and falling, I sat there staring, and using these old words I began to describe what I saw, together with the others, in this new world, I began to write down what I felt, that I was unable to comprehend, and the old sun began to set in the old world, darkness began to fall in the old way in my old room as I sat by the window, when suddenly some horrendous fear began to slowly creep over me, I don't know where it came from, I merely felt it growing, this fear that for a while did not reveal what it was, only that it existed and was growing, and I just sat there utterly helpless, watching this fear growing in me, and I waited, maybe after a while I would guess the nature of this fear, but that wasn't what happened, not at all, this fear, while continually growing, did not reveal anything about itself, it refused to reveal its contents, so that understandably it began to make me anxious about what to do next, I could not keep on sitting here forever with this fear that concealed its contents, but I still sat there, numb, by the window, as outside those two Towers kept falling and falling and falling, when suddenly my ears registered a grating noise, as if cumbersome chains were clattering in the distance, and my ears registered a slight scraping sound, as if securely knotted ropes were slowly slipping loose—all I could hear was this grating clatter and this scary scraping, and once more I thought of my ancient language, and of the utter silence into which I had tumbled, I sat there staring at the outside and as complete darkness filled the room only one thing was completely certain: it had broken loose, it was closing in, it was already here.

UNIVERSAL THESEUS

Now, at last: for Samuel Beckett
1:150

THE FIRST LECTURE

I

I do not know who you are, gentlemen.

I couldn't quite make out the name of your organization.

And frankly, I must confess I am not entirely clear about what kind of lecture you expect me to give here.

After all, you must be aware that I am not a lecturer.

I have given much thought to the matter, I racked my brains trying to find out what this was all about, just as I am trying right now, in front of you, but it's best if I admit that I haven't succeeded: I just don't know what you expect of me, and I have a lingering bad feeling that perhaps you yourselves aren't quite clear about it.

It had also occurred to me that possibly you are mistaking me for someone else. You had intended to invite a certain person, but he wasn't available, and only because of that did you select me, because I am the one who most reminds you of that person.

You are not saying anything.

Fine, it's all the same to me.

Mr. President, gentlemen—I shall speak about melancholy.

And I will begin by going way back.

During one of the later decades of the twentieth century, deep in the deepest hellhole of that decade, on a bitter freezing night in late November, a ghostly tractor-trailer advanced on the main street toward the market square of a small town in the lowlands of southeast Hungary. At a glance it appeared to be about thirty meters long, and its height ... its height, compared to its length and width, seemed to be far too great, and these gigantic dimensions naturally went with an enormous weight, all of it resting on two sets of eight double wheels. The sides were made of blue corrugated tin upon which an unskilled hand had daubed enigmatic figures in yellow paint, and although this entire ramshackle contraption should have been comparable to a freight train car, it did not resemble or recall any such thing in the least, not just because of its gargantuan dimensions and weight and wheels, nor because those crudely daubed figures and their alarming undecipherability instantly removed from this vehicle any resemblance to a train car, but chiefly because it had no doors, nothing that might suggest a door, as if the original plan had been to commission a subterranean workshop to build such and such a transport vehicle made out of blue corrugated tin with two sets of eight twin wheels but without any doors, there was no need for any doors, not even in the rear, that's right, no doors, not a single one, thank you, because if you undertake to do this, gentlemen, it will be your masterpiece as tinsmiths, that's what the commission must have sounded like, this will be your makeshift masterpiece, that must have been the sum of the sketchy instructions given to the subterranean workmen, you are building this conveyance not just for anyone to open and close, it will suffice if I, who ordered the work, open and close it when I want to, and if I do so then it will be from the inside, with a single gesture, by me.

It must have been somewhat like that, because at a glance, your first impression was most definitely that any amount of speculation about underground workshops, mysterious tinsmiths, and a customer whose identity was a complete enigma would be fully justified, since in addition to all that, one had to think of the inconceivable slowness of dragging it with a rickety tractor-trailer straining against the icy wind and the excruciatingly prolonged nocturnal journey this extraordinary contraption must have completed before it braked to a halt at the marketplace.

Not wishing to abuse your patience I won't go into further detail; suffice it to say it was an altogether ghostly apparition that, having fought its way against the wind, and, arriving at the square, ground to a stop with a wheeze, nor do I need to say that its ghostly air was first and foremost due to what lay hidden within, the cargo for whose transit it had been intended and built, and this ghostly air was also due to those who had accompanied the terrifying passenger in the vehicle, clattering along with it all the way from the East and over the Carpathian Mountains, meaning the crew, and finally it was also due to the significant and ominous entourage—roughly three hundred hulking forms drawn from the villages and farms of the region by this nightmarish vehicle as sleepwalkers are drawn by the Moon, and who, having arrived on pre-dawn trains, and guided by posters, had already trudged down the main street of the small town, to stand there at daybreak, all three hundred of them, apparently mesmerized.

The local townfolk had of course been informed not only by the posters but also the rumors that had arrived well ahead of this troupe, so that when in the morning they saw for themselves the strange freight on the market square all they said was, ah, then it was true after all and not just hearsay, so it wasn't mere baseless gossip, yes indeed here was the entire traveling circus with the whale and its whole retinue in fact indisputably arrived.

Esteemed Director-General, esteemed audience, they, the locals had found out just about all that could be learned about this troupe from all the stray talk going around—there was no need to reread the words on the posters—that here was the largest whale in the world inside that gigantic circus truck parked in the middle of the market square. They already knew about the frightfully obese Director and the permanently lit cigar smoking between his fingers that he raised from time to time in a cautioning gesture, and they knew about the immovable, impassive Factotum, as gossip had referred to the other member of the two-man staff, the one that looked like a wrestler, and that these two, plus the allegedly largest whale in the world, had already caused plenty of mischief along the way before arriving here.

So these local citizens knew quite a lot, and if I said they suffered torments of anxiety on account of this, no one would wonder, for, after all, the inhabitants of this town lived in a world where everyone, in a rising tide of hatred caused by their fear of human nature, was convinced that humanity would destroy itself. So that they were aware of a great many things, trivial details as well as essentials—namely, what lay hidden behind that wall of corrugated tin, they agreed that behind it lay a dreadful, enormous whale—but that this whale might be concealing something, that in fact the whale itself might be a substitute for something else, in other words this enormous carcass was simultaneously both messenger and message ... well ... the townspeople were entirely unaware of this.

Now began an excruciating, prolonged wait lasting into the afternoon hours, when the gigantic locked container was at long last opened up for the half-frozen audience. A slow, shuffling procession commenced, headed for the interior of the gigantic container, through an entrance suddenly created when from the inside the Factotum lowered the rear tin wall, and it all ended soon enough, because after circumambulating the interior, the spellbound flock of spectators was already once again assembled outside on the square. Yet none moved from there, not one of them set out on the main street back toward the train station, they remained there waiting, standing around and gawking at the open entrance to the whale, for a single glance had sufficed earlier: as soon as these three hundred drifters had cast a single glance at the whale's carcass resting on a low wooden platform, they were already on their way out, shuffling along, and then as a matter of course settling in the vicinity, in the vicinity of the whale, without budging an inch.

Esteemed Mr. President-General Director—pardon me if I use the incorrect form of address—and esteemed audience: in contrast to the local citizens, these three hundred, by way of this cursory inspection, and then their absolute refusal to budge, implied that the whale inside was merely covering up something, and that they had not come for the whale itself, but for what lay behind it.

There is a book explicitly declaring that from this moment on everything went wrong in the most infernal manner possible in this town, that is to say literally all hell broke loose, and the book intimates that it knows what this hell could be like, it knows what took place subsequently, what in fact this whale had been concealing on that market square back in the deepest hellhole of the nineteen sixties or seventies.

If you will pardon my arbitrary, presumptuous use of the first person plural, then allow me to put it this way: unable to find any ultimate meaning we feel crushed enough already to be fed up with a literature that pretends there is such a thing and keeps hinting at some ultimate meaning. We refuse to put up with a literature that is essentially, in its very fiber, so radically mendacious, we are in such dire need of an ultimate meaning that quite simply we can no longer tolerate the lies, we can no longer put up with this literature, and in fact it is not outrage, but boredom and the squalid level of those lies that make us gag; well then, given the above, in fullest possible agreement with you gentlemen, I myself can now announce that to claim there is a book that knows, that promises to reveal and narrate to us and only us all that breaks loose in the wake of one of these gigantic whales, is either an insidious effrontery or the vilest drivel, in a word, lies, of course, for nobody knows what really is unleashed at these times, no one, and no book knows that, because that certain something lies completely covered up by the whale.

Mr. Chief Counselor, esteemed gentlemen!

III

If all of this took place in the late sixties, then I would have been a boy of about ten, and if during the early seventies, about fifteen; in any case I clearly recall I was on my way to school that morning, shuddering briefly, and waving the whole thing off, thinking, what a cheap humbug, a stinking carcass, and fifty forints to boot, no way would I blow that much of my Easter allowance, I kept thinking, as I passed that tin colossus on Kossuth Square, parked right by the sidewalk where I walked on my way to school.

That was how it began, in the morning, but after school—it must have gotten dark rather early that day—I became more and more intrigued on my way home, until at last I too sneaked back to Kossuth Square, as did so many others, who, with the huge sum of fifty forints in their pocket, had scurried from home, slipping out stealthily to evade parental eyes.

I escaped back to Kossuth Square, and counted off my fifty forints into the palm of the Factotum, and even to be standing there near the Factotum produced a feeling that one had transgressed a certain boundary beyond which lay things perhaps splendid, perhaps ordinary, but in any case dreadful and dangerous. Of course I cannot recall now what I had expected to find back then; when stepping up on the planks I entered the interior of the conveyance, but I must have been certain that the spectacle would be perhaps splendid, perhaps ordinary, but in any case awesome and dangerous, and I must have had my own preconception of its clearly being completely one or the other; however what it actually turned out to be was utterly unexpected, not because the whale was too much like, or differed too much from, my expectations, no, not at all, but because I at once noticed how pathetic it was lying there on that low framework of hefty girders, vaguely looming in the light of a few dim lamps, and likewise, almost immediately, I understood that this mystery, the whale, resisted and would always resist any explanation whatsoever.

To get around the whale one had to get very close to it, especially near its head, where you had to turn in order to make your way out of there, and this proximity, the proximity of so much containment, nearly wiped me out by the time I reached the head and made the turn for the exit. My heart throbbed feverishly, something compressed my throat, and turning, I believe what I felt was compassion, shock, and shame, but then, after a few steps, already on the other side, I stopped for a moment amidst the general gawking and shuffling to just stare at the whale, trying to take it all in at a single glance, and when I succeeded, I no longer had anything in mind, I no longer wanted to, and anyway I would have been unable to put a name to what I was feeling, was it really compassion? what was it? and I disconnected my mind, my brain stopped functioning, only my emotions began to work in overdrive, the way a sudden wave of stifling heat, a swoon, a bottomless stupor can all at once overwhelm one. Back then of course I had been unable to stammer out a single word about this, not in there, nor outside, and after I tiptoed my way down the planks, I practically had to fight my way through the crowd of immobile people standing around in quilted jackets, boots, and lambskin caps, to make my escape from Kossuth Square. Incapable of uttering a word back then, now I am at last able to say what happened to me at the time and, I believe, to the others there as well, back in sixty- or seventy-something, because today I can unequivocally state that the whale, lying there on that platform of beams and girders in the feeble light, initiated me as it were, and perhaps the others as well, into a state of melancholy; as I stared at the whale and shambled around it in the putrid interior of that contraption, an infinite melancholy seized my soul ...what shall I compare it to, it was like honey—you know, the kind where a spoonful is enough to kill anyone.

Some kind of deadly honey, that's what this melancholy tasted like, but I would very much hope not to mislead any of you with this simile, because using it—this simile—I do not wish to imply that this melancholy is impossible to identify in and of itself, or that this melancholy, outside itself, carries some sort of referential content, some little anecdote, clandestine directions, or road map in a spoonful of honey, no, not at all, this melancholy did not require anything else in order to arise, it simply entered the soul, so that to liken it, as I did before, to the fatal sweetness of honey, to somehow connect it in retrospect with this spoonful of honey, only the fallen man within me can attempt to do this, the one who, beyond the fact of his disgrace, is well aware that everyone else here is likewise perfectly aware of the absurd necessity, and at the same time the unmaskable failure, of introducing a simile only to withdraw it.

Esteemed Secretary-General, esteemed assembly! like some deadly honey, in the sense qualified a moment ago, was this melancholy that swooped down upon me back then, on seeing the special attraction brought to our small town by the traveling circus that had arrived from the East, from somewhere in the Balkans, and by this I do not mean to claim it was here at this point that my especial sensitivity to melancholy originated, and that I have chosen this affair of the whale merely so that I can solemnly announce, lo and behold, that this by no means ordinary encounter marks the starting point of understanding for me, the understanding that the road toward "fundamental things," as I used to call them, leads through melancholy, because no, on the contrary, by no means was this the solemn point zero, the *fons et origo* of understanding for me, for it had already coursed through me in earlier times, this sensitivity must have been with me at birth, or perhaps it was born one afternoon when it grew dark too soon, and dusk found me alone by the window in a small room, or who knows, possibly even earlier when I was still in my crib, left alone one of those afternoons when dusk arrives too early—in the end it makes no difference when I first awoke to it—and I started to savor the deadly sweetness of this honey once I had awakened to it and it began, and from there on at various times and places it swooped down on me, most notably of course back in sixty- or seventy-something on Kossuth Square, behind that blue corrugated tin.

So its beginning is shrouded in a thick veil of mist, it could have been even before the era of the crib, who knows how early the occasion may arise for the onset of a sensitivity like this; in any case from then on the completely normal curiosity that develops in a person quite early—perhaps as early as the time when, with undeterrable gaze and nodding head, in order to explore something one first sets out on the floor crawling on all fours like a turtle, quite possibly beginning back then in the development of this particular normal curiosity, that is, the direction it took, and even its speed, had already been fundamentally altered within me. My suitability or propensity for melancholy had decreed a totally different path for this entirely normal curiosity of mine, so that I almost have to say this sensitivity had devoured my entirely normal curiosity by always aiming it at the same point, always directing it toward the same place, toward the world's *essence,* as I later called it, although in any case the curiosity, if it could still be called that, always came up against this same melancholy, instead of the world's essence.

Of course all of this can be stated in simpler terms, for instance, say, you set out and aim your attention toward this essence of the world, where—as still later I believed—angels and demons dwell together, whereupon at the first gesture, the first stirrings of intention to reach this essence, melancholy instantly seizes the soul ... yes, one may try to put this in simpler terms, but the thing that needs to be said does not thereby become any simpler.

I do not know what you will make of this lecturer cast in front of you indulging in a confession here, these things are always awkward, I realize, but esteemed gentlemen, esteemed General—and again I apologize if I address you incorrectly—please excuse me this one time if I make this confession contrary to your and my own ideas of good taste, yet I must divulge this vital information: all my life I have lived and continue to live under the cloud of this particular melancholy, with an uncontrollable impulse to look upon the very axis of the world, which, however, lies perfectly concealed behind this melancholy's all-consuming fog. This has ruined my entire life, and ravages me to this day, since from the very outset it wasn't as if I had tried to avoid it, to get rid of it, on the contrary, I practically ... how shall I say this? I hunted for it, even if it wasn't a hunt in the classical sense of the strong pursuing the weak, but more like the very weak hunting for the very powerful.

Yes, the axis of the world, Mr. Director-General, my esteemed audience!

IV

If I now assert that melancholy is the most enigmatic of attractions, drawing us toward the unreachable center of things, then you will have the right to smile, for you have already heard so much contradictory stuff from this lecturer: that melancholy is on the one hand the ultimate obstacle to seeing, and on the other, it is that yearned-for place in the afternoon dusk, and who knows what else, all heaped one on top of another.

I believe by now it should be obvious to you that this lecturer can tell you nothing new about the subject of his lecture.

Indeed, that was the case already at the time when you telephoned me and asked me to give a talk, announcing meaningfully that you would leave the choice of subject up to me, and adding, feel entirely free, whereupon I thought, great, as long as it's all the same to everyone, I will choose melancholy; but I never gave a thought to how I would acquit myself, because I kept racking my brains: why me, of all people why me?

And anyway, really, how could I say anything new when there is nothing new under the sun?

After all, the melancholy I am talking about—and which, for the sake of order, I will now recapitulate—is familiar to all of us, it can launch an assault upon the life it would wreck from three sources. The first and most inexhaustible source is self-pity, not just the kind about which even the playground aphorism claims "it stinks," but the kind where you pity yourself without any adequate reason. No one is harming you, you are fine, you sit in silence, alone in a desolate park after the rain, or in a cozy room abroad, before dawn or as darkness falls, and this self-pity ambushes and takes you by the rudest surprise, devouring and inevitable, because this is when you realize, without understanding it, that nothing exists.

A second source is the shift to a minor scale in music. Wherever and whenever I notice this moment, when in some musical composition the major suddenly shifts to minor, say, an A after a C, that music instantly rends my heart, I take it personally, as if it had happened expressly for me, my face becomes distorted by a grimace, as if by a painful pleasure; in a word, I plunge into melancholy and I sit there, listening, thinking, ah, the beauty—when it was only melancholy.

But the most lasting and most profound melancholy springs from love.

However I will say no more on this head now, I don't think any great surprises would ensue if I expatiated upon that theme.

And so, with your permission, I will now conclude my lecture.

V

I am done, although I can't tell if this was what you expected of this evening, or if I still appear to be the person you had in mind. I am afraid that I am not.

Anyway, it hardly matters. We went through with it. I have spoken, you have heard me out, no harm was done.

Gentlemen, my talk is over.

Your Highness! Esteemed guests!

This lecture was about melancholy.

THE SECOND LECTURE

I

I have been here before.

I recognize the building. Just as last time, this evening there is no one standing at the gate, the chandeliers are still unbearably brilliant, the stairs treacherously slippery.

I recognize a familiar scent here, and once again I have the feeling that just before my arrival an enormous bolt of lightning, herald of a frightful thunderstorm, has struck the place; one can never quite forget this emphatic quality of the atmosphere: acrid, dry, rather sweet, scorching.

And also ... I remember all of you as well. I have seen your eyes watching me on that earlier occasion, I have seen you in your seats under the searing brilliance of the chandeliers, all of you attentively leaning forward, staring ahead in this vague scent of lightning, as you wait for the lecture to begin.

The same thing happened when I was here for the first time. You all sat here exactly the same way and listened to me, taking it all in from exactly the same distance: deeply engrossed, motionless, with a totally inscrutable intensity. And even though quite some time has passed in the interim, what made our first encounter so peculiar hasn't changed either, since just as I hadn't known back then who you gentlemen actually were, neither do I know it now, as I stand for the second time on this podium-like structure, from where, as long as I can't find out what you want of me, then at least I would like to understand why I agreed to come here once again, I, the clueless guest you have so mysteriously elected to invite.

For now we resume at exactly the same place as the last time. I would never have thought that I would accept your invitation, yet here I am. On the telephone I said, we shall see, please call me some other time, we can discuss the matter then, but of course I was thinking all along, it's absolutely out of the question, what are these peculiar gentlemen thinking, once was more than enough for me—except this second invitation kept pestering me just as the first one had. You see, once again I kept thinking that surely you must be well aware of what I do, and how little I care for such performances, just as you must be aware that I am far from being an expert on any subject, for there is nothing, nothing whatsoever in my grasp that could be of the slightest interest to others, moreover I swallow the tail-ends of my words, and I talk too fast in a voice that's too low, almost to the point of rudeness, it's all babble-babble and mumble-mumble; so what could you want from me, I wondered, full of misgivings. And I had endless questions: What kind of organization was yours that—and I have verified this—doesn't appear in any registry, not even in a telephone book? And just what was it that led you to decide upon me of all people, what made you once again choose me, of all people? And why all the mystery about your identity? What was the sense of all this secrecy?

I could go on but I won't, this much should be enough to show that everything remains the same as on the first occasion, when I gave a lecture without knowing to whom, while you heard me out and applauded, and then, without a word, somehow simply dispersed throughout the building, as I stepped outside and set out for home, with a detachment of bodyguards behind me, whom I was utterly unable to dissuade from escorting me home—it was in the interest of my own safety, they claimed—in a manifestly professional manner, they kept ten steps to the rear.

Yes, everything has remained the same, with one exception, namely, this time apparently you are not letting me choose the subject, that is to say, you have asked me to talk about what kind of world I would like to live in.

Ordinarily what people request or ask makes no difference, my responses instinctively and unfailingly correspond to a request or question that was never made. As a rule, almost every time I begin with an apology about this, but this time I soon realized—in fact immediately after hanging up the telephone—that there would be no need to apologize. I realized that contrary to appearances you did not actually mean to restrict the topic, and I understood that by making a request for this subject—unvoiced by me for such a long time and all the more heartrending for not having been voiced for so long—that did not in the least mean that you wanted to tie my hands regarding the choice of topic, but rather that you were in the truest sense giving me a free hand to decide what I wished to talk about, since your asking me what kind of world I would like had in fact meant to convey that all of you gentlemen here were most concerned about the world—if I heard you correctly, what the world ought to be like.

I cannot deny that for several days following our telephone conversation I kept brooding about this astoundingly naive, one might say childishly simple, wording of this request embodying your particular interest: did this mean that you, for reasons unknown to me, imagined yourselves to be in a position where you could decide that, very well, the world *was* like this, but now it *would be* like that?

I cannot deny that this possibility had occurred to me, but afterward I quite decisively banished the thought, for in the last analysis I cannot believe that—bearing in mind your austere, unflinching, and almost alarmingly rigorous attention—I now find myself in the company of dreamers, nor do I believe there is the slightest need to elucidate (for you, of all people) how unbearable the idiocy of woolgathering is, given the current state of the world.

Realizing that I was on the wrong track, I dropped the notion, and gave up trying to decipher the actual meaning of your proposed topic; instead—and in no small degree swayed by the waves created inside me by the unresolved actual content of the topic you requested—I asked myself, what if, contrary to my original intentions, I nonetheless still came here once again? and, staring in front of me with the kind of bemused expression fitting the occasion, I thought all right, if I did come here one more time, what topic could I still talk about?

Could it be love? I wondered.

No, then it might as well be death!

At first I was sitting on the bed, near the telephone, then on a chair by the window, mulling it over, still not looking out the window (asking: love?), but then staring straight ahead (asking: death?), still wearing that bemused sort of expression suitable for the occasion.

It would be best—and here I stood up—to talk about revolt, about what makes an existing situation so intolerable.

I sat back down on the bed and thereafter my decision remained unchanged, so that this is what I will talk about tonight.

But before I begin I have a request to make.

When I entered this auditorium I noticed that the gentleman over there ... locked the door behind me.

I do not like to lecture in a locked auditorium.

So I ask for your understanding ...

And now, let us begin!

Honorable audience, most esteemed gentlemen! The question is the following: what can be said on the subject of revolt?

To begin with, please listen to a story.

II

In the summer of Nineteen ninety-two I was at the Zoologischer Garten station, a hub of the Berlin subway system, waiting for a train from the direction of Kreuzberg. The place for the front end of the arriving train, the spot where the arriving train was to pull up to, was—here as at all other such platforms—marked by the placement of a giant mirror installed on an aluminum pole, along with a variety of signal lights: this was the point where each train driver had to pull up with his train, while during a red light no train could move past this point. Thus far and not a jot farther, announced the mirror and the signal light attached below it, establishing the rule of orderly traffic upon a train's arrival, but this did not mean that the platform itself ended there; no, the platform itself ran past this signal and came to an end about a meter and a half beyond it. Thus a twice forbidden zone existed between the mirror and the actual end of the platform, from where the train and its driver were prohibited in the previously described manner, while the waiting passengers, among whom I too now stood, were doubly excluded in a most absolute sense, for even though the clear-cut and sensible traffic rules did not refer to us, and we were unaffected by the regular alternation of arrivals at the red light and departures upon the green, for us there was a transverse yellow line on the pavement at the foot of the mirror, as well as the prohibitory text in small letters on a sign on the back wall, and finally, as the internal mirroring of this line and this sign, a flawlessly functioning instinct that accepted this prohibition once and for all and thus shut us out twice over at the very least.

This was in August. I was waiting for a train from the direction of Kreuzberg, but the train was a bit late. I was observing the crowd of carefree passengers around me, and at first noticed only a certain tension in these so-called carefree passengers. I recognized the cause when I—probably the last in this tensely carefree crowd to notice—at long last, I too did notice that in the space demarcated by the yellow line, the space prohibited by the sign on the wall, there was somebody now standing in that forbidden zone.

An old clochard stood there on the platform urinating upon the rails, half turning his back to us, and somewhat hunched over, as one pained by this urination and these rails.

The particular instinct that prohibits setting foot in just this area doesn't only prohibit setting foot in it, but erases it from consciousness as it were—so that now when this consciousness suddenly became aware that an entire zone existed between the mirror and the end of the platform, it immediately announced: if some pedestrian were to claim that such a zone was surely superfluous from the viewpoint of traffic technology and utterly senseless from the viewpoint of traffic safety, it—that is, this consciousness—would protest most resolutely and reply that this was all a mistake; the perpetuation and maintenance of such areas has a significance with most far-reaching consequences. Any forbidden zone of this sort, such as ours here at Zoologischer Garten, not only explicitly communicates its unavoidable randomness, but offers exemplary proof that the regulations of our human world (including the simplest ones) are not just unfathomable but unchallengeable. These regulations, continued our consciousness, even the least significant ones, are impossible to separate from their invisible corpus; laws such as these—even the mildest ones—become visible solely when they are violated, and can be apprehended in operation only through a certain element of scandal, that is, via the introduction of a certain degree of danger; and to introduce danger into the process while they are operating is equivalent to deciding to launch an attack—no matter how mild—against ourselves, meaning the urination had to stop, this awareness commanded, the clochard had to go, the scandal must be nipped in the bud, and the regulation lifted out of the corpus into the light of day—in this case the prohibition to enter an area a meter and a half wide—it must sink back into that corpus, and the whole system must go on functioning truly invisibly, as far as I am concerned, and here the consciousness pointed at itself.

This was, therefore, more or less the substance of the prevailing mood in the ranks of the assembled passengers on this early afternoon in August, and I thought that this would be about all for this early afternoon, that is to say, when the urination stopped this forbidden zone together with the clochard would, as far as our consciousness was concerned, slowly sink back and get lost in the workaday obscurity; except at this moment on the other side, on the platform across from ours, designated for train traffic running in the opposite direction—that is for those members of the public traveling toward Kreuzberg—two policemen suddenly appeared, and with this the entire early afternoon in August, as usually happens the world over whenever the police show up, altered radically, at a single stroke.

I am truly reluctant to derail my audience from the menacing momentum of this narrative, but alas, I feel that it is high time to put on the brakes for a moment, and since it has obviously escaped your attention, to remind you gentlemen of my request regarding the locked exit of this otherwise captivating lecture hall. If the splendid baroque clock behind you shows the accurate time, then I have been standing on this podium sort of thing for about fifteen minutes, and these fifteen minutes for me—for a man who has spent his entire life either in fear of being locked up, or else in fear of not being able to lock himself in—are an eternity. I would not burden you gentlemen with this confession if the matter were otherwise understandable for you, in other words that I for one feel myself shoved straight into hell by the kind of automatic gesture such as this gentleman's, who showed me in here, and who, after I entered and turned my back, most likely out of absentmindedness turned the key in the lock, and presumably out of further absentmindedness, sank the key into his pocket.

My dear Sir, I think no one will make fun of your absentmindedness nor blame you if you don't wait until the end of my lecture and get up right now and unlock that door, nor do I think any further words need be wasted regarding this peculiar sensitivity of mine that really has nothing to do with our subject, for I can see from your gesture that you intend to comply with my request and with this said I can return to the Zoologischer Garten and continue where I had left off, that is I can continue with a brief sketch of the layout of this subway stop, which seems to be absolutely necessary so you can follow what actually happened upon the arrival of the police in the subway station on that early August afternoon.

The hub of subway lines at Zoologischer Garten is a system involving several underground levels. Dark and forbidding passages and corridors with stairways lead from one level to another, and the same types of dark and forbidding passages connect on any given level underneath it, the two platforms serving the two opposite directions of train traffic, so that if, let us say, you arrive at Zoologischer Garten from the direction of Ruhleben, but change your mind and decide not to continue on toward Kreuzberg but instead to return to Ruhleben, then you can't simply up and march straight across to the opposite side on your level, because the two sets of rails upon which traffic passes to and from Kreuzberg are sunk into a trench, a channel not too deep, but with a most strictly dedicated purpose, so that if you change your mind you must descend a set of stairs leading to a dark and sinister passageway under this twin set of rails, and make your way under the trench with its twin set of rails, across to the other side and another set of stairs that lead you up to the platform, which we may call our platform, from where you may return to Ruhleben, if that's how things played out for you.

It was in a sytem as complex as this that the two transit cops suddenly arrived opposite us, on the other side of the trench housing the twin set of rails.

As a matter of fact only one of them was a full-fledged policeman, while the other one—to judge from his youth and his face flushed to the very tips of his ears as he tried to control an unruly German shepherd that kept snarling at him—must have been some kind of novice policeman; in any case I could not make out their facial features, other than the greasy, shiny, pimply complexion and the regulation thin, merciless lips of both the old and the young one; no facial features therefore, because with facial features of this kind, even if you placed a thousand sheets of drawing paper in front of me, and after each spoiled drawing lashed me with a knout, still not one out of a thousand would turn out to be a true likeness. So only one of the two was the real thing, this was immediately obvious, the one who noticed the clochard urinating on the opposite platform—in the forbidden zone at that—and who sprang into action at once, stepping to the edge of the platform, the point where he was closest to the clochard, and furiously ordered him to stop what he was doing at once, or else—bellowed the policeman—the clochard would regret it.

The shortest distance between the two platforms was of necessity equal to the widths of two trains gliding past each other, meaning this shortest distance between the two men could not have been more than ten meters at most. But this ten meters' proximity wasn't enough for the clochard's fear of the police to override the certainty in his mind that to interrupt this uncomfortable urination would be even more excruciating, so that he—now turning his woeful visage partly in our direction, and as it were letting the officer's raucously official warning fly past his ears—thereby in the eyes of this policeman committed an act toward him that no one is allowed to commit toward a policeman: the clochard ignored him and kept on urinating.

I tried once before to write down for myself what happened after this, and I must confess that my failure to do so deeply affected me. Today I can see clearly where I made my mistake, but *to see* the mistake clearly is of course not the same thing as undoing the fact of the mistake. The mistake—the result of placing an emphasis on the wrong things—was a lapse in my own attention that made me miss the mark by seeking to grasp the pivot of the events in the wrong place. But this was not the most distressing aspect, it was not the actual mistake that left such a deep trace in me, but *its cause,* namely, that my attention had been led astray by empathy, my empathy for the clochard, because I preferred to see the essence of this early afternoon in August exclusively in his flight triggered by the pursuit.

Nor will I deny today that, as you may very well gather, the story I am telling here is the story of a pursuit and flight—what else would there be to speak about?—but that first written attempt was strictly confined to merely mentioning the pursuit, before devoting itself to a detailed, thorough analysis of the flight, confined in other words, mostly, if not exclusively, to the flight alone, as if ignoring the fact that preceding and accompanying it there was the pursuit, there were these two pursuers, and this fact, and these pursuers, should have been subject to the most thorough scrutiny. This one-sidedness upset the equilibrium and together with it the truth, so that I will not commit the same mistake now, especially in front of you.

The only thing the written version revealed about the real policeman (and even that in a great hurry, for it wanted to get to the clochard as soon as possible) was that, seeing that his warning had no effect, and noting the unceasing flow of urine upon the rails, he opted for the only possible solution: he zeroed in on the entrance to the stairway leading down to the corridor under the rails that connected the two platforms, and, more or less at a run, followed by the apprentice cop and the snarling German shepherd, off he went toward this stairway. Yes indeed, he zeroed in—I now append to this immediately and with disciplined restraint, granting that while making this absolutely necessary rectification, instead of appending I would like best to scream out, *sure, off he went, because he could not vault across that distance of ten meters.*

Esteemed audience—and let me say this to you today at last, on this second attempt, with a desperate insistence—it was this distance of ten meters, esteemed gentlemen, that constituted the focal point of those few minutes preceding the arrival of the delayed train from the direction of Kreuzberg that early afternoon—and I beg you to envision this for yourselves as sharply as if a hundred floodlights shone upon those ten meters in the subterranean platform of Zoologischer Garten!

That first version ... I have it here, just a moment ...yes, here it is, this written version says, and I quote, "enraged by this abyss separating them, they bolted ... for the stairway entrance leading down below the rails"—blah-blah-blah-blah, we already know that—"one could see," the text continues, "from the way they sprinted"—yes, this is it!—"how enraged they were by the possibility that the guilty party might some-how give them the slip while they were down below the rails, racing to-ward him. On their way to the stair entrance they were on tenterhooks for temporarily having to put greater distance between themselves and what they were dying to reach, and on their way, they kept casting tor-mented glances at the clochard on the opposite platform, for fear that he might somehow vanish while they crossed over below the tracks. By now, the old clochard had at last taken this in and stopped urinating since he realized"—this is still the first version—"that they would be there in a second to seize him. And so he prepared to run away, aiming for the exit at the center of our platform that led up toward freedom, that was his goal, but as he turned in our direction, to begin this so-called flight, it became instantly obvious to every commuter there that this flight would never happen, because the old clochard's entire body was quaking so violently that a sudden silence fell over the entire plat-form. Somehow his leg muscles refused to work, because even with the most tremendous effort, and flailing arms, it took him about half a minute to advance at most a few centimeters, in front of our eyes, as he struggled to totter forward, body quaking, arms sawing the air"—con-tinues the first version—"whereas in the meantime the policeman and his cohort with the snarling German Shepherd were approaching, swift as the wind. I watched the old man, his hopeless struggle to escape, and all the while I sensed the gimlet-eyed cop down below drawing ever closer, as yet unseen, but soon to heave into sight with a smile"—says the manuscript—"radiating satisfaction that all is well with the world, all is in place, and what's more, everything in this wonderful world is exactly where it should be, for this is how it has been decreed, that the guilty should quake and inch along, whereas the pursuer, swift as the wind in seven-league-boots ...," and so on, all of it breathless and hysterical to the end, so that I'll stop quoting here, this sample was perhaps more than enough.

I don't know whether you have noticed that this first version simply ignored the essence, this first version quite simply skipped the all-important ten meters, as if it had made no difference how the policeman's indescribable facial features hardened, then totally darkened, and at last became overcome by rage and the ensuing thirst for revenge, as if all of this had made not the least difference in this godforsaken world for the writer of the earlier text, that earlier me, whereas it was precisely this grim darkening and this thirst for revenge that revealed most clearly what had been transpiring inside the policeman on account of those ten meters.

This policeman, in his own eyes, was a creature of limited powers, in fullest measure authorized by society's presumable contempt for clochards to turn this limited power into *an unlimited* power in order to smite and crush especially such clochards, such ragged old pariahs as the one here at Zoologischer Garten, instantly and with the most resolute force, when such a pariah, illustrating by his mere presence in a prohibited space the rationale behind society's contempt, then practically threw himself through sheer negligence at the feet of the resolute enforcer of the law. The policeman's facial expression could be read to say that while these clochards generally spent the whole day avoiding forbidden spots (zones fraught with danger for them), that for these people there were only trails surrounded by such spots, such danger zones, as they staggered all over the place, meandering like civilians lost in a minefield, wandering among landmines, trying to scrape by, but they were unable to do that, because from time to time—presumably out of weariness, ridiculously exhausted—they strayed by mistake and managed to step on just such a landmine, and the mine exploded, and then these wasted good-for-nothings found themselves face to face with someone who promptly called them to account, and collared them, one who struck a blow at pariah-hood, just as this policeman was doing now—well, one could read all this and more in that indescribable face, when this full-fledged policeman, noticing what was happening on the opposite side, rushed to where the shortest possible distance separated him from the clochard and ordered him to stop urinating.

All of the foregoing could very well be an everyday occurrence, I know, but before you get too drowsy, and think, so what, a clochard taking a leak and a cop collaring him, before you say that to yourself, I would ask you to please consider that in *this* story, the one I am telling here, the policeman was unable to collar the clochard. There they stood, facing each other, the distance across, as you know, was no more than ten meters, and at ten meters each could see the slightest swerve in the other's eye, without being able to touch that person, well, there they stood facing each other, the complete pariah and the complete policeman, and this complete policeman turned into a helpless policeman, and the complete pariah turned into a disobedient pariah, and that was how they stood there facing each other on one of the underground levels of Zoologischer Garten.

In the eyes of a policeman, a helpless policeman is even more insufferable than a drunken pariah, so it is small wonder that this policeman, seeing this noncompliance on the opposite side, grasped his truncheon, then realizing it was useless to swing it—there was the distance, those ten meters—well then, his facial features really hardened, those brows definitely darkened. Unlimited power meant that *this* unlimited power had to produce an immediate and absolute effect, as long as that pariah was supposed to be thus deprived of the minimum of protection, rights, or recourse guaranteed by society. But this unlimited power suddenly lost all of its effectiveness, the clochard simply ignored the cop and kept on urinating, with a pained grimace, meanwhile to be sure turning this woebegone face slightly in our direction, whereas he, the policeman, merely marked time there on this humiliating stage while being ignored, and was forced to take notice of how all his unlimited power could turn into plain helplessness; moreover, since after all, he was unfortunately not permitted to fire his revolver at the man, you could see that he felt himself positively disarmed, and this condition of being disarmed—his darkened brow indicated—was especially intolerable for a policeman with a sidearm in his holster.

A policeman usually divides the world into good and evil, and I could see in this policeman's eyes that he thought no differently. There could be no doubt as to where he placed himself, and even less doubt about where he placed the old clochard, and so from his own point of view here was an instance where the good would set out to wreak vengeance upon evil. I do not want to become entangled in this issue of good and evil, and I evoke it from the policeman's eyes only because it is precisely such a policeman-like simplemindedness that sheds the brightest light now, and at the time it had cast an even brighter light, on that truly unbridgeable gap of ten meters separating the two of them, and the remarkable thing was not—as the first written version attempted to convey by inciting emotions—the manner and mode in which the pursuit and flight took place (that all happened, by the way, more or less as the rough and ready wording of the first version described it), but that in spite of the pursuit, and in spite of the flight, the policeman did not succeed in bridging that gap of ten meters, those ten meters persevered, or rather: in vain did the policeman at last collar the clochard about the same time as the arriving train roared into the station, in my eyes those ten meters had proved to be insurmountable, because what my eyes had seen in this pursuit and this flight, to employ the simplicity of police language, was that good can never catch up with evil, because with the gap between good and evil there is no hope whatsoever.

This was what had moved me so, and not the clochard inching and quaking, the policeman flying in seven-league boots swift as the wind.

Gentlemen, you have probably guessed by now why I brought up this story.

III

You might say now, fine, fine, but let's hope this man isn't saying here that the smell of urine should waft everywhere, and we ought to plant a kiss on the lawbreaker's forehead?

Before speaking about essential matters I usually wait and procrastinate as long as possible, but at this time I consider the following announcement so important that any further delay is out of the question; I beg you to understand, the policeman was ready to kill that clochard *because of that distance of ten meters,* and I dragged up this story to make it clear, standing in front of you here: evil exists, and the good, sad to say, can never catch up with it.

Then I boarded one of the trains at Zoologischer Garten, the light under the mirror turned green, and we glided past that zone measuring a meter and a half where by now of course there was no one. I was thinking that the world was intolerable, and felt like leaping out onto the dark rails, but of course did not do so, instead I mulled over when the last time was that I had spoken the words "good" and "evil."

Was it in childhood? Or when I was in high school?

Anyway, it was a long time ago, I concluded then, hurtling along from Zoologischer Garten in the direction of Ruhleben, and now I would like to request you gentlemen not to believe, not even for a moment, that by alluding to this "evil" dragged up from the murky depths I am referring, say, to the clochard and the policeman! I hope you will understand that back there we were talking about the drama of good and evil, and about how, sad to say, there was no communication between the two, and how a single decisive detail in the world is, sad to say, enough to make the whole world intolerable.

On the train ride toward Ruhleben I recalled that quaking body, those flailing arms, and I mused about that clochard and the other pariahs—when would they revolt, and what that revolt would be like. No doubt most violent and dreadful, I shuddered, they would take turns massacring each other, but then I stopped and said to myself, no, no, the revolt I had in mind would be something else, an all-out revolt.

Revolt is always all-out, I thought, suddenly sobering up, and I looked on tensely as one lit-up station after another flew past, and saw the clochard in front of me again, and understood that for him not only that meter and a half between mirror and platform's end was forbidden, his forbidden zone included the whole platform, stairs, streets, buildings, what was above the ground and underneath, everything.

By then I was watching with alarm those lit-up stations gliding by as I realized, stunned, that a point existed from where it was forever forbidden to enter this city, this country, this whole continent—and I gaped outward, at Bismarckstrasse, Theodor-Heuss-Platz, and finally Ruhleben.

Esteemed convocation: yes, evil exists.

IV

Look at me, I am tired.

How are we doing with that door?

Forty-two minutes I have been talking and that door is still locked.

I should look again, you're saying, because it is open now? Very well, but what about this security detail? Again? To escort me? Where?

I just want to go home.

Hospitality? What kind of hospitality?

The lecture is over.

This time I spoke about revolt.

THE THIRD LECTURE

I

I am here for the last time.

For the final time I am standing in front of you to give a lecture.

And I will ask no questions. I understand that I am supposed to give a lecture. I won't ask what its purpose is. I don't want to know.

The only reason I won't remain completely silent is that given my situation I am forced to speak, which you may take to mean that I shall speak like one who remains silent. This talk, consequently, will not metamorphose into inquisitiveness—that is, I will not start making inquiries to find out about your ultimate identity nor about the somewhat ominous ambiguity of your intentions regarding what is to be done with me. I will keep my word, so that those worried-looking gentlemen in charge of security who conducted me up here from the subbasement and to whom I gave my word that I wouldn't ask—nor would I expect to receive an answer to—any questions, yes, you gentlemen may rest at ease and exhale a sigh of relief right here at the start: I will not inquire—not even up here in this splendid auditorium, under the possibly sheltering auspice of your most unusual public presence—I will not ask what your intentions have been over the past weeks regarding me, you see this . . . how shall I put it . . . lecturer is totally ridiculous as a public speaker because he's totally absorbed in exploring the dance steps of *saying goodbye to the world,* and he is incapable of anything else; no, I will not badger you about why you happened to select and invite me here, only to frog-march me, after my second lecture, into a subbasement suite and deprive me of my freedom; just as, finally, you may be absolutely certain: I will not try to pry into what the point is of a so-called farewell speech, when one is taking leave as I am, that is: when the departing one doesn't need an audience, nor does this audience need the departing one, for by now they have nothing further to share.

For in my case, no doubt, my leavetaking is actual and definitive; and this lecture of mine will be a true valedictory. The first statement is explained by an inner impulse (enough said about that for now); and the latter is explained by your third invitation, or shall I say your nonappealable summons, as will be immediately seen from the following brief—although for some of you perhaps not superfluous—outline of events.

You see, today at daybreak—which by the way was the seventh of my detention here—I was woken by the house telephone ringing at my bedside. A voice of sparse, measured elegance informed me that this evening I was to appear once again in front of you. Thanks to our memorable encounters, said the voice, we were able to get to know your views on melancholy and revolt. This time we would like to hear what you have to say about possessions, and here the voice grew softer, and added that I—this "I" referred not to him but to me—had earlier hinted more than once that my inner state could be likened best to that of someone taking leave, and therefore he, the voice, would now like to reassure me not to worry: the people sitting in the audience this evening are also nothing but leave-takers, and since this evening it would be leave-takers on both sides, I would be fully justified to consider my lecture as a valediction. Then something was said about a great expectation, but the sentence broke off halfway, the voice left off, the line was disconnected.

Esteemed gentlemen!

Until this morning the house telephone had been inclined to function exclusively in one direction only, when I asked for food or drink from the "service" staff that showed up only on these occasions. Never the other way, that is, during seven days no one had anything to communicate to me regarding my situation or yours. So thanks to this one-way traffic only now am I able to inform you: I have no interest in what you want from me, I'm not interested in your intentions, nor what you are saying farewell to, for in all likelihood not only does an unbridgeable gap exist between our respective interpretations of a valediction, but the content of our valedictions is far from identical. I would emphatically like to make you understand that after the monotonous senselessness of my subterranean sojourn, I am giving this lecture, apart from my own amusement, not because of some baseless, putative shared trait, but solely because by complying with your request, I wish to be granted, in addition to my two daily walks (morning and afternoon), a third and a fourth walk, an early morning, and a so-called evening one.

You see I desperately need air, my body, ever since a sudden illness a few years ago, cannot do without fresh air, so that airing, especially frequent airing in my case is, as they say, most desirable. Therefore I will offer you a lecture in exchange for fresh air, and since I take your nods to indicate there are no serious obstacles to the implementation of these two additional walks, the only thing left for me now is to clarify what kind of lecture we are talking about here.

By now you ought to be used to my never promising anything, in fact each time I have done my best to cool down the ardor of your expectations. This time, too, I must do the same, nay, this time I promise even less than before.

One week ago the same gentlemen who brought me here tonight escorted me from here down to the sub-basement through an emergency exit (you may recall there was a spot of trouble with the doors), and these gentlemen, who back then, a week ago, told me not to ask any questions and not to worry, if at first glance this looked like confinement—actually I would enjoy the most auspicious hospitality during my stay here—these same gentlemen, while escorting me now from the sub-basement, kept saying the same as before, that I should still refrain from asking any questions, not to worry, just calmly concentrate my attention on the subject of mutual concern to us, after all we—and here the gentlemen pointed at themselves—are here so you can accomplish this without any hindrance. These aberrant interpretations of hospitality and captivity clearly illuminate how profoundly mistaken these gentlemen were on the way from the sub-basement to the lecture hall, and how radically we differ in our assessments of the situation, and how utterly different our interests are under the apparently dying flickers of the constellation of our "subject of mutual concern." If I conclude correctly from the extreme little I can surmise regarding this castle and your circle, you are most concerned about the predictability of the world, in other words, your own security. All of that, however, is merely of tangential interest to me; on the contrary, what concerns me (as mentioned before) is the sequence of steps enabling one to back out of the world. Please don't misunderstand me, I do not dispute—since I too must endure the same—that the world in question indeed lacks certainty, but while you gentlemen, I suppose, lament the absence of security in the universe, I lament the absence of beauteous meaning in the human world, or—inasmuch as we measure our differences by our disillusionment—your disillusionment comprises the so-called universe, whereas mine is limited to so-called humankind, by which I mean that you gentlemen have in fact been disappointed by failing to discover the keys to the universe, while retaining this universe itself; whereas I have been disillusioned by human intelligence after realizing the key to it is commonplace prostitution, and since I have found nothing else, I am left with nothing.

It probably sounds peculiar that without even trying to disguise it by some artful stratagem, I openly admit that in my case I am discussing something so trivial. Peculiar it is, possibly a bit ridiculous as well, and I would certainly understand if you yelled at me: Hey Mr. Artist, you should have dusted off this trivial insight before tossing it at us, because this story is at least a hundred fifty years old, in other words, it's musty; so what, you're disillusioned by human intelligence, why not by all of humankind? Please, please spare us that sort of thing. Meanwhile, what am I to do? A hundred fifty years, well, it's been a hundred fifty years; the same thing happened to me as to someone a hundred fifty years ago, probably it went down this way because I have traveled backward, for me everything has gone backward compared to the way—I imagine—it has gone for you in this world a hundred fifty years later. Because here and now, the customary course of the intellect's choice of a theme is that in the wake of earlier experiences and ensuing disastrous traumas, that human intellect, rising above resignation vis-à-vis the human universe, becomes fed up with this world mired in the monotony of hopelessness, and transcends it, at last leaving it behind and identifying this particular theme in some enigmatic grandeur—some indecipherable, mysterious majesty, that is to say, in the universe, or in the deity of the universe.

From here on—sad to say, but I must add, predictably—it, the intellect, cannot thrive, because its attention can never reach beyond itself, and, as attention-paying subject, it forever remains a prisoner in its own security. It is not interested in the universe as much as in its own special status in the universe, interested not so much in the universe's divinity, as in the likelihood of its own chosenness, in a word this theme becomes a sacred but regrettably unattainable goal, and yet the dignity of this theme, the high level of attention paid to it—in contrast to the rank, the worthiness, of the subject paying it attention—continues to exist, and will always exist.

For me, all this went down very differently.

It began with what it usually begins with: my very first act of consciousness, practically on the way out of my mother's belly, was wanting to know everything right away about this universal plenum I was a part of; and about its existence I learned not from the experiences of others but from allusions made by others, beginning with the first cursory, skimming glance finding the human world around one devoid of interest—imbecilic, insignificant, and therefore negligible—and since this judgment was at least as recklessly appealing as it seemed convincing, after this first cursory glance I quite simply ignored the human world and, as if ashamed of it, skipped it and immediately darted toward another world where, or so I believed, I would face the dramatic presence of majesty and eternity. The process itself was most like daydreaming, for the *universe* that I had believed to have found (to call it by its name here) ultimately by its very nature had no need of any confirmation and depended exclusively on the imagination. This imagination embellished a limitless and impartial nature with a totally unjustifiable force of attraction, and then it experienced this embellished nature as the universe; yet when ultimately a more thorough, searching investigation, aiming as a matter of course to establish a so-called ultimate meaning, ran aground and deprived this so-called universe of its attractive power, all that remained was nature itself with its maddening neutrality, its untamable, prodigal omnipotence—and of course came disillusionment, a most extreme collapse, the bitter recognition that, instead of a thirst for knowledge, all along this had been about the primal desire for possession, and taking possession had failed to happen. I don't wish to temporize here, so in summation all I have to say about this collapse is that its gravest consequence turned out to be the collapse of the imagination, of free imagination, after which the only possibility was to retreat, and here we are speaking of a global retreat where one cannot expect a favorable turn of events—and this being a well-established case, allow me to be redundant: there cannot be a favorable turn of events ... But regardless of how this happened, no matter how instructive the sad tale of my downfall may be, the tale of gradually awakening to the realization that what I had been gazing at with such wonder and yearning did not exist, for it was glued together solely by this wonderment; let's skip the details now; suffice it to say that I had fallen back exactly to the place where presumably you, the shrewd ones, had started out from, the most prosaic setting, a world bogged down in the boredom of hopelessness.

And here I truly mean the most banal realities of life, the world of table salt petrified in its container, shoelaces thinning in spots knotted day after day, street assaults and lovers' vows trickling away into the sewer, a world where even a bouquet of violets carries the definite odor of money. This was the place I had fallen back into with a crash, where it would have been of vital importance to somehow discover the joy of so-called little things, and find, in the principle controlling the workings of the human world, the unmistakable traces of grandeur, of the eternal, in other words, a more spacious existence.

Keeping in mind what you may have gathered about me from the foregoing, surely no one will be surprised if without further ado I confess that in this most banal reality of the world I found, instead of the joy of little things, a loathing of little things, rather than discover the unmistakable traces of the grandeur of things eternal, I found instead irrefutable evidence of pettiness and the drive for instant gratification. So that by now nothing prevents me from deriving special enjoyment in using hackneyed expressions, and saying for instance that I have been engaged in a desperate struggle, searching for a most subtle form, given my situation in this disenchanted human world, which is confined to tangible realities graspable by the hand. I was dreaming of a form capable of conveying the hopeless situation of an age in which people ... how can I put it in the most clichéd manner possible ... are forced to live amidst a dreadful absence of ideals. But quite soon I came to realize that not a single mode of expression, no form whatsoever, not even the most infinitesimally subtle, can derive from sheer will, insofar as thinking itself is unfamiliar with a freedom that has no object. Therefore I imagined that my form and mode of expression must refer back

64

to a sensibility rooted in the aforementioned principle that controls the workings of the human world.

Well, that was precisely what I failed to find, that certain sensibility in this controlling principle, and the fact that I couldn't find it—namely because there was no such thing—filled me with such bitterness that to this day I have been unable to get rid of it, no matter how much I imbibe—sweet or sour, pungent or salty—no matter what I try, nothing works.

I am telling you all this—the story of the differences between our respective disillusionments and intellectual choices—so that you will understand what I must announce now: it is with a *bitter* taste in my mouth that I stand here before you, who expect to hear some kind of informative talk from me, a bitter taste that is independent of the oppressive feeling caused by the captivity that is imposed for the sake of my own safety. I speak about the matter in such detail in order to make it impossible to simply glide over this bitter taste, and to emphasize just exactly how *bitter* it is, so that you will truly understand what I mean when with this *bitter* taste in my mouth I repeat: it is barely a smidgeon better than zero that I can promise to deliver as your lecturer this evening. In my experience, it makes no difference if the topic be melancholy, revolt, or possessions, a lecture such as mine will somehow fail to engage the attention of today's audience, probably not because, in spite of all of its commonplaces, it is still too "difficult," as listeners claim, but because everything coming from this quarter (which, you will recall, I have admitted could be as old as a hundred fifty years), everything arriving from this quarter bores this audience, because it can't understand why anyone, such as this lecturer, especially after a hundred fifty years, couldn't get over the fact that the human world is either vulgar or mendacious, or both.

Of course now I could reply that this is just it, and how should this hundred fifty years be reckoned? What if we can't be sure if this century and a half is still ahead of us, gentlemen! Maybe it isn't for me—that is to say, starting from my kind of disillusionment—that we should trace back a hundred fifty years!

Yes, I could say that, and ask questions like that, but it wouldn't change the fact that even so, I wouldn't get over what makes the world of human intelligence so vulgar and so forth, not even if one hundred fifty years were still ahead of me (or behind you). I am incapable of overlooking the vulgarity and mendaciousness, I keep looking, and I just can't see past them, so that both the universe and any god of the universe disappear from my field of vision; and as for my range of sight, if I may put it that way, it extends only as far as this frightening quality of the human world, I might even say point-blank that I have lost my range of sight in the relentless fog of the vulgar and mendacious.

There was a time when all of this first became obvious to me, and the rather alarming condition compelled me, in my heart of hearts, to give all of this some serious thought. Following these cogitations, or rather in their course, one day I awoke to the fact that I was nauseated, and this was a nausea radically different from all other nauseas.

It lacked an object.

I well remember the day; there I sat hunched over on the edge of the bed, contemplating a spot on the floor before me where the sun happened to be shining, and I waited for the nausea to pass. But it refused to go away, and when it occurred to me that perhaps it never would go away, it became joined by a sort of lightheadedness that I had trouble identifying at first. This lightheadedness was unlike liberation or relief, didn't resemble them at all, it was rather a nightmarish weightlessness, like when you want to pin things down, but no go, because nothing has any weight and nothing can be pinned down. It was the kind of nightmare where you realize that the missing weight of things is sitting right there on your chest, like some kind of succubus, but before you can shove it off, it gets sucked away through a mysterious process into the unknowable realm of your cells, and from there on you are defenseless, your cells already weigh a ton, while your whole body is so light it almost floats, and that's how it goes until you can only wonder how the cells could be so unbearably heavy when the body is so nauseatingly light, and in this nauseating lightheadedness things gradually recede from you just as you too begin to gradually recede from them, in a word it is like when a person lugging a load becomes exhausted by all this lugging and suddenly looking down at his hands sees that there is nothing in them, there never was, that he had been lugging nothing—that is, when you suddenly realize that something is no longer in your possession, just as nothing ever had been.

Esteemed gentlemen!

I am that person!

And the reason I promise you so little is that I have nothing to make promises with.

Behind you gentlemen stands the universe, even if it doesn't exist. And behind me, even if I claim it exists, there is only nothing, nothing but nothing.

But I will no longer abuse your patience.

My assignment is to speak about possessions.

Please grant me your attention.

II

One autumn day, back in the time when I could freely move about on the streets without permission or escort, I had to go to the post office for some reason. I no longer recall precisely what my business was, maybe it was letters, or a few small packages, I am not sure, but I remember that both my hands were full as I turned toward the post office entrance on the main street.

Back then as you know, these types of buildings were not yet protected by security, so that anyone could pass unhindered through the entrance. One could go inside to send or collect money, buy postage stamps, pay bills, then leave, or even go back in case you forgot something, in other words people were free to do as they pleased, and that was how it was on this autumn day as well.

I entered, and once past the throng of arriving and departing people I found the service window I was looking for, which wasn't difficult, because you chose a window marked according to the kind of business it handled: by a sign for money or a sign with an envelope on it. Since I had envelopes, or small packages, I had to stand in front of a window with an envelope sign, or rather, take my place at the end of the line, for I have neglected to mention that people were waiting in rather long lines in front of both types of windows. For the sake of a complete description of the scene—I know the circumstances of those days should be familiar to you—for some strange reason, no one was standing to the left of the entrance, where one could send large packages; and one other thing, opposite all this—opposite the section for sending large packages and the service windows with their various designations and the people standing in line—there were tables of different heights with shelves; there were counters for writing and desks with chairs, so that to simply affix a postage stamp you did not need to take a seat (ergo the countertop), whereas in order to write a letter or postcard you could sit down (ergo a desk and chair).

Well, there I was, standing in line, looking at the back of the head of the person waiting in front of me, but in reality I wasn't looking at that head but constantly checking the distance between me and the given service window. I wasn't watching the back of that head my eyes were absentmindedly riveted on, but was counting how many people were waiting ahead of me, one, two, three, four, five, six...seven, I decided, but maybe those two people there, the man and the child, were to-

68

gether, so it was only six, and at that moment, really quite by accident, I suddenly recalled where I was. I could see myself from up above, as if I were looking down from a cloud as I stood in line, and I was able to see how the whole thing worked, and work it did, not quite smoothly, but in fits and starts. Still, it worked; after all things were clearly demarcated at the post office, you knew what was expected of a person waiting on this side of the service window, or of the person sitting inside behind that window; it all had been arranged so that letters, small packages, amounts of money, and larger packages could move about, the function of stamps was understood as the dues paid for this traffic, in other words, all in all, this post office was working, I certainly don't know what use a dysfunctional post office would have been. The prevailing mood was not quite merry, but neither was it dour, the postal clerk (I had quite a good view of her if I turned my eyes from the back of the head in front of me and looked through the panel of glass separating the clerk from us) was not working with alacrity (which would have made her instantly sympathetic) nor was she working at a snail's pace (which would have made her obnoxious), and taking in the situation, on the whole, with all of us together, the way we stood there in line, one would have thought that things would remain that way.

Six, I said to myself, or if the man and child are together, five.

A ray of sunlight filtered in from the outside.

Quite a number of people came and went in and out; some just stood about, looking around before deciding on one line or another, while others practically ran from the door to the end of the line they were destined for, lest one of those standing and looking around, or possibly some later arrival, a sharp customer, should squeeze in front of them. If you stood in line, you counted, looking at the backs of the heads ahead of you, and kept recalculating the distance remaining, as I did, actually caring about one thing only: how long it would take to reach that window. Those who took their place in line kept tabs on every person standing in front, it made a difference if it was five, or six, so that for a new arrival to insolently cut in at the head of the line instead of joining the end would have been inconceivable. That would have counted as a clear-cut case, easy to condemn; there was, however, another, sneaky kind of attempt, where, ignoring the line, someone stepped up to the window, claiming not to intrude, he wasn't there for the same reason as the others, but merely to ask a question, he just needed some information, one question and he'd be gone.

I will not continue analyzing the potentially unfriendly scenes that might ensue while one stood in line, not wishing to overdo things and let a tormenting stylistic inanity heighten the tension to the breaking point, while at the same time I do intend to give a taste of the small-minded attitudes prevailing at the scene, in part to convince you that this post-office version of existence had indeed been bleak on that day, and also to make it clear: the woman who at this point in the story suddenly stepped up to our window and thereby gave a decisive turn not only to the particular day but in a certain sense to my whole life, this woman in no way fit into this post-office version of existence.

She came in through the door as if she had never been in a post office before: confused, terrified, extremely distressed, it was evident that it took tremendous effort for her to enter, and to stay cost her tremendous effort as well. Regarding her exterior, she seemed insignificant, her clothes revealed almost nothing about her (an unbuttoned light-green cotton jacket, under it a knit cardigan, a black skirt, and she wore some kind of kerchief on her head, I don't recall its color or material, actually it could have been a knit chapeau, I really don't recall). Only her eyes betrayed something about her, and her posture, for they instantly made it plain that this woman . . . was completely shattered.

After much hesitation in the doorway she went over to a writing desk, sat down with her back to us, put her handbag in her lap and began nervously rummaging through it. Clearly, she failed to find what she was looking for. She shut her handbag and proceeded to rummage through her coat pockets, without any success, because the object, a ballpoint pen, as it eventually turned out to be, was hiding in the left pocket of her cardigan. That's where she pulled it out from, only to look around, with this pen in hand, still frightened and confused, and given the nonstop coming and going around her, there seemed to be precious little hope she would find a way out of her frightened confusion. Yet she did, on her own, for it seemed that little by little she began to figure out what all these various windows marked for payments and envelopes were for, and she stood up, to advance rather unsteadily, with stops and starts, to the right window designated by a sign with an envelope, and, amidst visible signs of displeasure from those standing in line, she leaned close to the window, and in a very soft voice said to the clerk, "Pardon me . . . I would like to send a telegram but can't find one of those . . . papers."

Across the cubicle's glass panel we had a clear view of the clerk giving the woman a sullen look and shoving a blank telegram form at her through the opening.

The woman took the form but did not retreat from the window, she merely stepped slightly to the side. She gazed at the sheet of paper, turning it over and examining it, but if she had intended, as I believed she probably did, to draw attention to herself and be given advice about how to fill out the form, it was a wasted effort, for the postal clerk refused to acknowledge it, in fact she utterly ignored her and with what amounted to ostentatious heartiness she turned to face the next patron. Those waiting in line, especially the ones closest to the window, probably felt like shoving the woman away from there, and maybe even—accidentally—treading lightly on her foot, to make her come to her senses, and stop holding up the line; on the other hand these same people waiting in line were somewhat perplexed, for it was really impossible to decide what this woman's problem was, and I believe I was not the only one to whom it had already occurred that perhaps her problem wasn't so much the telegram form but that nobody had told her to go away, to forget about sending that telegram, yes, I was more and more inclined toward that conclusion, while noting that only five, or perhaps four, were left ahead of me, and I would soon find out whether that man and that child were together; I had a growing suspicion that the woman was at least as much expecting to be dissuaded forthwith from sending that telegram as she was expecting to be reassured that the telegram should definitely be sent.

You may think it peculiar if I now assert that it had not occurred to me at all that, say, this was about some ongoing family or romantic drama; this whole thing might seem rather weird, and somewhat suspect, if after the event, all these years later, I tried to shift the highlights of the incident to point in a direction that was to my liking. But it is not like that, not only because any interference of that sort has for a long time now been distasteful to me, but because truly assuming to interfere with the emphases of the story would predicate quite a different one. Therefore it seems self-evident that one should not even try to guess what lay behind the woman's unusual behavior, that is to say, the woman herself and her story became the obvious reasons for not interfering with the story's emphases, inasmuch as it seemed to make no sense to imagine in connection with her—her of all people!—some sort of romantic or family drama.

It was equally impossible to imagine anything else there, impossible to tell what sort of background lay behind her, because her confusion had a certain indefinable ethereality, her alarmed eyes emanated a particular, perfect innocence, and in that disconsolate posture, as she lingered by the window, and then returned to the writing desk and again sat down on a chair, there was a certain kind of purity that I, and no doubt quite a few others who stood in line—precisely because of its inappropriateness to the place, its near-otherworldliness—wouldn't have been able to explain (without embarrassment) in terms of sober, worldly considerations.

I don't mean to claim that the woman, given all her sorrowful purity, was an angel, nor would I want to say that she was not an angel.

If nonetheless I must still say something about this, it would be best if I said that although the writing desk and chair couldn't have been more than eight or ten meters away from me, even if I had wanted to make the attempt, I could not have bridged this gap of eight or ten meters. It would have been impossible to just walk over to her, startle her by a light touch on the shoulder, and then speak to her; one had to admit: this woman, the way she sat there with her back to us, in that cotton jacket that somehow got so rumpled or twisted around at the waist, was utterly unaccostable and unapproachable.

And she was left-handed.

I watched her as she wrote, while I noted the latest change in the line, three, I said to myself, and now concluded without the least satisfaction that the man and the child were together.

Then the woman rose from her chair and with the telegram form in hand came back to the window. She waited until the person standing there concluded his business, then she leaned toward the opening, pointed at the form, and said, "Pardon me again ... I think I made a mess of this one ..." The postal clerk, no longer even trying to hide how burdensome she found these repeated interruptions, as if to express her solidarity with the common cause of those standing in line, petulantly slammed down another blank form in front of the woman, who thanked her, apologized to the people in line, and returned to her desk. She took out a wad of tissue paper from her handbag, blew her nose, folded up the tissue, put it in her coat pocket, and began to write once again.

I watched her writing.

She gripped the pen spasmodically, holding it all the way down near the tip. She limned each letter slowly, and after each word she paused to think it over. At times she raised her head as if to look out through the window, or rather as if she were contemplating the sunbeams streaming through the window of the post office, bemused, seeking after something in the incoming light. Then she bent over the form again, very close to the paper, and resumed writing.

Only two more, I noted in the line, and saw the man and the child leaving together as they pulled the door shut behind them.

Then the woman rose again and came to the service window for the third time. "Please forgive me for disturbing you again ...," she began, anxiously. "I'm done ... Except ... I'd like to add something. I don't know if it's all right like this ..." She handed the telegram form through the opening. "I would like to add one more word ... But I don't know ... Do I have to write the whole thing over?"

For a while the postal clerk said nothing, she just stared straight ahead with a severe look on her face. You could tell that she detested this woman. Then, like one who has counted to ten and calmed down somewhat, she spread her arms helplessly, cast a conspiratorial, chummy glance at the next in line, a young soldier, and making a face that said "What can I do?" took the telegram and bent over it. "You tell me. What is the word? I will write it in. Let's get this over with."

The woman replied in a barely audible voice.

"I would like to add here, 'useless.'"

And she pointed out on the telegram form exactly where.

The postal clerk raised her eyebrows, nodded, and wrote the word in the desired place, counted up the syllables, quickly added it all up, took the money, returned the change, and kept her eyes on the woman while the latter, practically on the run, left the premises, and the door closed behind her.

Then she spoke in a voice loud enough for everyone to hear.

"I just can't take these loonies. I've had it up to here with them. If I see one more ... Just take a look at this!" she turned to the young soldier, and in her disgust pounded her palm down on the telegram. "Now what am I supposed to do with this?!"

"Why? What's wrong with it?" the young man asked.

With an infuriated gesture the clerk held out the telegram to him and crumpled it up in her fist.

"There is no addressee."

Esteemed gentlemen!

III

I think at this point we may take a breather.

Every train of thought has its own tempo, including my own, and I have to confess that at times I cannot even keep up with my own, much less with others'. Think of it as when some vigilante street patrol, maybe the Hajnoczy patrol (it doesn't matter which one of many), is pursuing somebody with authorization to kill, or capture, it really makes no difference now, and the hunted man quite simply runs out of breath, and the patrol lags behind as well, and both parties maintain that the manhunt is still on even though it is not, this is actually the moment for taking a deep breath, seeking to regain the tempo in a doorway or in a backyard among oil drums, just for the duration of this shortness of breath, panting, regaining our tempo, for that is what the hot pursuit is actually about, regaining that tempo that both parties—the pursuer and the pursued—had lost at the same time. Well, that's how I, too, find myself now, forced to interrupt my lecture. You know what comes next during this interim, in a suitable doorway or backyard among oil drums where one can catch his breath; however, I promise you that this is the last time, there will be no further so-called interruptions, or detours, that is to say, just this final one, and then from here on, trust me, all will go smoothly, like a well-oiled machine, unhindered, making a beeline to the finish, never stopping until the final sentence—where not only this lecture but my entire engagement will come to its definite conclusion—at which point I too once and for all can retire from the spotlight of your attention, that has been all along so ambiguous and is now perhaps becoming rather ominous.

Yes, we pause here for a moment, and meanwhile, to make the panting less audible while this "I" inside me regains its proper pace, let me return to the mundane locale of my sojourn in your sub-basement, and beside reminding you not to forget the additions to my daily allowance of walks, let me bring up another matter that I have been meaning to mention.

Because of some decisive turn in the prevailing situation that's been kept hidden from me, your designating this lecture as my valediction, I fear, does not necessarily guarantee that my final appearance here will be the first step toward my liberation. That is, it looks very much as if I might have to stay here, possibly exempt from being the focus of your attention but not from the protective custody you have decreed for me. If that's how matters stand, I can count on a prolonged stay here, but you must understand that such a sojourn is the same for me as embarking on the *Titanic*, meaning that my requirements become radically altered, the rational ones are reduced to just about zero, whereas my irrational needs, the ones that kick in, now become all-important, I might say vitally important, so that one day this past week, as I lay on my bed flicking back and forth among TV channels (those indicators of business as usual), one day this past week I suddenly realized that something was off about these TV channels, ah but of course, I realized what I was watching was nothing but so-called canned material, indicating that outside, in the real world, something had radically altered, something irrevocable had occurred, that impelled one, gentlemen, to a desperate decision to settle in for a lengthy siege, and now I would remain your special captive for the duration of this siege. It became clear to me that quite possibly I would never leave this fortress, your splendid but lethal domain. I suddenly understood that—if I may put it tersely—*here we go once again, here we go aboard the* Titanic.

I am not saying that the whiteness, the pure whiteness of the sub-basement—the whiteness of floor, walls, and ascetic furnishings, upset me, as my guards, or whatever you want to call them, believed on more than one occasion—no, the problem isn't this whiteness, which for others may indeed be truly blinding, nor for that matter the total absence of any color whatsoever, no, as long as we are on this subject, for me this universal banishment of all color into whiteness constitutes an elegant summation of the actual ongoing events, so that far be it from me to protest against that; it would make no sense at all.

It's about my honorarium.

Up until now I have not broached this subject, nor would I do so at this time, had I not felt myself now aboard the *Titanic,* but since that is where I seem to be, I must inform you that even though I lay no claim to monetary considerations, nonetheless since those particular near-zero needs of mine I have referred to have now indeed arisen, they are as follows—and I ask you to take note of them. I would require:

1. Any and all documents and objects that survive from my childhood.

2. Two hundred and twenty thousand meters of yarn.

3. A revolver.

As for the first, suffice it to say that here I am thinking of diaries, report cards, certificates, photographs, school notebooks, storybooks, coloring books, drawings, dolls, toys, collections of napkins, postage stamps, insignia, and matchbooks, in other words anything that a special commando sent out by you would be able to retrieve from this labyrinth of my childhood. (If he finds the house I was born in, he should by all means search the attic, the entrance to which—possibly you don't have this in my file—is found in the back, on the side next to Uncle Feri's house . . .)

About the second requirement it will be enough to say that for my purposes the yarn can be in a ball or in a hank, it's all the same to me, the important thing is that it should all be in one piece, that is, I require a single length of yarn two hundred and twenty thousand meters long.

As for the third item, I believe no comment is necessary, since the issuance of permits for weapons of self-defense has been extended to include middle school students.

This would be all, and I trust you will dispatch that commando at the earliest opportunity, just as, I trust, you will not question my reasons; for all I care, you may consider this to be my last request, after all it makes no difference to me what you take it to be, since we are dealing with an absolutely private matter as far as why I need these, what they have to do with each other, and why exactly these three. In any case bringing up these documents and objects of my childhood comes at a most opportune time for you gentlemen as well, since this is exactly what will now follow: a reference to these things, for we have now reached the end of the detour where I am able to disclose everything I could tell you about possessions as the cornerstone, the supporting pillar, the foundation, the most profound essence of our world or should I say our former world; all of that by now can only refer to the absolute *loss* of all possessions, although the roots reach all the way back to my childhood, where all of these requested documents and objects originate. This is the same childhood—of dolls, report cards, and matchbox collections—that belongs to the story that is of concern to you, gentlemen. You see, the story that follows, and which you have been obviously very much anticipating after all of these seemingly incidental and trivial tales and analyses, began back there in my childhood, and its starting point was a love of possessions. As for its ending, it can be summed up briefly as being about the absolute disgust evoked by possessions. Of course what intrigues you is what could have possibly happened between the beginning and end of this story. Well, I must say that the matter is a lot simpler than you would think; and can be recapitulated briefly.

In the beginning I had only one doll and I loved it very much.

Then I was given a teddy bear and a lion, both made of imitation plush, and I loved them very much, too. After that I was given a castle made of wood, complete with tin soldiers, and after that came school, and I was given a soccer ball, a backpack, a blue sweatsuit, and love slowly turned into liking, I was glad to have all these things—soccer balls, backpacks, sweatsuits. And the hoard of my possessions grew, and kept growing, and as it kept on growing, my gladness turned into a hunger for owning more of these things, or at least for these things that I owned to remain mine forevermore in the strictest, most undisputable sense, and for this hoard to keep on growing and growing.

And so this hoard grew and kept growing, just as I did. Then I grew up into man's estate with all the usual: wife, child, house, car, TV—all of which of course really amounted to a hunger and desire that all I possessed should remain mine.

But there came a day, in my adulthood of course, when I stopped in a tavern and lingered the way husbands usually do on the way home after shopping, and when it came to leave-taking and someone asked who belonged to that full shopping bag, being somewhat tipsy I said nothing, even though it belonged to me, but nobody knew it, my words simply refused to come, so I said nothing and allowed the befuddlement over the absent owner turn into a powwow among my drinking buddies, ending in a dividing up of the contents of the full shopping bag, each of us taking home whatever he liked, given that some unknown drunk had obviously failed to keep a watchful eye on his belongings. (I seem to recall that I got to take home a tomato.) Later I proved unable to come up with a serious reason for remaining silent, but that particular day proved to be fateful: from then on as if the devil had gotten into me, I kept doing that sort of thing more and more often, I seemed to have acquired the habit of distancing myself from my possessions, of denying that things were mine, and this distancing and denial, although it started with tangible things—the proper objects of ownership—did not stop there, but began to metastasize to things that were not proper objects of ownership, and spread from, say, a shopping bag full of goods to a head full of ideas, from tomatoes to thoughts, and finally to language itself. For instance it became increasingly difficult to say, "Come here, my love!" or "Please pass me my hat!" and I began to have trouble even with such innocuous expressions as "Oh my god!" or "Your mother . . . ," that is, I just started to have trouble with any and all possessive language—adjectives, pronouns, suffixes—especially when it involved the first person singular, while of course I had every reason to keep using these, for after all I did have my love, my hat, my god, my mother.

Perhaps I hardly need say that eventually, along with this transition, though not connected to it, I did lose everything: my god, my mother, my love, and ultimately even my hat; but do not for a moment think that this explains the baleful crisis of possessive adjectives and pronouns, no, not at all, this explains nothing whatsoever; years of this crushing duplicity went by and I found no way out. Duplicity I call it, but I could say it was total anarchy, because even as I was trying with all my might to say no to possessions, at the same time I also said yes to them. Let's take, for example, the street, where, you see, I had noticed a peculiar fact, namely that people went around, not with their eyes straight ahead in a normal manner, but sidling aberrantly, all of them, without exception, twisted, with sidelong glances at shop windows; that is, while I recognized and recused myself from the fact that I was living among people blatantly unable to resist the hypnotic attraction of acquiring possessions, at the same time I found myself from time to time unable to resist casting the occasional glance at these shop windows. And at times, fighting off my nausea, I even entered some store or another to purchase, say, a new hat to cover my head. I can only characterize my situation as the most abysmal anarchy, riven as I was by possessive pronouns and nausea, actual possessions and actual disgust, the mendacious, or at the very least unclean, foundations of my life, while I hadn't the slightest notion of what was tearing me apart, what was confounding me so thoroughly when I had to apply the first person singular to the world.

You already know what ended this anarchy for me.

Yes, gentlemen, it was that telegram at the post office on that autumn afternoon.

I cannot claim that everything became clear to me right away; first it was only that single word, "useless," that pierced my heart, then that "addressee unknown." There I was, my heart pierced, walking homeward, meandering, and if I may take the liberty of putting it this way for you: teetering between a lethally sweet melancholy and the necessity of immediate revolt.

I no longer recall how long this lasted, possibly days, even weeks, until one morning I was sitting by the window, looking out at the unconsoling light, and outside, below the kitchen window, a band of sparrows burst upward from the dry twigs of an unclipped hedge only to almost instantly swoop back down again.

It was as if a veil had been plucked away, then lowered, so swift was this bursting upward and swooping back down, and even though there couldn't have been an immediate connection, still to this day I believe that some connection must have existed between the swift impulse of the band of sparrows and my enlightenment, for it was enlightenment-like, the way I awoke to the realization—as I had on that earlier day of nausea (I recall that succubus)—that I did not possess anything, and never would, nor was I the only one like this—and I imagined my eyes taking in this entire world mired in the desire for possessions—all of us were and would be like this forever.

By now you may have gotten used to the fact that, other than repeating evidence, nothing much can be expected of me, so that you
should not be surprised, hearing for the second time, although coming
from deeper down, that "I possess nothing" and that "You, too, possess
nothing." All the same I would like to make sure that you understand
what I mean.

You gentlemen are well aware that there once was a world where—
quite apart from qualifying its contents—it was possible to ascertain
clearly, even if only in a limited sense, the meaning of possessions, and
this meaning was ascertained only as long as peace reigned in both
human as well as natural relations. Looking at those dry twigs in front
of the kitchen window, I suddenly understood; that is, the band of
sparrows bursting upward and swooping back down, flicked aside the
veil from the fact that this world, whose existence by the way many
would characterize as notional, was finished, the conditions of peace
no longer obtained in human and natural relations, because now a state
of war prevailed in these relations, in short, a decisive turnaround has
taken place, whose chance of occurring and our progression toward
which we have of course been aware of all along (we even kept saying
to each other, blinking, that there was no way to hold it back, everything was being swept unstoppably toward the brink, etc., etc.)—except we didn't realize that the change had already occurred.

Just as on a train journey, when emerging from a forest or the gently swelling hills, we suddenly find ourselves out in the middle of a
bleak desert, that was how this had happened, from peace into war,
the only difference being, in this case, that it was far more difficult if
not impossible to draw the line where one ended and the other began,
because no borderline sets these two apart, instead one gives rise to the
other, is somehow wedged into the other, that is why—in contrast to
an actual train journey—in the war/peace-situation everything happens almost unnoticeably, one moment we glance out the window and

it's still woods and gently sloping hillsides, then we look again, and it's the desert.

Please don't mistake my meaning; when I say state of war I'm not thinking of ...I don't know ... say, gunfire in the streets, or something like that ... No, it is not shots fired in the street, or the fear that we might be shot at, obviously this may happen at any time, but that is not what makes war, not at all, it is not manhunts on the street and such things. But when ...how should I put it ...time passes, the world goes on its way, and arrives at a road sign, along the way, and this road sign points nowhere, the road ends here, the going cannot go on, everything seems to converge here, and then ... for some reason—and we may call this the one and only true and unexplainable mystery—a demon is released from its bottle.

This most maleficent demon is not the same as the angel of death, for it is not the spirit of peace but the demon of war, of delight that everything in existence can be ruined. This is the most intense delight, supreme, unsurpassable—and nothing and no one is exempt from its sway.

You can say no to everything except this, because it seeps in everywhere unnoticed, because it is the be-all and end-all of every real utterance, the inimitable ecstasy of power over things, where the depths of dominion are utterly limitless.

This demon is driven by an inexplicable hatred, and it compels us to destroy ourselves. And once it is actually released, the defensive perimeter around us, the empire of things outside us, everything we lord over, from a collection of matchboxes to a kingdom, all that is ours, suddenly loses its meaning and collapses into itself.

There I sat by the kitchen window and that flurry of sparrows made me understand.

That, actually ... We possess nothing.

IV

Esteemed gentlemen!

Before I take my final bow, allow me to share some news with you, perhaps you haven't heard it yet.

In 1981, on Okinawa, one of Japan's southern islands, known primarily for the American military base there, and which is a part of the East Asian faunal region—after the dismantling of the American base and the return of the Japanese, the local government decided to build a road. Till then there had been no road connecting Okinawa's southern portion—where thanks to the American base, a relatively extensive civilization reigned—and the island's northern part, which had remained entirely in a state of nature. The road to be built was meant to establish a connection between the southern and northern parts, between civilization and nature.

The work began, and bulldozers, excavators, and work crews arrived in the subtropical jungle until then undisturbed by humans, and one fine day, namely on July 4, 1981, in that realm of previously untouched nature, workers with their bulldozers ran over a beautiful bird. This bird was about thirty centimeters long, its back was olive brown, its chest and belly had black and white bars, its long bill and legs were a bright coral red. The workers themselves thought it was beautiful, and thanks to this, the carcass fell into the hands of a scientist investigating the fauna of the island in the wake of the road builders and American troops, and this scientist beheld the carcass with astonishment.

The bird belonged to an unknown species.

No one had ever seen one before, none of the ornithological monographs mentioned it, and the scientist, whose name was Mano, realized the magnitude of the discovery. But he refused to monopolize the glory, and offered the honor, in the customary Japanese manner, to

Professor Yamashina, director of the ornithological institute in Tokyo, insisting that the distinctive honor of describing the species belonged to the professor.

The unspoiled nature of the island's northern portion of course did not exclude aboriginal inhabitants who had been living there for centuries, so that, given the presence of this aboriginal population, the bird had still evinced such perfect skill in keeping its existence invisible for endless successions of generations, and well, this fact understandably created considerable worldwide interest.

Professor Yamashina, on the basis of Mano's observations, determined that the new species belonged to the family Rallidae, and since because of its long bill it could not be classified among the short-billed crakes, he opened a lateral branch in the classification, and named it the Okinawa Rail, *Yanbaru-kuina* in Japanese. Unsurprisingly, in the description of the bird's behavior, Professor Yamashina's first sentence noted that the Okinawa Rail leads a most reclusive existence.

Now all that remained was to explain how it could have happened that this secretive mode of existence was such a resounding success.

The observations concluded that we were faced with a regrettably small population, and it was precisely this, plus the extremely limited range of the species, that in part explained the success of this invisible mode of survival. One theory was that the birds inhabited a terrain where small predators must be relatively few in number, or entirely absent, and they considered the fact that humans hadn't presented a danger—miraculously the aboriginal population had refrained from hunting them, the birds had managed to stay out of sight, so their paths never crossed.

These observations, inasmuch as we may speak of observations in the case of such a shy creature, were thorough and wide-ranging, while leaving room for a few intelligent guesses that didn't come any closer to solving the mystery.

Subsequent inquiries brought up the possible significance of the flightlessness of the Okinawa Rail.

You see, the newly discovered species subsisted on the ground and was unable to fly.

The phenomenon of flightlessness is known in the avifauna of both the continental land masses and the oceanic islands, but in the latter instance the explanation is even more obvious. It is more obvious, but leads to a pitfall that, as it turns out, puts off the solution of the posed question toward the infinite.

Given that for island-dwelling birds one great danger is being swept away by a storm, some species attempted to defend against this by simply refraining from taking to the air. The defensive reflex of not flying became hereditary, and especially in the case of larger birds that were poor fliers to begin with, within relatively short periods this resulted in the total loss of the ability to fly. This in turn demanded a stealthy mode of existence, for the ground-dweller is completely at the mercy of predators. This is exactly what must have happened in the case of our Rail, the loss of the ability to fly led to extreme shyness, the two scientists concluded, but in view of the fact that the avian world contains several similar cases, we must note that not one has been as successful as our Rail.

The professor and his co-author did not hide their unbounded admiration for the Okinawa Rail, this great artist of seclusion, on account of its perfect defense mechanism.

I, too, render my tribute to this bird, which is why I told the story, but at the same time I feel myself trapped.

You see, my point of view is different from Professor Yamashina and his fellow researcher's. In my eyes the Okinawa Rail is simply: a bird that cannot fly.

V

Well, so much for my news, and there is nothing else I can think of at this time.

I have kept my promises, and said all I intended to say.

Will I have the same guards on the way down?

Is that a yes?

In that case, gentlemen, I am ready.

The lecture is over.

Let's be on our way.

ONE HUNDRED PEOPLE ALL TOLD

I t took twenty-five hundred years, by and large twenty-five hundred, that is approximately one hundred generations, for the fact to become obvious and identifiable with indisputable precision, that was how much time it took to get this far, to reach our days, but we could also say that roughly twenty-five hundred years sufficed for the teaching to crumble, to waste away, for its message to become dim and inverted, for the complete and irreparable breakdown of its original meaning via an endless chain of misinterpretation and incomprehension took a hundred generations, we may also say *all it took was one hundred people,* including the first, who understood it, and bequeathed it to tradition, and the last of the hundred who definitively abandoned the unsurpassable realm of knowledge relating to the fact, that is someone who—from another viewpoint—proved to be capable of constructing a humanly conceivable world based on a *distortion* of this unfathomably deep knowledge since it was not only impossible to recover the original teaching but it is no longer of any interest to know what was lost, because this is what has happened, a hundred people, a hundred generations, twenty-five hundred years, and we have forgotten what the world's most original philosopher had thought through and proclaimed between 450 and 380, or between 563 and 483, B.C., in the environs of the Isipathana Deer Park and Kushinagar, it took only a hundred people, so that we of the early twenty-first century no longer have the foggiest notion that *the fact* simultaneously creates and destroys

itself, that words and ideas cannot say anything about the world—
about the immense cosmos containing so-called self-evident facts—
other than positing nothing; a perfect and sparkling nothing, while
on the other hand by the time the way the world works was set down
in writing, this had most definitely, once and for all, escaped from our
memory, it had escaped with a finality, irretrievably, although not for
a lack of facts or reality, but because to procure a primitive spiritual
state, to take the most obvious path to obtain control over the humanly
conceivable world and thereby establish the security of a being in the
realm of nature, this forgetting appeared unavoidable, nothing else was
needed, the only indispensable requirement being this renunciation in
the cramped entryway to a spacious and slowly disseminating chain of
thought, so that, ditching our awareness of an extraordinarily complex
universe, we could now spend our lives amidst the barrenly beating
waves of an ever more clear-cut, simpleminded, brutal logic, thus giving rise to a reflexive human existence, this via a pathetic misunderstanding of the mechanism of causality, to a bewitchingly crude guiding principle based on the correlative system of fact-reaction-fact, or
rather symptom-reaction-fact, which in its own way does not hinder,
in fact it assures that the operation of the law is hindered by nothing,
least of all by this creature destined for so much although not for everything, who persists under the illusion that he has at last gained intelligence in exchange for the vehicle of seeing the deepest interrelation
of things, which he has discarded as faulty while most mysteriously it
still keeps its occult functioning; thus self-deprived of the command-
ing power of true intellect, laid low by this self-inflicted wound, wal-
lowing in the arrogance of a knowledge, that has never been knowledge
unless it be the fool's knowledge insisting on being led back to the fact
of the inviolability of his role, that is, of his presence, i.e. his *existence,*
and within this mysterium that is so inconceivable, to become what he
in any case must become within the simultaneously existing and dis-
solving context of trillions of tangential facts.

A mere twenty-five hundred years, and there is no one left who is fully aware of what the second one of the one hundred had heard once upon a time at the Deer Park and at Kushinagar, every single link in the original chain of thought has been turned into the most egregious error, every single item in the texts is erroneous, every single item in the commentaries erroneous, as is every single item in the corrections and alterations, clarifications, and revisions, nothing but errors, errors upon errors, so that only one thing saves us from the insanity of cynicism, only one thing gives rise to an assurance more feeble than the faintest breeze, namely, that in every created and existing phenomenon it is possible to f e e l that the original teaching indeed existed once upon a time, and that the world, the cosmos, the universe, in other words something and everything—*somehow, that is to say, in a not communicable manner* still exists—is it possible to feel this for a brief moment, regardless of what exactly is world, cosmos, and universe; it is plainly ineradicably embedded within us to feel that everywhere at all times facts exist in all their ungraspability and uncapturability, what's more, trillions and trillions of facts exist released in the stillness of time, because amidst the ceaseless lightning bolts of doubt, the feeling is indeed indestructible, that for instance where it is spring now, springtime buds burst forth and whatever must turn green is greening—we feel this for a brief moment, regardless of what exactly a bud is, and green, and spring; here we stand now, utterly abandoned, having lost the one who could enlighten—because he had once upon a time understood—and we are slapped down to be here, without the one, simply to be, like springtime and buds and all this greening, here in the profoundest cluelessness about what it means that this must certainly be springtime, with buds and things about to turn green, that therefore there must be direct experience, i.e., occasion for direct confrontation and experience, or more precisely: that is all there is occasion for—

to stand there in springtime, where there is spring, and observe buds and everything greening, to stand and stand there when springtime is come, to stand and observe this, amidst the most calamitous immediacy, abandoned to our own devices, nursing a dismal suspicion that someday after all we ought to see how it is possible that simultaneously with all these existences, all these trillions upon trillions of facts, nothing whatsoever exists at all.

Perhaps it was really a hundred people all told, that was how many it took, and there is no hope there will be a hundred and one, because a life based on incomprehension and misinterpretation and erroneous ideas must end just as springtime must end, budding and greening must end, and everything will be just as incomprehensible as it has been since the beginning of time immemorial, with no help whatsoever along the way, and even this end brings no enlightenment, since the one who could have delivered it delivered it already, once upon a time, except that no one grasped what he had declared: away with reasoning and away with meaning, away with the thirst of desire and suffering; there was no one who truly grasped and embraced it, surely that's what should have been done back then, after 380 or 438, embrace what would be grasped of the words spoken by the ascetic prince of philosophers, and find a form, some brand new form, to embody this heartrending state of being touched, and not hand it over to so-called understanding, not fling it down for so-called interpretation, not leave it at the mercy of the mind that could not help but destroy it immediately, retaining it for itself or relegating it to the realm of religion, it makes no difference which path the mind chose to do away with the princely message, it was blindness in broad daylight, the mind snatching the message from the addressee, so that now somewhere presumably we have a message, while there is this woeful, incurable blindness, and after those one hundred, no one appeared who would at least recognize that what refers to another can never actually touch that other, so that only words are left now, for another twenty-five hundred years, human words that will never be—just as they have never been—good for anything, because not only have they not deciphered what has been and is still inscribed in the unmediated sacredness of trillions and trillions of facts, not only have they detoured us from where they should have directed us, but they haven't even been suitable, and never will be, for truly consoling us for the loss, for there being no way back to the one, nor can they ever even warn us: we must listen very carefully to what is spoken, if it is spoken at all, because it is said once and only once.

NOT ON THE HERACLITEAN PATH

Memory is the art of forgetting.

It doesn't deal with reality, reality is not what engages it, it has no substantial relation whatsoever to that inexpressible, infinite complexity that is reality itself, in the same way and to the same extent that we ourselves are unable to reach the point where we can catch even a glimpse of this indescribable, infinite complexity (for reality and glimpsing it are one and the same); so the rememberer covers the same distance to the past about to be evoked as that covered when this past had been present, thereby revealing that there had never been a connection to reality, and this connection had never been desired, since regardless of the horror or beauty that the memory evokes, the rememberer always works starting from *the essence* of the image about to be evoked, an essence that has no reality, and not even starting from a mistake, for he fails to recall reality not by making a mistake, but because he handles what is complex in the loosest and most arbitrary manner, by infinitely simplifying the infinitely complex to arrive at something relative to which he has a certain distance, and *this is how* memory is sweet, *this is how* memory is dazzling, and *this is how* memory comes to be heartrending and enchanting, for here you stand, in the midst of an infinite and inconceivable complexity, you stand here utterly dumbfounded, helpless, clueless, and lost, holding the infinite simplicity of the memory in your hand—plus of course the devastating tenderness of melancholy, for you sense, as you hold this memory, that its reality lies somewhere in the heartless, sober, ice-cold distance.

II. NARRATES

NINE DRAGON CROSSING

The future, the same old.

He had always planned that some day he would travel to see Angel Falls, then he had planned to visit Victoria Falls, and in the end he had settled for at least Schaffhausen Falls; one day he'd go and see them, he loved waterfalls, it's not easy to explain, he would begin whenever he was asked what his thing was about waterfalls, waterfalls, he would begin, and would immediately interrupt himself, how can I say this? giving his interlocutor a bewildered glance, as if expecting that person to help him provide an answer, what exactly it was with him and waterfalls, but of course the one who asked the question never rushed to help with the answer, why should he, after all he had asked the question because he didn't know the answer, so that this usually caused a bit of a confusion that either increased or else immediately ended, because either after some temporizing or else right away, he would somehow manage to close the matter, for at these times when they tried to extract an answer from him he would either gradually or with a sudden movement literally turn away from the interlocutor, he did not intend to be rude, but it made him very nervous that this was what always happened, that he would get embarrassed right away, this whole thing got on his nerves, to be asked, and to become embarrassed because of it, just standing there like one smacked on the head with a frying pan, while his interlocutor obviously didn't know what was going on, what was this with a frying pan?—so that those among his acquaintances who knew about the thing chose to drop the matter, even though the question would have been justified, everyone around him knew that he liked waterfalls and that he had always planned on traveling to see at least one, as they say, at least once in his life, first and foremost Angel Falls, or Victoria Falls, but at the very least Schaffhausen Falls; whereas things happened quite otherwise, in fact utterly otherwise, for he had arrived at that time of life when one no longer knows how many years remain, possibly many, perhaps five or ten or even as many as twenty, but it is also possible that one might not live to see the day after tomorrow, and so, one day it became clear as day for him that at this time of life he would, as they say, never get to see either the Angel, or the Victoria or even the Schaffhausen Falls, the sound of one of these falls, by the way, was constantly in his ears, after fantasizing about them all these years he had started hearing one of them, but which one it was he couldn't know of course, so that after a while, around the time he turned sixty, he was no longer sure why he had wanted to see the first or the second or at least the third of these waterfalls, was it so he could at least decide which one it was he had heard all his life, or more accurately the second half of his life, whenever he shut his eyes at night? or because he had actually wanted to see one of them, if not one of the first two, then at least the third, he was now past sixty and this actually terminated the hitherto always open-ended aspect of the matter, what is more, it somehow made it clear that he would never get to see the first or the second or even the last one of these falls, not because it would have been so impossible, why would it have been, he could have easily gone to a travel bureau when he happened to have the money, even now that he was past sixty, and he could make a payment for a trip to the Angel, or to the Victoria, or at least to Schaffhausen; on the other hand, he had always thought that just for this reason, just because there happened to be a waterfall there, he would not make the trip after all, but wait until one of his work assignments would take him somewhere in the vicinity, except this never happened, by a grotesque twist of fate he who in the course of all those years had been sent to just about every corner of the globe had never been sent near a falls, there had never been any interpretation job in the vicinity of the Angel, the Victoria, or even the Schaffhausen Falls, and this is how it happened that he, who all his life had wanted to see the Angel, the Victoria, or at least the Schaffhausen Falls, he of all people, who had this thing with waterfalls, one fine day, and for the umpteenth time, found himself in Shanghai again (the occasion was of no interest, he had to interpret for one of the usual series of business meetings), and he, for whom all his life waterfalls possessed such a special role, now in an utterly astounding manner precisely here in Shanghai had to realize the reason why all his life he had yearned to see the Angel, or the Victoria, or at the very least the Schaffhausen Falls, precisely here in Shanghai where it was common knowledge that there were no waterfalls, for it all began with his finishing up his work for the day, and he was exhausted, he had been a simultaneous interpreter ever since he could remember, and of all things it was precisely simultaneous interpretation that exhausted him the most, especially when it happened to be for a business meeting in Asia, as was the case now, and especially when, at the obligatory dinner afterward, he was obliged to drink as much as he did this evening, well, what's done is done, in any case, here he was by eveningtime, a wrung-out dishrag, as they say, drunk as a skunk, a used up dishrag, this dead drunk, here he stood in the middle of the city, on the riverbank, soused, dead drunk, a wrung-out dishrag, speaking sotto voce and not being terribly witty: so this is Shanghai, meaning that here I am once again in Shanghai, he had to admit that, alas, he found the fresh air had not been all that beneficial even though, as they say, he had nourished great hopes for it, since he was aware, if we may speak of awareness in his case now, aware that he had drunk way too much, he had far more than what he could handle, but he had been in no position to refuse, one glass followed another, too many of them, and already in the room he had felt sick, a vague notion churning inside him that he needed fresh air, fresh air, but once outside in the fresh air, the world began to spin around him even more, true, it was still better here outside than indoors, he no longer remembered if he had been dismissed or had simply sneaked outside, it was alas no longer meaningful to speak of memory in his case at this moment as he stood in a peculiar posture near the upper sector of the Bund's ponderous arc of buildings, he leaned against the railing and eyed the celebrated Pudong on the other side of the river, and by this time the almost disastrously fresh air had come to have enough of an effect for his consciousness to clear up for a single moment and abruptly let him know that all this did not interest him the least little bit, and he was terribly bored in Shanghai, here, standing on the riverbank near the upper sector of the Bund's ponderous arc of buildings, this was made evident by his posture, and what was he supposed to do now?—after all he couldn't remain leaning on that railing till the end of time in this increasingly calamitous condition, he was alone, his consciousness blurred once again, his head was swimming, obviously a restaurant was not an option in this instance, he could not bear the thought of eating, in this unsteady state even the thought of moving on and sitting down in a restaurant just to get through the evening appeared unbearable, and anyway he was not in the mood, not in the mood for anything, but then his consciousness drifted back to inquire, what now, was he going to stay here forever? shouldn't he take in a movie? or some sort of night club, but were there any night clubs around here? he shook his head on the riverbank, but instantly stopped, because shaking his head made his nausea even worse, so he stared strictly straight ahead, as one contemplating the Pudong, although all he saw was the filthy water of the river, and he was getting totally bored with the scene, yet he was free for the entire evening, in fact to be more accurate this was the one and only evening designated as free time for him by the interpretation service that had flown him out here for a total of three days, only one evening; this thought began to revolve in his head, this was his only free evening, and he did not know what to do with it, he kept his stare fixed on the scummy surface of the river, while his conscious mind whispered to him that all right then, he would not do anything on this free evening, quit agonizing here about what to do, he should pick himself up and sober up, go back to his hotel, lie down in his bed and watch TV, back in Europe he had rarely watched Chinese TV programs, his room would be pleasantly cool, he would call room service for a ton of ice and perhaps a bottle of Perrier, yes, a big bottle of real Perrier would be great, the thought electrified him, so that he no longer felt it was so terrible that inexplicably the world continued to spin around him worse than before, and even though he hadn't succeeded through sheer willpower in sobering up, he somehow managed to find his way to Fuzhou Road, so things seemed to have taken an auspicious turn; however after a few steps, a dreadful nausea overtook him, yet he did not stop to throw up, he kept walking, that is he managed to walk all right, his face had turned red and his hair stood on end, although he was blissfully oblivious of this, it would not have interested him anyway, only walking interested him, and the hope that this nausea would soon start to let up and he would soon be back in his hotel; he envisioned the hotel room, he could feel the cool of the air conditioning, as he walked on up Fuzhou Road, it was out of the question that he squeeze himself into a tight taxi cab, or take the subway, both of which would have been immediately on hand especially here on Fuzhou Road, he had to keep to the surface, the wide-open surface, this thought rumbled within his head, and he kept breathing as deeply as he was able, great gulps of air deep into the lungs, deep into the lungs, this thought kept rattling inside his head, but he did not feel any better, in fact he began to feel worse, even though the weather, now that it was getting near ten p.m., could be said to be almost pleasant, he walked on, had to stop and throw up while alarmed pedestrians gave him a wide berth, then he set out once more, time and again staggering and regaining his balance at the last instant, then staggering and regaining his balance once more, and he kept on marching, marching unstoppably on Fuzhou Road; of course at the time he did not yet think—for the time hadn't yet arrived for thinking—that this was how he would go on, on foot, far from it, in fact the thought kept bobbing up that he would like to, as they say, *seize the next available opportunity,* but he did not seize the next available opportunity because he didn't know what it was, as it happened he just kept walking until he arrived at the corner of the square with that most suggestive name, Peoples' Square, where all of a sudden, as if he had planned on this all along, without the least hesitation, he turned left, and his movements might have been read as intending to cross the square diagonally, but that was not what happened, because his feet came to a different decision, and even though his upper body had been inclined toward this diagonal crossing, his feet kept him on a course straight ahead, so that there was nothing else to do but advance making a beeline now that his nausea seemed to abate a little, however by now he started to feel rather spent, and began to regret setting out on foot, he scolded himself, you are an idiot to be gadding about in Shanghai, where every distance is ten times and a hundred times the usual, especially when they had given him a coupon for the taxi, and, had he chosen to take public transportation, his ticket would have been free, the firm had a relatively liberal policy in these matters, but by now it made no difference, he waved off the thought, but the broad gesture forced him to halt, whereas he had to be moving on; a conscious voice inside kept reminding him that he had to be on his way now, so he set out once again, and walked on, for on top of everything else he had arrived in a place where a blurry awareness dawned that he hadn't the faintest notion of how to find the bus, the 72, which was his only chance; he was now falling in love with the 72, he had always been very fond of it, and would always love it, because of the route of this bus, although momentarily unavailable in his head, nor was much else readily available there, only the desire to find the 72 at any cost, because only the 72 could solve his problem, only the 72, repeated the voice of consciousness inside him—for this consciousness knew that ordinarily this bus and its route were quite familiar to him, this was a popular, far-ranging bus line that he had used on countless occasions whenever he sojourned in Shanghai, that is why, thundered a voice inside him, you must find this bus—and so he trudged on, keeping the cardinal points in mind, because even in this condition he was approximately aware of them, he never made a mistake determining which way was north, south, east and west, basically, and he was sufficiently familiar with Shanghai by now not to really get lost anywhere in the city, as long as it was the inner city, the central parts taken in a broader sense, which was the case here, he was walking in the park at Peoples' Square, although he wasn't aware of this, and then his feet led him in a southerly direction, walking down the entire length of a smaller side street, and he suddenly found himself in the former French Quarter, in that old French Quarter that had undergone such an incredible rebirth; a reawakening consciousness within him made him gawk, the place had come to life since he had last been here, a little Saint-Germain-des here in Shanghai, he tried to pronounce the words, a Saint-Germ … a Saint-des, or at least it had a slightly similar character, he gave up trying to pronounce it, now this main street here, this Huaihai Road, in contrast to that other one, was exaggeratedly long, and the crowds far too thick, it was Friday evening, the shops were still open, the restaurants and all other imaginable places of entertainment still open, everything was still open, life was never allowed to come to a standstill here, the milling crowds were simply insane, the traffic tremendous, and everything at a speed exactly one size greater than one's sanity could withstand, this was the opinion beginning to take place in him, one size too big, thought the reviving consciousness inside him, for if you were to label what is bearable a size 3X, then only 4X, and that alone, would fit Shanghai's size, or how else to put it, he thought as he elbowed his way forward through the crowds in front of the brilliantly lit store windows, this speed was appalling, sweeping him away who knows where, and evidently no one was aware that it was so awful, come on now, his steps slowed down, this time his feet obeyed him, letting him pose the question: come on now, people, where are you off to in such a rush, really, and anyway why is everyone in such a rush here, and he turned his head left and right, but because of the instant vertigo, he quickly stopped doing that, and once again as if his head were propped up, balanced on his neck, he fixed his stare on a single point, it is Friday night here, and furthermore if I pick any one person to look at, for instance this well-dressed woman here, her hands clutching two shopping bags from elegant stores, one cannot claim that she is in such an insane rush, but the moment his gaze returned to take in the entirety of the crowds passing on the sidewalk he once again felt the senseless chaos of this tempo to be unbearable and insane, why couldn't they just stroll? he stared provocatively at one face after another, all over the world it is Friday night, ten-thirty or eleven, it makes no difference, the air is pleasant and getting more and more so, as if the air had stirred slightly, it was not quite a breeze, no, not quite, after all this was Shanghai in August, an inferno, but it seemed that a breath of air had ever so slightly caressed them all, all of them milling chaotically about on Huaihai Road, for now he felt himself capable of perceiving even this, that it was chaos, and this perception may have been the first sign of his recovery, perceiving that these people, all of these people here, were chaotically and utterly insanely rushing and milling about, forward and back, across and in and up and down, an insanely humongous hurly-burly, this was Shanghai, and elsewhere all over the world about this time, people would be slowing down, it was the end of the week, people—he craned toward the oncoming faces like some prophet struggling to make fools see the light, here you are on Huaihai Road, fine, so you do a bit of shopping, that's good, then a bit of dining out, or a bit of chit-chat, or whatever, okay, but no, these people here acted as if they had gone haywire, the place was truly like a madhouse, so he took an abrupt turn to the right, that is, in a semicircular arc he crossed over to the other side of the street thanks to the successful action of automobiles rushing to his aid with screeching brakes, he managed to just barely fit into the fraction of time that helpful drivers provided for his free passage among their vehicles, across and up and away; that seemed to be his apparently resolute plan, to take Madang Lu toward the north, this had suddenly flashed inside him like some traffic light, because I've had enough of this, I'll go up here, this way, and indeed this maneuver worked, ah, this will mean only a slight detour, here I am in this little street—as it happened it was a narrow little side street, a tiny European-sized passage, one might even say it had tight Parisian dimensions, he said to himself, so that alongside the car traffic the pedestrians only had a narrow sidewalk that was anything but commodious, true, but that frantic rush on Huaihai Road, at least that had been left behind—here he no longer felt the desperate scramble that reigned back there, over here people somehow weren't in such a hurry, after all this street had a truly European, almost Parisian coziness, this somehow seems to work, he nodded, this Parisian notion, and he marched on, slightly relieved, until he glimpsed the end of the street and saw that there, where the street ended—in fact quite near him up ahead—the grim hulk of a highway spanned across above street level, just like some monster, he thought with a grin, as if some Golem was lying on his back there, his sprawling body inscribing a neat arc between two building blocks, he said to himself on glimpsing it, for from here on he was capable of saying things to himself, such as: *oh no, not this;* these superhighways in Shanghai assumed such proportions that it was basically impossible to walk over to the other side, and he was just too tired for this, or how to put it, this just wouldn't work for one so soused, he was too exhausted to struggle with an expressway like this, a pedestrian, he now thought quite lucidly, in the vicinity of an expressway like this simply doesn't stand a chance; as they say, *his fate is sealed,* and once more he thought of the bus, what was he doing here wandering around on foot, his feet were burning with weariness, to say no more of the rest of him, he cautioned himself, in a word, the feet have had it, he decided, and instead of quickly looking for a bus stop, for the 72, here he was trudging on, and why was he still on foot? he asked himself, but then he remembered that he was probably in the best location to find a way out, for let's see now, as his two precious feet put on the brakes, here I am on Madang Lu Road, with Huaihai Road behind me, and in front of me Jinling Xi Lu, therefore it must be right around here, near precisely this expressway, there has to be, there actually was, a bus stop for the 72 around here, he recalled, and the outlines of his whereabouts gradually became more and more familiar—where he stood and where that expressway was and the nearest bus stop—as long as he now stood on Madang Lu, oh yes, and he set out again, he should be advancing right alongside precisely this expressway, the Yan'an Gaojia Lu, so this had been the reason for his not turning back when he glimpsed that grim hulking mass, this was the reason for his walking on, across from the Yan'an, and this was why, when he reached the edge of the sprawling monster—he grinned again, for he hadn't the slightest notion why but he found this monster amusing—this was why when he reached the edge of this famous superhighway and ascertained that there was no sign of a bus stop, not here, there, or anywhere, that he started to walk on, these dear precious feet, he glanced down at them, as they went, one after the other, and if his eyes were not deceiving him, which could just be possible, he thought—or his memory played him false, which would not be surprising—then his instincts—his vision and his memory—in sum his instincts would find what he was looking for, because it had to be there, he thought, making a wry face, it would have to be there, therefore onward, take a left here and onward along the Yan'an, and he looked at those precious feet down there, his feet, the way one went after the other, and he was certain now that everything would be all right, and if he continued on the Yan'an, straight ahead, persistently, then it was only a few hundred meters, at the most five hundred and there it would be, the longed for, the redeeming, the homeward-bound 72, as he eyed proudly those two feet down there, and he was positive that with them along, all would turn out well.

I do simultaneous interpretation, he said aloud, and paused, to see if someone had heard him, but no one had at all, and so he couldn't count on getting help, whereas he was in desperate need of help, of immediate rescue, instant intervention, urgent angelic miracle working, oh well, of course, how could he have imagined that his announcement, in the Hungarian language, and in Shanghai, would be of any help, yes, that would be a tough one to explain, but to explain anything in his situation would have been a chore, I do simultaneous interpretation, he repeated therefore, while to the best of his ability he kept his head—that is the skull where the pain originated—completely still as he pronounced these words, his whole body went completely rigid, that was how he managed to contain the pain up there, trying to keep this pain from growing any more intense, for this was an intense pain that kept getting more and more so, it was getting so intense, so powerful, that it simply blinded him, and somehow it had become detached, an alien, he refused to acknowledge that it was his, because this pain, this infernal pain, inexpressible in words, could not be acknowledged, it was such torture, and descended on him so swiftly, it struck him like lightning, or to put it more accurately, he was suddenly aware that here he sat stone cold sober, here, somewhere, in a location impossible to identify for the time being, all around him the roar, rumble, thunder of traffic that was insane, everywhere, overhead, down below, on the left and on the right, yes, that horrific din simply everywhere, and here he was sitting right in the middle of it, but where this here was he had not the faintest idea; blinded, he could not see, and for that matter he could not hear, for the din he was hearing was just as powerful, and was increasing at the same rate as the pain inside his skull, so that he heard nothing, thus he was deaf as well as blind, and now he could only imagine saying who he was but could not actually say it, for he had become dumb as well, in order that the pain should not increase, the question was of course: could anything that hurt so bad that it was unbearable manage to hurt even more, the answer was yes it could, he concluded, and something throbbed mightily beyond this pain, therefore he just sat there, keeping still, his pose unchanged, here, somewhere, all around him, that roaring, rumbling, thundering, and there was nothing else to do but remain like this, doing nothing, saying nothing, not moving, not thinking about where he was and what was going on, yes, especially not thinking, not even about why he was quite sober now, hadn't he been dead drunk, drunk as a skunk, yes he had been extremely drunk, but stop remembering, he admonished himself frantically, for obviously to remember was to move, and his only chance now was to renounce all movement, to come to a full stop, so that this pain would lessen inside his head, no speaking, no hearing, no thinking, no remembering, no, not even any hoping, for to hope was also to move, and even that could jog this completely paralyzed state he tried to maintain, coming to a full stop, so that the pain should diminish, should subside, and this strict discipline had its effect, albeit after an immeasurable length of time, after the passage of days? nights? and more days? and more nights? all of a sudden, pow, it began to subside, diminish, and it stopped, and the moment arrived when, after days and nights, nights and days—he was able to open his eye only a slit, at first only a slit, but it was enough for him to establish that he had never sat in the place where he was sitting, and perhaps no one had ever sat there before, for he immediately realized that he was sitting in the middle of expressways curving every which way, or to put it more accurately, expressways arching in various directions, he was surrounded by expressways, no mistaking it, the image seen through the slit told him: expressways overhead, expressways down below, expressways to the left and finally expressways to the right as well, naturally his first thought was that he was not well, and the next thought was that not only he but this whole thing around him was not well, elevated expressways on many levels, who ever heard of such a thing, in this manner he shrank for a while from the recognition, reluctant to acknowledge it, because as a simultaneous interpreter he possessed certain areas of specialization, one of these being traffic and transport systems, and since he was a simultaneous interpreter with a specialty in traffic and transport systems he had a good hunch by now about where he found himself except that he refused to believe it, for after all there was no way he could be here; he shook his head metaphorically, for of course he couldn't actually shake his head on account of the pain, no human being could possibly be in the place where he now was, notwithstanding the fact that he could see the famous pillar down below with the dragons winding around it, oh no, he thought now, oh no, I am inside Nine Dragon Crossing, but how can I possibly be inside it, that is the question, Nine Dragon Crossing, or as the locals say, *Jialongzhu Jiaoji*, is not something a human being can be inside of, and the moment arrived when that slit became a full view, because by now he dared to open one eye, the pain persisted with a dulled reign inside his head, dulled, so that he thought the hope that might now rekindle in him would not be entirely unfounded, and he peeked out through this one eye, for he had opened only his left one, he opened it wide, or one might have said that the eye simply popped wide open, for he was not hallucinating, he was indeed inside Nine Dragon Crossing, or as the locals said *Jialonzhu Jiaoji,* he was deep inside it, with his back leaning against the railing of some sort of pedestrian bridge, as if someone had propped him up against it, who could have done that, he hadn't the faintest idea, in any case here he was, propped up, because this what do you call it, pedestrian bridge, had a plexiglass railing, a waist-high plastic siding along its full length, obviously to prevent one from toppling and falling among the cars screaming by, to prevent you from toppling, he repeated, and now his other eye popped open most boldly, for this was the moment when he realized that he was high up, that this pedestrian bridge as its name indicated was a real bridge that rose in the air above ground level and was not merely bridging over something but in fact conducted the pedestrian at various levels of elevation among the expressways that ran up above and down below, running this way and that, was this a sane thing to do?! he asked himself, no it was not, he answered, so that after all—and here he lowered his glance to look in front of his feet—then I must be crazy, this is how it had to end, I got royally drunk, *perfectamente* drunk, so drunk that I ended up here, in this madness, I am imprisoned inside this madness, for it was obvious that he was a prisoner, he was unable to budge, and now it was not that the courage to move was lacking, for after all that pain in his upper atmospheric region had considerably abated, he still lacked the energy, he was weary, so weary that even this eyeballing had exhausted him— the way he had first opened the left eye a tiny slit, then fully, and then the other eye too to look around—but of course this hadn't involved moving his head, no, at first he had cautiously rotated only his eyeballs, without moving his head, it took a while before he dared to do that, and then he did, and it was a success, the pain did not increase, it stayed at the same dull level, then he once again opened both eyes, to take in once again where he was, and he spoke, and this time he did not say who he was, but instead said, I am stone cold sober, my head is clear, I am able to think, I can see and hear, but I wish I could not see and hear, because now that I can see what I see and hear what I hear I can also think about where I am, and that is impossible, it is not possible that I am inside Nine Dragon Crossing, and it is quite another matter that the well-known pillar upon which Nine Dragon Crossing symbolically and not so symbolically rests, stands there down below in plain view, nonetheless it cannot be that I am sitting inside Nine Dragon Crossing, or as the locals refer to it, *Jialonzhu Jiaoji,* for a person cannot sit inside Nine Dragon Crossing, one may drive through it in a car, and that's it, this is an intersection after all, a world-famous hub, a so-called metropolitan divided highway intersection, this much he could recall at a pinch from the specialist vocabulary he carried in his head, and a person could not climb inside such a metropolitan highway whatchamacallit, especially not so that he ends up with his back propped up against the plexiglass siding of a pedestrian footbridge, and he is half toppled over and therefore leaning on his left hand to keep from sliding any more, no, not this way nor any other way, this is absurd, I'm probably not insane, he reassured himself, but only hallucinating, it is not unusual when one gets as drunk as I did, which was *perfectamente,* as Malcolm Lowry says in *Under the Volcano,* and I can remember walking on the Huaihai, and I can clearly recall the Madang Lu, and the Yan'an, oh yes, the last image flashed up for him, he saw a man, his shirt soaked in vomit, his cotton pants soaked in vomit, light summer leather shoes soaked in vomit, and that was himself, and now he was here, sliding downward inside Nine Dragon Crossing, for that left arm, that left, was getting weaker, it could no longer support this body, that shirt soaked in vomit, those pants soaked in vomit, and those light summer leather shoes soaked in vomit, he would slide all the way down, he realized, and he slid down and instantly fell asleep as if hit over the head, when in fact he was simply tired, horribly and inconceivably tired, right here in the middle of Nine Dragon Crossing.

*

I am a simultaneous interpreter, and I have perfect recall—he rose
from his humiliating supine position on the pedestrian bridge—everything that needs to be known from a transport-systems point of view
about an intersection like this is in my head down to the last detail, and
he stood up, and although he had to grab on to the handrail at first,
after the first three or four meters he let go of it and took some unaided
steps relishing the full dignity of his balance, thus setting out on the
pedestrian bridge toward somewhere, but as the bridge right away
curved into a turn, leading toward a future that was too uncertain for
him, he decided it was wiser to stop, and so he halted, then looked
down into the depths, after which he looked up at the heights, as if to
make sure that all was well in his head, and by now all was well, his head
was clear, his head no longer ached, his head was capable of quite lucidly making inquiries into existence, namely his own, which he proceeded to do, to wit; if he found himself here as the passive subject of
some sort of obscure history by now forever destined to remain obscure, obviously there must be a reason—and meanwhile he kept
glancing down into the depths and up into the heights—and this reason must be none other than the fact—this realization tore into him—
that I have come to a point in my life where I must now declare what I
have learned about the world in the course of sixty years, nearly forty
of which have been as a simultaneous interpreter, and if I don't then I
will take it to the grave with me, but that, and he continued his train of
thought, that, however, will not happen, and I am going to make my
declaration right here, and these sentences followed one another in his
head smoothly enough, except at this moment he took another look at
the depths and another at the heights, in short he looked in every direction that this Nine Dragon Crossing, or as locals called it, *Jialonzhu
Jiaoji,* had extended its innumerable parts, these expressways winding

pell-mell in all directions, divided into various levels, shuffling them up and dispatching them on their way, well now, at this point he rubbed his eyes, dug his fingers into his tousled hair a few times, then smoothed it down, and just stared ahead at a certain point in the thick of Nine Dragon Crossing, even as his glance already informed each and every particle of the pedestrian bridge—the handrail, the plexiglass siding, and the entire surface of the walkway—that indeed, he would gladly declare himself here and now, but the problem was that he had learned nothing about the world, and so what was he to say, what indeed: that he was a simultaneous interpreter who had lived close to forty years devoted exclusively to his profession, something, and here he raised his index finger, that made him realize that he was speaking aloud on the pedestrian bridge, which as a matter of fact he had always liked to do, I—and he pointed at himself, as if he were addressing an audience—have always loved simultaneous interpretation, true, it is exhausting—he would be the first to admit, it was very exhausting, in fact for him nothing in the world was more exhausting than simultaneous interpretation, yet he loved doing it; he was not claiming that, for instance when he looked at, say, a deck of cards, he did not have some unanswered questions, because for that matter he did have some, particularly regarding that deck of cards, because aside from his profession he also loved card games, and his question was, well now, was this a full deck of cards, or was it merely any forty-eight individual cards, but they were only those kinds of questions, the one particular question regarding the world itself, which, he was well aware, might be expectable from an experienced simultaneous interpreter in his sixties, that one particular question, no, it had never occurred to him, so that if fate had now cast him here to make a declaration about that then he was in a fine pickle, for he didn't know anything about anything, there was nothing he could say about the world in general, nothing that he could put in the form of a philosophy of life, no, nothing like that, here he gave a slight shake of his head, what spoke to him is what he saw here, from this pedestrian bridge, but about life in general, alas, he could say nothing, because let's take this place for instance, here was this pedestrian bridge where he was standing, from here—and his arm inscribed a sweeping arc including the entirety of Nine Dragon Crossing—looking at it from here the whole thing had no meaning whatsoever, none, in fact seen from here this Nine Dragon Crossing gives the distinct impression that the whole business began like this: let's say, he said, first there was one highway, say, from the west to the east, and that meant the highway also ran from east to west, so that here in our example there happens to be—and he looked down from the bridge—Yan'an Road, well then, this three-lane highway—that is three lanes in each direction—had come to reach this point where its passage was intersected at right angles by a highway arriving from another direction, that happened to be, he went on, in the case of our example, the famous Nanbei Lu, that is to say this meeting created an intersection, but since we are dealing with expressways here, in a metropolitan setting, in the case of such an intersection we may very well count on the arrival of automobiles with a variety of destinations, automobiles that will not necessarily choose to race on straight ahead in the same direction, but, for instance, one might want to turn; instead of heading straight on, one of them might insist on turning, say, to the left, and this sets in motion the whole calamitous rigmarole, since other automobiles with similar intentions will arrive in great numbers at this intersection, thus creating a traffic control problem given the four cardinal directions, isn't that so, and he looked around and up and down in the midst of the insane din, theoretically four times three, that is twelve different directions that become possible, that is to say, and he spread his arms momentarily, let's take it from the beginning, here comes an automobile on the Yan'an from the west, with its own individual destination, it may on the one hand keep going straight, or else it may turn at a right angle to the left, to proceed in a northern direction on the Nanbei Lu, or of course it may take a ninety degree turn to the right to continue its journey south on this stretch of the Nanbei, so that's three directions, and this automobile might have three little siblings, because in addition to itself there are three others in the four approaches to the intersection, therefore we may conclude, he went on with his chain of thought, that altogether there are four automobiles, and for each we must guarantee three possible choices, thus giving birth to twelve possible directions, thus creating, he gave an anguished sigh, an infernal clash, for we cannot call what has been created here anything else than infernal—because a simple, straightforward situation gave rise to an infernal structure of a degree of complexity such as THIS, and with increasing horror he now eyed from the inside the concrete mass of manifold expressways arching all around him up above and down below and this way and that, an infernal structure without any rational explanation whatsoever, what else should he, a simultaneous interpreter unqualified to provide answers to the great questions, call it, he was not an expert on transport technology, only a simultaneous interpreter specializing in this, among other things—and he wished to emphasize *this among other things*, in other words, how should he put it, given that simple starting point, that single automobile approaching from the west and intending to go in one of three possible directions (straight ahead, left to the north, or right to the south), well then, there were three others like it, in a word, given such a clear-cut situation why do we end up with something like THIS?! and once again his eyes swept over the horrific cavalcade of ponderous expressway ramps stretching and arching above and below each other, and he could only gape this way and that way, he tried to follow individual stretches of highway in order to find out what direction they went in, but it proved impossible, at least from here, from the inside, the entire thing had ended up so bafflingly complex, so impossible to survey at a glance that if you looked at it, as he did now, then sooner or later not only your eyes, but your brain started to hurt, because it was all exactly as he had just described and demonstrated on the basis of the technological vocabulary of transport he had proudly referred to, for indeed in the beginning there were only two basic directions, and these two have remained—the east-west directions of the Yan'an Lu and the north-south directions of Nanbei Lu—that is, two major metropolitan traffic arteries intersecting each other at ground level, the vehicles moving on them were regulated by traffic lights and if one arrived as a pedestrian at this intersection, his fate would be relegated to a so-called elevated pedestrian crossing, well enough, this was down at ground level, however oncoming vehicles arrived with various other destinations that could only be provided for by infernal regulations, in other words on top of this straightforward ground-level intersection they had constructed a so-called "complex," a so-called "stelliform" metropolitan expressway monster, naturally only after performing the in this case indispensable seven-day Buddhist ritual to pacify the Nine Dragons that had been disturbed down below and after this ritual, the builders could go ahead first of all with the central pillar representing the nine dragons, then proceed with the reinforced ferroconcrete columns supporting individual sections of the expressway with their cantilever brackets, braces, buttresses, beams, and half-beams, the superstructures and underpinnings, after which under the alarmed, watchful eyes of the citizens the construction progressed and expanded and sprawled and progressed some more and rose higher and expanded even more and sprawled wider until the entire project was finished, so that today it looks like this: progressing from the bottom up, the first level above the ground-level intersection carries a divided expressway going north-south and south-north, thus replicating what transpires down below in two opposing directions, well enough, but on top of this they were obliged to add another elevated level that was designated, not by simultaneous interpreters specializing in transport technology, but by the traffic design experts themselves as the "first level of intercardinal directions," by which they meant expressways composed of north-west and south-east indirect connecting ramps and the south-west and north-east *direct* connecting ramps, which is far from the end of the story, since now we come to the third level, named again not by simultaneous interpreters but by traffic design experts "the second level of intercardinal directions," meaning the north-west and south-east direct connecting ramps and south-west and north-east *indirect* connecting ramps, only to crown all this on a fourth level with a so-called "alternate direct thruway," which means none other than the high elevated replica of the east-west and west-east highway that had already been built in a rational manner at the ground level that was our starting point, so there you see what happens when the experts succeed in creating a solution, namely in this case Nine Dragon Crossing, or as they themselves named it, *Jiulongzhu Jiaoji*, when they create it and not for instance simultaneous interpreters, which he happens to be, he said this underneath the expressway, eyeing that notorious pillar, the Nine Dragon Pillar, and in his opinion what happened here had started with a sound concern—automobiles arriving from four cardinal directions intending to depart in twelve intercardinal directions, all these automobiles demonstrating that they were unwilling to wait, unwilling to be slowed down by traffic control lights that alternately permit and prohibit passage in the twelve directions, they (the ones arriving from the four basic directions) were too numerous, and in time would be even more numerous, and with such a multitude no system of traffic control lights would ever be able to cope—and therefore all of you, the devil said to them, will be paralyzed, all of you, the devil grinned at them, will not go anywhere from here, you will remain at ground level as eternal prisoners of traffic lights now red, now green, therefore allow me to suggest, said the devil to the traffic-control designers, that you build Nine Dragon Crossing in light of the above, or as you would call it, the devil said with a shrug, *Jiulongzhu Jiaoji,* because this is the sole solution that makes possible the speed at which the city is able to operate, and of course the traffic-control designers conceded that building a Nine Dragon Crossing was imperative to handle the increasing speed and so they built it, after which on Nanbei Elevated Road alone, that is on Nanbei Gaojia Lu alone, they constructed seven or so others similar to this, and the situation on Yan'an Elevated Road, that is Yan'an Gaojia Lu, appeared to be no better, in a word, the desired speed was attained, and only he—and here it was the simultaneous interpreter speaking again, the livid-faced condemned man of Nine Dragon Crossing—only he alone didn't understand why we needed such speed, speed that moreover would soon have to be increased, god is there no one, he now cried into the artificially illuminated firmament of Nine Dragon Crossing, no one who understands that we simply don't need such speed?!—and he waited a while, but nobody responded, therefore he shoved himself away from the railing against which he had been leaning for the last few minutes, and taking the utmost care he nonetheless set out in the dark on that pedestrian bridge curving away into an uncertain future, until after taking exactly seventeen steps his form disappeared beyond the bend, and thus shortly thereafter all human presence ceased within the interior hell of Nine Dragon Crossing which is no place for a human being in any case, because human beings have no business to be there.

Your Perrier, sir, said the room-service waiter outside the door, but then he had to send him back for an additional bottle, and he had to request that the first bottle be exchanged for a larger one, then he had two or three fresh pitchers of ice brought up because after he at last arrived in his room and toppled onto the bed, it was not so much that his head began to ache immediately as all of a sudden there was a large bowl of mush in place of a head; he had entered the room, taken off his clothes, kicked off his shoes, and thrown himself on the bed, arranging for everything from there, the phone within reach: his room service order, the modification of the order, the repeat of the order, and so on, meanwhile lying on his back and not moving, resting his head—that bowl of mush—against the pillow, his eyes closed; that's how it was for a while, until the horrendous stink he himself emanated began to bother him, whereupon he crawled to the bathroom, brushed his teeth, turned on the shower and scrubbed his body with soap and remained under the shower for as long as his strength held out, then toweled himself dry, sprayed frightful amounts of hotel deodorant on himself, pulled on a clean t-shirt and underpants, and before lying back down he took the soiled garments and his light summer leather shoes, stuffed them in a plastic bag that he tied with a tight knot before placing it outside in front of the door, then stretched out on the bed, turned on the TV, merely listening to the sound without watching, for his head continued to remain a bowl of mush, and this was all right, things were all right now, his eyes shut, the TV on, the sound not too loud, and a voice was telling him on the Hong Kong channel last used the night before, the Whole had no purpose, because there was nothing outside the Whole from where anything could lead to here, for there was no place from where … and there was no outside, nor could it be its own purpose, for the goal was always beyond the point where someone desires a goal, but the Whole had no meaning, if it had one, the Whole would be subsumed inside a narrative that always possesses one essential feature, that it must have an end, whereas the Whole cannot have an end, and therefore we may say that it has no narrative, thus no meaning, and thus no aim or goal or purpose, and if this is so, then there is no existence either, because there is actually no Whole, this was a man's voice, softly droning, a singsong voice, on and on, but as he listened with eyes closed, lying supine, close to drifting off, with a full load of mush inside his head, he listened to this or rather let himself hear it, he had the feeling that the voice was not so much trying to say something to him as to lull him, rock him with the southern, musical sound of Cantonese dialect, to smooth away everything inside him that was rough, everything that might spill out, everything that was aching, the sound cautiously enfolded, cooled, and cooled and cooled again that serious load of mush inside his head, and it felt good, and this was precisely what he needed so that he let them keep telling him via this South-Chinese musical instrument dipped in a Cantonese dialect that the Whole had no aim, no meaning, since the Whole could not be enclosed within the causal web of goals and rationality, for then the Whole would of necessity become entangled in a narrative, whereas among other features a narrative has one characteristic, namely that it has to have an end, didn't we already cover this? that large load of mush now inquired inside his head, no, a voice replied and continued, *the Whole cannot have an end and endless narratives do not exist, thus it has no goal, thus it has no meaning, from which it follows that all that we call the world, the universe, the cosmos suspiciously lacks any palpable content, in other words, it does not exist, in other words the Whole has no existence, it does not exist, because if it existed, if it did exist, then every reference to the smaller wholes and to the relationships between these smaller wholes would refer to it as well, but it does not, therefore the Whole does not exist, but at the same time it is also true that from the everyday experience of something always giving rise to something else, that gives rise to something else again, we cannot conclude that from all discernible present, past, and future wholes it follows that there must exist a grand totality of these, this does not agree with the concept of the Whole, and not because there is no infinity, that is not the reason for its nonexistence*—here for a few moments someone must have plugged in an electric razor or some other appliance in the adjacent room behind the TV set, because for several moments the TV began to buzz, but really only for a few moments, that was all, and then everything came back as before, the program with the man's voice in a singsong drone, but it was more than just singsong and droning, it was downright insinuatingly mellifluous, and constantly, during every least fraction of an instant, aiming to persuade, continuously and melodiously seductive therefore, and vivid, as the Cantonese dialect always is, and it was just in the middle of saying, in this sweetly persuasive, ever vivid Cantonese dialect, that *the entirety of the Whole is not a sum of the smaller wholes but simply exists ... if it existed, except that it does not, therefore there isn't any sense in talking about it, which would be all right, except for one problem, that now the belief in it also has no sense, however, without it our entire way of thinking collapses, for we cannot coexist with a Whole that does not exist, a Whole that does not amount to the sum of its parts, we cannot bear the thought that there is something that does not exist, something we cannot conceive of, something in front of which all our thoughts, all our intuitions, all our ideas collapse into sheer meaninglessness, because the merest thought of it is false, wrong, misleading, stupid, but on the other hand if this is how things stand, and there is no single ultimate Whole that contains all the other wholes, then there are no wholes that are the sum of their parts either, and this is how it could happen that it makes no sense to inquire about the meaning of the smaller wholes, even if, and especially if, we are unable to do without the causal-experimental, that is with the extraordinarily persuasive power of "if I drop it from above, it falls," the extraordinarily persuasive power of which lies in its simplicity, in its so-called obviousness, this is what we are obsessed with, antecedents and consequences, this is the fashion,* said the man's voice, *this is the latest fashion of the mind, the latest fashion of the imagination, the pattern for our thinking and imagining how things are, that is to say we work from patterns, just like trained workers, the only problem being that we have a need for encountering the Unapproachable, and that is how things that are unapproachable come about, and here, at this juncture, alas, faith is least helpful, because faith is the mode of handling our fears, and so our God, our*

gods, the so-called higher regions, the transcendent, all of these are pro-
duced by the outrageously complicated web of errors stemming from our
fears, based on our faith, and toppling us into calamitous stupidities, all of
that in such a miraculous manner that we could never give them up, we
continuously manufacture them even as they keep on creating us, it is a kind
of division of labor, the wages are considerable, we receive the Infinite, we
receive the Eternal, even though, as Buddhists remind us, these are nonex-
istent in two ways: on the one hand, they have no reality, and on the other
hand they have no unreality either, I must tell you, the TV set droned on
in that Cantonese dialect, *it is high time I told you, it is late enough that*
you can bear this thought, the TV set tried joking, *that in fact Such Things*
Do Not Exist, not only do they not exist, they are impossible, and not only
impossible, but any speech, thought, imagination, feeling and belief refer-
ring to them, that is to It—for It does not exist, is meaningless, after which
the only sensible thing to do is to remain silent, to refrain from speaking,
that is the only worthwhile thing to do, to refrain from speaking, that is the
only meritorious thing to do, so that someone, said the TV set, *was not act-*
ing meaningfully, worthily, or meritoriously ... and this was the point
where this senseless, unworthy, non-meritorious, melancholy, brooding, but all the while sweet-as-honey and vividly convincing prophetic
proclamation began to dissolve into a sound of an entirely different
order, the words, sentences, voice, speech, morphing in slow gossamer-
light increments into a so-called eternal sound of running water, but
no, not really the sound of water plashing, and he pulled the blanket
over himself for he was starting to shiver because the air conditioning
was set too high, no, this was not water plashing, it was a roar, like the
ocean, but no, not the ocean really, reflected that sizeable load of mush
inside his head, this was something else, this ... this sound, he now
recognized, before sleep swallowed him up, was a waterfall.

He woke immediately, as if jolted by electric shock, suddenly, instantly
becoming as alert as a mongoose; he looked at the TV set in disbelief,

but it was still the same man who had presumably been speaking all this while, and he was still having his say, but without the sound of his voice, only the waterfall sound could be heard, he leaped from the bed, sat down on its edge, and leaning forward stared at the TV set, the man was not a priest, not some kind of evangelist, he had a dark blue suit, metal-rim glasses, low forehead, thin lips, he stood on some sort of podium, as if this were a university lecture, he stood on that podium and he kept talking and talking without a voice, only the sound of the waterfall, which was exactly the same, oh my god, he clenched his fists in his lap, it was exactly the same as the sound of the waterfall that he had never been able to identify among those three, a nightmare, he thought, and pinched himself, but he was awake, it was still the same image of the man with the glasses on the podium, yet the soundtrack was a waterfall, but that couldn't be; he watched the TV screen panic-stricken, then less and less so, at last he calmed down, thinking that he would once again go over everything soberly, not that it would get him anywhere, he got nowhere, but all of a sudden the man with the metal-rim glasses disappeared from the screen, and the image now showed a cascading waterfall, and he slowly grasped that this was not some nightmare, it was simply that at four fifteeen a.m. in that Hong Kong TV studio no one gave a crap, they might have all fallen asleep, it was suddenly clear to him, they must have fallen asleep without switching the video and the audio was already coming on, that was it, that was the only possible explanation, there was nothing peculiar here, if you thought about it, he leaned forward even closer and watched the waterfall on the TV screen, and spoke out aloud, well then, this is it, here is that waterfall, coincidences do exist, it is not impossible that such a thing happens to you once, and now it has happened, such things can happen, he reassured himself, and then he just kept staring, staring at that waterfall on the TV set, he saw no subtitles whatsoever that could have helped to identify which one it was, the Angel, the Victoria, or possibly the Schaffhausen, all they showed was the waterfall itself, the sound was a steady roar, and inside his head, obviously still powerfully dazed by the long time he had spent listening in his sleep or half-awake to the man with the glasses, a flurry of words began to whirl again, that the Whole exists in its wholeness, the Parts in their own particularity, and the Whole and the Parts cannot be lumped together, they don't follow from one another, since after all the waterfall for example is not composed of its individual drops, for single drops would never constitute a waterfall, but drops nonetheless do exist, and how heartrendingly beautiful they can be when they sparkle in the sunlight, indeed how long do they exist? a flash, and they are gone, but they still have time in this almost timeless flash to sparkle, and in addition there is also the Whole, and how lovely that is, how fantastically beautiful, that this Whole, the waterfall as a Oneness, can appear—if only someday he were to make his way to the Angel, if someday he were to find his way to the Victoria, if he were to get at least one chance, the words whirled on inside his head, at least to visit the Schaffhausen Falls, because this was just like his own life; a new train of thought opened for him, his life, too, included the great problem of the Whole and its Parts, meaning that the two could not be superimposed or projected upon each other, for although it was true that his life had its moments, hours, and days that existed as these moments, hours, and days—and when they became the past, they did not get there from the present—his life, too, had its own Wholeness, his life would obviously sooner or later come to an end, but it would one day reach its own fullness and not be coming from the future, and thus there was something still in store for him—parts as well as the great Whole, this great Whole of his life, that would attain its shape and form at the moment, at the sacred moment when he died, the moment of death—that was what this waterfall roared, as he stared at the TV screen, leaning as close as possible so as not to miss a single droplet, and he let it roar on, his clenched fists tightened in his lap, he let it sing that fullness exists, and it has nothing to do with the past or with the future—it even has nothing to do with what happened to him yesterday, or happens today, or will happen tomorrow; he watched each and every drop of the waterfall, feeling an unspeakable relief, and savoring the taste of a new-found freedom, he understood that his life would be a full life, a fullness that was not made of its parts, the empty fiascos and empty pleasures of minutes and hours and days, no, not at all, he shook his head, while in front of him the TV set kept roaring, this fullness of his life would be something completely different, he could not as yet know in what way, and he never would know, because the moment when this fullness of his life was born would be the moment of his death—he shut his eyes, lay back on the bed and remained awake until it was morning, when he rapidly packed his things, and checked out at the reception desk with such a radiant face that they contacted the staff on his floor to check if he had taken anything with him, how could they have possibly understood what had made him so happy, how could the cab driver or the people at the airport understand, when they were not aware that such happiness existed, just as he himself was unable to disguise this happiness, he radiated it as he passed through the security check, he glowed as he boarded the plane, his eyes sparkled as he belted himself into his seat, just like a kid who has at last received the gift he dreamed of, because he was in fact happy, except he could not speak about it, because it was impossible to speak about what he had learned in Shanghai, there was indeed nothing to do but look out through the window of the plane at the blindingly resplendent blue sky, keeping a profound silence, and it no longer mattered which waterfall it was, it no longer mattered if he didn't see any of them, for it was all the same, it had been enough to hear that sound, and he streaked away at a speed of 900 km per hour, at an altitude of approximately ten thousand meters in a north by north-westerly direction, high above the clouds—in the blindingly blue sky toward the hope that he would die some day.

ONE TIME ON 381

In memory of the middle-aged Amalia Rodriques

H e would go away from here, take off for the south.
       There had been no wind since dawn, and there he stood among
the others in the swirling clouds of marble dust.

The white protective helmet was no help, and the black goggles
were no help, the kerchief tied to cover his mouth was no help, nor
was the cap with earflaps, none of them was ever any help, and so he
stood there with his white helmet, black goggles, kerchief covering his
mouth, waiting for his turn. There were still three adults with wheelbarrows ahead of him, the line advanced slowly, always just a tiny bit,
one small step at a time, then the wait until the line moved up another
shuffle, and at these times he too shuffled ahead in the line, because behind him were another four or five, all adults, so they all shuffled forth
in unison, he in the middle, bending forward, giving the wheelbarrow
a push, straightening up, waiting, then once more the same, always
the same, and while he waited he could only look on, look on at the
machine working up ahead. He looked on, without a thought in his
head, as did the others, for what was there to think about while looking at the machine, and what was there to look at in that machine one
gave no thought to, anyway, it was enough just to be in a permanent
state of dazed fatigue, just to be not thinking, only looking on, blindly,
like a statue, at the machine working in the sifting marble dust, at the
blade of the diamond saw cutting, with a force that was light as breath
and brutally powerful at the same time, one after another, thin slabs of

marble from the enormous blocks hoisted by the crane and left there in a heap. Farther away, a large rolling machine lumbered along atop the rocky cliff and its diamond saw blade was hard at work, except that it was a giant rotary cross-cut sawing machine rocking back and forth on rails—but that was truly not at all interesting to anyone, for who would be interested in seeing how it hacked its way into the wall of rock and how it hacked out the next block which would be conveyed by one of the cranes to somewhere in their vicinity, to be sliced into slabs in the midst of this snow-white inferno? Nobody was interested in anything here, and so there was nothing for them to look at, yet they still had to look at something lest they go mad in the din and dust, and so they looked at the machine in front of them cutting slabs as it sliced marble with a grating, screeching, agonizing siren scream, as that dreadful diamond-studded steel band revolved round and round, and advanced through the rock like a knife through butter.

He trundled the wheelbarrow a little further along and then he was once more at the head of the line. He adjusted the gloves on his hands, grabbed the slab of marble, swinging it slightly to find the necessary balance, until he could stagger back with it to his wheelbarrow, and then grasping the grooved rubber lining of the wheelbarrow's two handles he pushed it over to where the other slabs lay—eight times nineteen rows of Estremoz Crème thinly sliced—that he and his companions, working since dawn, had stacked so far.

He would leave this place and set out for the south.

They paid four euros for loading by hand, he had been doing this for eight months without a raise in pay, four euros and ten cents, that was it, in the sweltering sun, the suffocating marble powder, for four-ten from six to eleven a.m and four to nine p.m., and it's time for a break, he said under his breath, time for a break, and although he took his place in line again, and remained in this line for a little while, the others might have noted only that he no longer stood there, having shoved the wheelbarrow to the side, and only his back may have been visible, if at all, and then moments later his small thin figure vanished in the haze of the quarry.

He would never become a *canteiro*, don't even dream about it, the overseer at the mine told him. Be glad you get four-ten, put your shoulder to the wheel, like the others, and put on some weight, because skin-and-bones kids like you don't have very bright prospects at the quarry.

I'm going away, was what drummed inside his head.

He knew that he would be back, because he knew that there was no place for him elsewhere in the world, but he would go away now, no matter what happened, he would set out and head south.

He left the line and headed for the quarry's exit.

No one called out after him, perhaps no one had even noticed.

The town lay to the left.

He had to keep away from houses, because meeting anyone would instantly mess up the whole thing, and so he kept away from them, and taking quick steps past the lower edge of the town he soon found what he was looking for.

He was looking for Highway 381.

It ran from Estremoz through the forest to Redondo.

But he was not trying to get to Redondo.

He wanted to be on 381.

It was an asphalt-covered highway, paved in '61, and since then re-paved several times in the eighties, so that you couldn't find a single crack in the road, it was smooth as a mirror. As small kids they only dared to venture a little ways, as far as the river, and so Ribeira de Terra had somehow become the boundary, as if it were a road sign, thus far and no further under any circumstances.

It was an asphalt-covered highway and now, after ten, it was practically steaming in the heat—even through the thick soles of his boots he could feel it was hot as hell.

The dust and the din were the worst. Eight hours solid in the white stone dust, when already after the first half hour this white marble dust completely coated them—not even their eyes could be made out distinctly behind the protective goggles, only the grimy circles created by constant wiping, through which they could barely glimpse each other, and no one bothered anymore to crack the old joke, what's up, millers, did you lose your way and end up in a quarry?

No one had seen him, no one passed this way at this hour. He hurried past the intersection of Primeiro de Maio and N4. He was walking on 381 now. The sun blazed with horrific heat. He had ditched the protective helmet, gloves and kerchief back by the quarry's gate, but the cap with earflaps remained on his head.

What should he do with it now?

The noise was just as bad as the dust, there was no escape from it. The caterpillar forklifts, shovel excavators, band saws, the enormous trucks, and giant cranes, those giant cranes! All of them, each and every one, with their horrible howl and clatter, roar and shriek, they came and went, hacking and lifting and lowering in order to lift and lower again, so that they, the ones with wheelbarrows, or as the *canteiros* and truck drivers called them, the "pedestrians," never had a moment's relief.

The drone of the highway winding toward the Spanish border was audible in the distance, but the boy still wearing his cap and earflaps could not hear the noise. Anyway, his brain was still buzzing with the dreadful din of dump trucks, forklifts, band saws, bulldozers, and giant cranes, those giant cranes! His lungs were filled with the dust of the white marble, but he had long ago given up trying to hawk it up. When they hired him eight months earlier they made it clear to him that there was nothing to be done against the noise and the dust. When he stopped in the doorway on his way out at dawn on that first day and looked back at his mother, all she could say was that it couldn't be helped, Pedro.

And there is really nothing else to do, Pedro, you will work in the quarry until you grow old.

He walked under the overpass, and detoured to the left into the fields so they wouldn't see him from the quarry, then he returned to the highway to continue walking on 381. His way led past farmhouses, but there was no need to worry that people would see him. At this time of day not a soul stayed at home, everyone was working in the fields.

He hid the cap under a large stone, not daring to just throw it away. If he came back he would find it there.

If he came back.

So far not a trace of a shadow could be seen anywhere, there was nothing to be done about that, but at least he could keep to the shoulder of the road where the heat didn't burn the soles of his feet so much.

From here on things began to be different. The farmhouses were left behind, and more and more trees appeared, standing pale under the scorching sun. The noise of the autostrada did not reach this far, but no birdsong could be heard either, obviously the birds must have been taking shelter in the thickets, lest they be toasted within minutes.

The forest wasn't far from here, he could see the first eucalyptus trees, and from there things would get better.

He took a deep gulp of air and was seized by a violent fit of coughing.

He arrived at the river.

Practically no one ever used Route 381, hardly any of the locals did, since people from Redondo had no reason to be in Estremoz nor did those from Estremoz have any business in Redondo, whatever traffic there was consisted of a few tourists, mostly ones who had lost their way in Evora or on the way to Spain, other than these no one, ever; everybody knew that the road was in fact superfluous, they knew this in Estremoz and they knew it in Redondo, but of course no one had mentioned this in '61 before it was built, when they could have said that it was not needed, they said that it *was* needed, how would it not be needed?

and so it was built, the asphalt a perfect job, and ever since then hardly any cars ever drove on it, maybe one a day, and now, as Pedro looked up at the sun, you could be certain that not a single car would pass this way, no one went anywhere in this wretched heat, it had always been like this, you could count on it now, and so he did, no one approached from up ahead and no one came from behind, I am alone and will remain alone, now he could feel the road beginning to rise and head uphill, soon he would reach Serra de Ossa, at least the foothills; actually he hadn't the slightest idea where Serra de Ossa began, he had never gone this far on 381, and of course he had never been to Redondo, but he had always known about the forest, sometimes when he woke in the middle of the night he would hear it in the distance, just as he did now, more and more distinctly, although the birds remained silent, the forest still had its own kind of silence that one could hear, a sustained mute sound from the direction of the south, of course not really a sound, nothing but an undercurrent, tidings, a sigh that never ends, coming from the south, where Serra de Ossa lay somewhere in that direction, where the world ended, and now he was heading that way.

He wasn't expecting anything to happen to him once he arrived up on Serra de Ossa, no, not at all, in fact Pedro was certain that nothing would ever happen to him, nor had he been longing to come here, he had simply known all along that he would come here once, that he would seek out this place, and go down the length of 381, and now the time for this has arrived, the precise moment had been when he lifted the slab of marble from the wheelbarrow and placed it on top of the stack, that was when he thought, well then, time to put this wheelbarrow down, put it down and set out on 381.

So he had put down the wheelbarrow and here he was, winding his way uphill, he trudged on in the torrid heat, keeping off the asphalt to avoid burning the soles of his feet, staying on the narrow strip between the asphalt and the scrub that grew alongside the road.

He didn't hate the quarry, he did not hate anything. He had no expectations, he had no desire for anything, nor did he hope for anything. He accepted things as they were. He had to put up with the dust, had to put up with the noise, he had to pull on those coarse gloves, push that wheelbarrow, shuffle along in line, lift and then put down the slab of marble that at first had seemed unliftable, do all that and look on at the screaming progress of cutting blade in stone. All of that he endured without questioning and without revolt, and he considered all of it as the way things were, inevitable. Nothing ever cheered him up, nor did he feel melancholy either, he saw things as tolerable and therefore all right. When he closed his eyes in bed at night, and tried to imagine the world, the world too appeared to be covered with dust: everything white, everything stiflingly white. Once, just before sleep overcame him, he imagined that the world was just like himself and the others at the quarry: it was only a ghost. He never had any dreams.

Now the first sounds of birdsong reached his ears. He was walking at a high elevation, most likely he had been on Serra de Ossa for quite a while now. The parched eucalyptus trees standing on both sides of the road still had some leafage, so he abruptly left the road, found an older tree, and dropped to the ground. He propped his back against the peeling tree trunk. He was drenched in perspiration. The birds fell silent.

Estremoz Crème is the world's finest white marble. Although in his childhood he had heard *canteiros* say that this marble had to be appreciated on the first day, he had never understood what they meant. Then when they hired him, and his first day of work arrived, he was so intimidated by everything that he was supposed to learn all at once, and he had to muster so much of his strength in order not to collapse every hour from exhaustion, that it never occurred to him to pause in front of a slab for the sole purpose of seeing for himself what made it the most beautiful marble in the world. And anyway, each moment he felt himself watched by the supervisor, and wouldn't have dared to take a single step without the man's authorization. Estremoz Crème became for him another piece of stone, an anonymous chunk of stone he had to struggle with again and again, a hundred, a thousand times, day after day. The overseer's eyes were always on him.

A terrible thirst began to torment him.

He scrambled to his feet and set out across the forest, to see if he could find one of the innumerable streams he had heard were on Serra de Ossa. He didn't want to get very far away from the road, and seeing the rough ground parched and crisscrossed by many fissures, he soon realized the search was hopeless. He stopped, looked around, but saw nothing; it was obvious he would not find water among the eucalyptus trees. He walked back to the road. Sooner or later here in the woods alongside 381 he was bound to find a farmhouse, a shack, perhaps a hunting lodge, anything, where he would be able to drink his fill. He quickened his steps but fairly soon felt tired. After all he had been walking for hours in the blistering sun. He might as well sit down again. But thirst was more powerful than fatigue, that damned thirst, it must have been because he was so preoccupied with it. Yes, he needed to quench his thirst.

How far could it be to Redondo?

He passed another turn in the road, then another and another.

Redondo was at least another two hours away.

If not three.

He stared hard at the next bend in the road and resolved that when he reached it he would look for a shaded spot and rest a while.

But after he reached the bend he did not sit down, he merely slowed down his pace somewhat. He pivoted his head and stopped. He had heard something before he saw it.

He hardly believed his eyes.

A barely noticeable trickle of water gurgled among the rocks on the hillside, a thin little rill of water running down to the roadside where it almost instantly evaporated in the sun.

It was a marvelous sensation, to be drinking at last.

It would have been untrue to claim that he did not know what Estremoz Crème was like, but had someone asked him, he would have barely been able to stammer out a single word. Perhaps he would have said: it was white. However on rare occasions, when in the middle of summer he climbed up on the roof of the house and lay down, and, blinded by the sun, he closed his eyes, then, at those times, even though he didn't know what he was seeing, nonetheless he could see it. It was like a soft blanket of snow, or as if colorless flaming clouds were billowing on its surface. But he knew that in reality it was nothing, a mirage.

He could tell by the air that he was now quite high up on the mountain. A forest of cork oaks had replaced the eucalyptus. On the uphill side of the road was a wall of rock and on the other side, on a slope descending toward lesser valleys, cork oaks were everywhere, their bark stripped to the height of a man. Twisted, gnarly trunks with barely any foliage above. Should he keep walking? Which way? To the left he saw a path, and he took it, leaving the road.

Or was it really a path? Evidently no one had used it recently, nor were there many signs of its ever seeing much traffic in the past. Perhaps, he thought, it was a path, because to the right, on the sharply rising mountainside, four or five old eucalyptus trees stood in a row, and they seemed to indicate a way and a direction. To the left prickly succulents grew out of the mountainside and hung down to the ground. The wall of rock cast a shadow.

After another hundred steps he was forced to clamber on all fours. The path, if indeed it was a path, led to some kind of summit. He advanced with head down, extremely tired. Head lowered, in the cool of the wall of rock's shade, he felt empty and exhausted. What could be waiting for him up ahead? Another springlet? The previous one was now far behind, he could use another drink of water.

He sensed it before he actually raised his head.

He sensed something waiting up ahead. The path turned sharply to the left, and the sharp bend concealed it. He knew that after rounding the bend he would see what it was. It happened very quickly.

An enormous building loomed in front of him, up on the heights.

One could not grasp its dimensions right away.

It was too huge, way too huge, but completely blended into the landscape.

It seemed as if it had sprung from the rock, burgeoned like the vegetation that had almost completely overgrown it.

Or as if it had come into being simultaneously with the forest.

Unable to move, he stood there and stared, he had never seen anything like this.

The Pousada back home in Estremoz would have been dwarfed next to it.

He had never heard about this.

What should he do now?

He started to dust off the work clothes he was wearing, but instantly created such a cloud of dust that he quickly stopped. He eyed the arch over the entrance, and the vacant niches of the bell tower up above, the narrow embrasures—he dared to view only the details, avoiding the whole. The whole thing was really too vast.

Why had no one ever spoken about this?

He vaguely recalled hearing about a monastery, a *convento* hidden deep in Serra de Ossa, but that should have been much farther away, below Redondo. And Redondo was still so far away. This could not be the *convento*. But then what could it be?

He took one timid step forward.

Nothing happened.

Soon he realized that he had nothing to be afraid of: there was not a soul here.

His courage returned.

The heavy gate wasn't locked, it was easy to get in.

Why had they abandoned such a … such a beautiful palace?

And who had abandoned it?

Holding his breath he entered the first hall. This was no vestibule, but a great hall with a high vaulted ceiling, the flooring made of dark slabs of marble from the mine at Borba, with deeply recessed windows, and running along the entire length of the walls at a height of about a meter and a half were a series of wondrously beautiful painted tiles depicting saints and landscapes and scenes with inscriptions, none of which said anything to Pedro.

He entered the next hall, and the next, and the next after that, a rapturous look frozen on his face. Everywhere he saw those saints and landscapes and scenes and inscriptions painted in cobalt blue on the walls and everywhere he saw the floors of dark marble from the Borba mine.

Maybe he was dreaming for the first time in his life.

But barely anything was left intact. Many of the tiles had fallen and lay broken on the floor. The walls and the once elaborately painted ceilings were fusty with mildew. The door frames buckled, the doors had rotted and crumbled into fragments that lay scattered all over the floor. The windows' external shutters hung in tatters. He felt drafts here and there, but the pervasive smell of moldering decay defied these occasional gusts of air. The devastation was universal.

The palace lay in ruins.

The palace?

In fact it was an enormous heap of ruins.

In a daze he wandered from one hall to another. He stepped out into an enclosed square courtyard completely overrun with weeds, then he reentered the building and went up a broad stairway to the floor above, and for a spell he was once again immobilized by stupefaction, for not only had he never seen, but he could never have imagined a corridor of such length. To top it all, this corridor at its center was intersected by another one. At the end of each corridor light poured in through a large window, but this brightness sufficed to light up only a few meters, all else lay in darkness or a dim half-light ... Cells opened from the corridors—that is, some did, and quite a few others he found wouldn't open when he tried to push the door, as if someone had nailed them shut from the inside.

And everywhere, no matter where he roamed, upstairs or on the ground floor, he saw these fantastic *azulejos,* these wondrous walls of tiles! In one place he recognized Jesus Christ carrying the Cross, at another, he saw the Angel of Annunciation and the Virgin Mother, but in most cases he could not tell what was depicted along this seemingly endless succession, as one picture followed another with apparently no end in sight, an almost countless number had been painted on these tiles, as if in this vast palace they had intended to narrate everything that had ever happened in the history of humankind from the beginning until now, everything, and he could see it all, his eyes were already dazzled, overwhelmed by all those blue saints and scenes and landscapes and inscriptions, although it was quite clear to him that even though they were telling their stories, each tile its own story, narrating everything that has happened from the beginning until our day, they were not addressed to him, they were not speaking to him.

For hours he roamed the halls, the stairways, the interior courtyards, he even came across a chapel that opened directly from the palace, then once more upstairs, and once again down, he surveyed every accessible space.

And even though the whole structure stood in ruins, the building even in its mute desolation made you feel that in spite of having been abandoned it still belonged to someone, to some distant world, perhaps to heaven itself, or to the even more distant Lord in the endless distances, in eternity.

He had no business being here.

He could not explain to himself what he felt.

He looked on at all this possessed by a frigid, distinct alienation.

He went in search of water.

A cunningly carved marble fountain stood in each of the interior courtyards, but no water had flowed from them in a very long time. He tried to locate the kitchen, but found nothing. He discovered a passage leading to the cellar which he scoured from one end to the other in case some liquid still sloshed around in the bottom of an abandoned bottle, but no luck. Finally he came outside to the terraced gardens that formed an extension of the longitudinal axis of the building and there he devoured the fruit that had still not withered on the pomegranate trees, that the birds had not picked apart completely, and then he found water as well. A wall of rock rose at the far end of the garden, and there he once more heard the sweet sound of gently trickling water.

He drank his fill, as much as he could stand, and then lay down under the broad boughs of an oleander. Now that he saw the building from the rear, from a fresh angle, he noticed that the different parts of the palace were built upon various levels of the ground and all came together in an open elevated terrace facing him. Sleep overcame him and he woke only when the tinkling of some sort of bell startled him. He regained consciousness at once, but there was no reason for alarm: it was only a flock of sheep approaching, slowly, very slowly from somewhere lower down, peacefully grazing their way uphill, from the direction of Redondo. He waited for some time under the oleander, but the flock had strayed all this way unshepherded.

The sun was no longer blazing, in another minute the nearby mountain crest would block its light.

He climbed up to the elevated terrace. Approaching it from the side proved to be child's play, the rear of the building was braced against the rocky cliff. It took only a few strides, left foot here, the right over there, and he was up on the terrace.

Broad, spacious, and open in all directions, the terrace rested upon stone pillars. Running around its perimeter was a hefty, nearly a half-meter thick, stone balustrade formerly clad in tiles, and this balustrade on each of its three sides had a bench recessed into it. He sat down on the central bench, settling into a comfortable pose, leaning on his left arm. In front of him the landscape stretched away in the direction of Redondo down below.

The lazy and tranquil landscape completely filled the panorama, all the way to the horizon.

A world so wide could not possibly exist.

He heard birds twittering, and the bellwether of the flock.

In front of him, down below, the incredible expanse of forest stretched away; there was infinite calm all around, above the woods the vast sky's vault, and in his ears the twitter of birds and tinkling of bells—and it all grew quieter, and more and more peaceful.

One after the other the birds flew home to their nests.

The sun began to set.

Peace reigned over the land, and this peace was so deep that Pedro, as he sat there contemplating it, now remembered the line at the quarry, where he should perhaps still be standing even now, and this made him think of his wheelbarrow, and how when he had to bend down to grab the grooved rubber lining of the handles, even through the work gloves he could still recognize his wheelbarrow among a thousand others.

Yes, he could.

He climbed down from the terrace, walked through the gardens to the path, and from there down to 381, and set out toward Estremoz.

And although the sun went down, and darkness fell, there was always some light left for him to see where he stepped.

On the way back the trip was shorter.

GYÖRGY FEHÉR'S HENRIK MOLNÁR

In 2002, the year of his death—I no longer remember the exact date, not even the month, but it was sometime in the spring—the film director György Fehér phoned me from Budapest to say that he had a project he'd been lugging around in his baggage, a film project, as a matter of fact this was the only thing he had really wanted to do in his life, but it was a very complicated matter, he would prefer to discuss it in person. In the course of recent years I had grown to like him more and more, and just around that time this affection was at its peak, and so I was prepared to meet with him whenever. I don't yet know when I'll come, he said, I'll let you know beforehand, but in the meantime I'm sending you a cassette in advance, he said, a documentary film, sort of, so that you'll have some idea what this is about. It was such a long time ago when I shot this footage, it must have been sometime in the late sixties, I'm not even sure any more if it actually happened, he added. I can barely recall the circumstances now. At the time I worked as a cameraman for the state TV station, they sent us out to document a trial, but it turned out to be a fiasco, the whole project was dropped and this is the only copy that survived, purely by accident. But if you take a look at it you'll see there is something there. Perhaps originally they'd planned it for a news program, a segment about the trial, edited of course—I no longer recall. And of course they never used it for anything, and no one ever went near it. This cassette is the only existing copy, the original was lost. So this is what our film should be based on.

I was really surprised. The two of us? Make a film? Of all people he ought to have known better than anyone how much I disliked making films. Furthermore whenever—before he launched into a film, or during a shoot and between shoots—I brought up my dislike and the reasons for it, he always replied that he believed me and understood that I hated the whole process, but I must understand that no one hated it any more than he did himself.

He had given many signs of nurturing friendly feelings toward me, possibly because in those days I was considered to be the greatest simpleton in the entire Hungarian film industry. Whenever we spoke, whenever he looked at me, or happened to be present to hear what I had to say before, during, and between various film shoots, he always had a strange little light flickering in his eyes, a flicker of fascination, of disbelief: how could anyone be so utterly clueless about where he was and what was he doing here, in the first place, with film people. We met more and more often, and I could feel that behind his sympathy there lurked a curiosity to find out, to see for himself once and for all whether I was really as half-assed as I appeared to be. He spoke to me about his favorite writers and his favorite literary works, but never said a word about working with me. To make a film with me? I was certain that he would never want to take advantage of my half-assedness, not to mention that I was convinced he was one of those few who knew my secret: I hadn't the slightest clue about film and filmmaking. He assured me that he hadn't either.

Anyhow, I lapsed into dumbfounded silence. "A film, did you hear me?" he resumed. "Just you and me …" He spoke the words emphatically. "It occurred to me that after all these years you and I could do something together." "And just what did you have in mind exactly? What kind of film do you intend to make?" I inquired. "Ah well, you know … a film," he replied in the slightly affectless voice he used whenever he found a strange question amusing. What kind of film, he asks?! Well, a film. There is only one kind of film—that was the sort of thing implied by the lack of affect in his voice. "Anyway, why don't you take a look at the cassette," he added. "See if you can think of something. I'll mail it tomorrow."

He said goodbye, hung up, and I never saw him alive again.

After his funeral I ran into several people who had been at the graveside. We realized that we all shared a deep affection for the deceased. Sometime later one of these people told me that not long before his death Gyuri had contacted him and asked, as a sort of last request, for his help in working together, just the two of them, to make a film. Gyuri told this person that he would send a cassette. And what do you know, the cassette never arrived, this person now told me. Subsequently I came across another fellow, and after we had a few glasses of wine it turned out that both of us had our own little stories about Gyuri, so he motioned me to lean closer and in a lowered voice narrated how Gyuri's last wish was to make a very special film exclusively with him. Just you and me, he told me, this fellow went on, that was what Gyuri had supposedly told him. Finally a third such person popped up in my life, with the same story, the same waggish reality so typically Fehér, and this too ended the same way, the promised cassette never materialized.

I refrained from disclosing that I was also involved in the affair. And I certainly did not reveal the fact that I, on the other hand, did receive the cassette.

I have a distinct memory of the occasion: instead of leaving it in my mailbox the mailman had brought it to the door of my apartment. I took the cassette inside, placed it in the VHS player, watched it to the end, then watched it again.

Next I took pen and paper and wrote an old-fashioned handwritten letter to my friend. After I was finished with it I placed it in an envelope, sealed it, affixed a stamp, and mailed it to his mother's address, since he never had a mailing address of his own.

Dear Gyuri!

I see the camera jiggling in your hands, as with your eyes glued to the door of the courtroom you are angling for the suitable momentum with which to zoom in on him the instant he enters, although I can also tell from the way that camera is jumping around that you will not be able to predict just who will be entering next, and that is what happens, your hands make a mistake, for the camera leaps at someone who enters ahead of the awaited one, and you track him for a bit, this person of no interest whatsoever, but the hand holding the camera already knows that this was not the right one, and quickly abandons him, both the camera and the hand holding it are rather abashed, one senses this as the camera slinks back to the entrance, sort of admitting that it does not know its business—the camera is not the right one for this job, it is too much of an EVERYDAY CAMERA—*the whole thing is rather like the devil playing a little prank in order to demonstrate that although he is not the rightful director here, in any case* HE TOO WILL BE PRESENT ... *then abruptly the scene turns serious, because the one we have been waiting for now enters, he is unmistakably the one, not even this everyday camera can mistake him, the camera trembles in your hands, it trembles because the moment the man entered the courtroom the camera, too, entered reality, moreover a reality where an extraordinarily important case, one of reality's truly dreadful stories, is about to unfold. Not merely a story that is part of reality, but one that would reveal what that reality, in point of fact, is.*

I lean forward to watch the VHS image, and the first thing I note is that something is not quite right about the way he thrusts his hands forward.

At a superficial glance, it seems perfectly natural that a person being led somewhere with his hands cuffed in front would, in order not to stumble as he advances, thrust out his hands somewhat forward and up, in order to see where he is stepping, and as a matter of fact this is what he is doing, thrusting his hands forward and up as he enters the courtroom without slowing down at the threshold, behind him guards on each side hold him by the arms, directing him. Making his way through the people standing near the door, he enters the courtroom, tilting his head forward slightly, to see where he is stepping—I already realize at the moment of his entrance, the way he is holding his manacled hands up ahead of him, tilting his head down slightly to see where he is stepping, that he is giving us early notice that the main point here is not that the handcuffs on him are an injustice in the legalistic sense, but that the greatest injustice here is that any legalistic sense exists in the first place, for in his case the matter does not have a legalistic sense, his case is not a legalistic case, he is not "indictable," since he is only a man fallen into the most primitive sort of trap about which here, today, it is impossible to say a word, there is no one to speak to; the one and only person—every move he makes conveys this—the sole individual in this courtroom who is his equal is he himself, and underneath his formidable discipline one can sense his terrible fragility, that he is handcuffed, that he is alone, that it is scandalous that no one else wears handcuffs in this courtroom, for in this manner the whole thing has the appearance of a chained animal being led here, I watch him advance with rapid steps, he knows precisely where he's heading, knows more precisely than anyone else where he has to go, and why; directly behind him are the two guards, his look is shut off, it is not possible to have a more shut-off look, I can see his terrible defenselessness, the way he takes his seat, the way he holds his hands out to one of the guards to unlock the handcuffs, I note the precise movement, he knows exactly what the guard must do, the way he turns the handcuffs up with the lock toward the guard, all this makes everything clear, and I can't help but watch as the handcuffs snap open, and the way *now with hands freed—very different from a moment earlier, when he had still been handcuffed!—he plants himself on his chair, and you can see how disciplined, how focused he is, he doesn't look around, but looks once to the right, once to the left, and at the end, when you can hear someone entering on the judge's platform facing him, I see him glancing up, actually this is the first time that I see his gaze, I see his eyes as he regards the judge.*

Good Lord, I know that glance from somewhere!

The judge's voice, harsh and rigid with antagonism and indifference, tells me with deadly certainty that this is not a trial, nothing will be decided here, this is a horrendous travesty, with actors who are in their way perfect for their roles; he knows—hearing the judge's voice, especially in places where he recites file numbers, dates, refers to transcripts from former hearings, in other words, the exhibits—that all is preordained here from the very first, and no one knows this better than the prisoner himself, whom from here the camera in your hands will never leave, or only for a moment, as if your clumsiness had compelled you to stay glued to his face, to his gaze, as when one simply CANNOT TAKE ONE'S EYES AWAY *from something, this explains the viewer's strange feeling that he is one with the camera, just as clumsy, just as mesmerized, just as incapable of believing his own eyes, of comprehending how it could have happened, whatever happened, as is the camera, through which he is now seeing this; for I cannot believe my eyes, that here sits this handsome, intelligent, fragile, exceptionally sensitive man, steeped in this superhuman concentration, and I am looking on helplessly while it will happen to him! What that will be of course I cannot know at the outset, and because of the extraordinary clumsiness of the hands hold-ing the camera I can only gradually and with difficulty begin to understand the story, and while piece by piece I try to solve the mystery, as piece by piece I try to assemble from the heard fragments what in fact the accused has done, and what came before and what followed later, as all this is going down inside me while I watch the horribly inward gaze of the prisoner—for I cannot do otherwise, since you do not give me anything else!—I must also keep thinking about how is such clumsiness possible, how is it possible that now the audio, now the video keeps failing, what is going on here, how is it possible that something is always going wrong, one thing after another, and again and again, and at times I am outraged, this simply cannot be true! you're doing this on purpose, precisely now, when I want to hear or see this or that, oh yes, I must keep thinking this, why this clumsiness, why this constant error behind the camera, I must wonder who the hell is operating that camera, who can possibly be so unaware of technique, or if he isn't then why was such a defective camera placed in his hands—then after a while I decide to reject this line of thought, and I am impelled to think that no, on the contrary, the crew on this shoot are doing their best, they are honest, decent folk who are doing everything humanly imaginable within their power, but the camera, the machine, simply keeps malfunctioning, they are utterly helpless, it is not a matter of their being careless, or irresponsible, or their playing around with the camera, but simply that there is no other alternative, and what is going on here is a struggle against helplessness, an extraordinary trial is in progress that must be documented, otherwise the world would fall to pieces, documented, while constantly being sabotaged by the equipment on hand, so that this is a battle between the crew and the camera, a battle between the camera and the world, I can practically envision it in front of me, even as I watch the face of the prisoner, all of you out there, the cameraman, the man who does the lighting, and the director, all trying to communicate by means of mute gestures, first one, then another pokes in exasperation at some part of the camera, trying to point out to the other what to do in order to restore the absent audio or the vanished video, I catch myself paying at least as much attention to this imagined dumb show as to the ongoing event itself, only to have every such imaginary intermezzo one after another wiped out by some new fact that is heard just then, a fact that lets me understand something about the events that had transpired, a fact that slowly, step by step, acquaints me with what had happened in the past and what is happening now.*

That murders were committed.

And that they intend to kill a man here.

This first trial session has throughout possessed its own internal momentum, as well as its internal pace, so that I, the viewer nailed to the prisoner's gaze, steadily sink deeper and deeper into his story. It becomes increasingly obvious that the charges alleging that this man had committed murder are absurd, that the forces opposing the defendant (this judge, these jurors, the two guards, all these people here) are every last one of them despicable, murderous scoundrels whose greatest crime is not that they brought this unfortunate man to this pass, but the fact that THEY DO NOT UNDERSTAND HIM. AND THAT THEY WILL NEVER UNDERSTAND HIM.

By now I feel more and more helpless as with truly heartrending despair I watch the prisoner's face. I would like to tell him: No matter what you may have done, I can understand you. Those people cannot, but I, sitting here, can. Your story won't vanish without a trace, they cannot do this to you without further ado, because I am sitting here and I can see you and I empathize with you, and in my mind I have acquitted you of all charges, while at the same time I am giving unequivocal notice that everyone around you is rightfully indictable.

I must duly consider, while your face is constantly before my eyes, and while your story is gradually assembled in my mind, that this is the fate reserved by the world for one who is sufficiently sensitive and "intelligent" (in the special sense of the word), which embodies the essential reality of human society and his own inevitable defeat at its hands.

This whole thing has been going on for a horribly long time, it feels as if I've been watching the cassette for hours and a definitive opinion is forming within me about what I am seeing. Staggering evidence of a fatefully doomed intellect and high-soaring spirit. And I myself become a prisoner, merely looking on, unable to help the accused. For the most horrible thing in all of this is the compassion rising within you even as you see that no one, plainly no one in that entire courtroom will cry out: Enough of this! While you, the viewer, are plainly present, as close as can be—This is no film! you howl deep inside, you could lean closer and be a millimeter away from him, you could even bring your face to touch the screen showing the other man's face, and still, you are unable to defend him … No, you must watch to the bitter end as they bring about his undoing.

Because by this time, toward the end of the first trial session, you don't even deliberate much when you explain to yourself what has happened: you have come to love this man, Henrik Molnár. Even to say his name has become so weird now. As if you actually knew him. As if you needed to prove that you knew him … One cannot love one's self, one can only love one's child this well. Who is meanwhile not your child. Who is meanwhile a murderer.

Your child is a murderer.

You are beginning to get used to the atmosphere of the trial, the courtroom is beginning to look familiar, as well as the judge, the guards, and of course the defendant. You get the feeling that you are somehow acclimatized, everything is self-evident, and will continue to be so.

And now the second trial session is here, and you stumble upon a peculiar new sensation. You are unable to endure the fact that this man in front of you—at times you can only see, or only hear him, for the camera and the crew haven't gotten any better, it is still the same nerve-racking struggle now with the sound, now the image, and you, the viewer—that is, me—you are constantly praying, MAY THE SOUND RETURN or else MAY THE IMAGE RETURN, and that is where you are when you must confront the fact that this man, the accused, actually is a murderer.

You shrink back slightly from the TV screen. You are incapable of reconciling all that you feel with all that you know.

That this man, Henrik Molnár, after telling the girl that she was going to die, had indeed turned around and stabbed the boy in the chest with his knife?

But that is impossible.

You cannot imagine him doing that.

As you keep watching his gaze you are unable to detect the slightest change in it. This unchangingness stuns you, and you must pose yourself the question, do you truly understand the man. If his face can remain so unchanged while you yourself have changed so much, then this face is shut closed and inaccessible to you too.

He stabbed that young child with a knife? He plunged a knife into a living person?

Can you envision that? Can you reconcile that with all that you have come to feel toward Henrik Molnár?

Would you be capable of plunging a knife into a living person?

Into that judge?

Yes.

Into the guard?

Yes.

And this young child here?

Possibly.

But where does that leave Henrik Molnár?

And where does that leave you?

You are aware, as you keep watching the events on the screen, that you must test yourself to see if you are truly capable of plunging a knife into a live person's chest.

The judge's?

No.

The guard's?

No.

This young boy's here?

No way.

When you force yourself to imagine the gesture, that you are actually doing it, the whole thing becomes impossible. You will never be a murderer.

You cannot perform the act of stabbing.
And now you scrutinize the face of the accused again.
It is the face of a murderer.

You look at Henrik Molnár, alarmed by the prospect of what would hap-pen if we did not act to stem murder, if we had no laws and no prisons, no judges or guards of any kind, in other words no civilization of any kind. Therefore you make an effort to imagine that you UNDERSTAND *the judge, the guards, the jurors, the prison, the whole horror. So that no one should kill anyone. You try to imagine that you understand this judge, these jurors, these guards.*

But you simply cannot do it. This judge, these guards, and these jurors: they are impossible to understand. When you think of Henrik Molnár, they all seem to be monsters.

And there he sits in his infinite purity, this most guilty of men, this prisoner.
And this is the final fact you understand about him: what it means to be perfectly solitary. You have watched for hours his unchanging face, his gaze. It is unbelievable, but it has remained the same all along, although months, possibly years, have gone by. Henrik Molnár does not change. It takes a while before you understand: he isn't changing because he maintains a state of concentration that simply defies comprehension from here where you are watching. You guess that they will probably sentence him to life imprison-ment. He, the luckless victim, and you, the powerless viewer. You are getting weary, and look forward to the finale. You weigh the chances that perhaps he won't be sentenced to life after all. The whole affair is so drawn out that you think it might all end here, more or less. Perhaps it won't be life, but

you fear that's what it will be. Nothing less is to be expected from this judge and this pack of guards and jurors.

By now you believe that indeed this thing will draw to a close.
Then you hear the sentence.
Death.
So they will kill him.
This is dreadful.

The film crew is once again visibly confused. By now it isn't merely a question of the sound being on the fritz or the image vanishing. By now all of you, the whole crew, must be certain that you have recorded something extraordinarily significant. AND THAT EVERYTHING YOU HAVE FILMED HERE IS A MATTER OF LIFE OR DEATH! *And this once again creates disturbances in the camera work. Once more the camera starts to wobble, the whole crew is palpably jittery. A death sentence.*

That's what must be running through your minds. While in your hands the camera is rolling, a bit jumpy because of the tension.

Again it is just as clumsy as it was at the outset.

Naturally you must follow him as he leaves the courtroom.

Keep shooting as long as possible.

But nobody expects that there will be something else to film in the hallway. EVERYBODY IS STUNNED BY IT.

Through the camera, you too admit no one had counted on this.

That Molnár had everything planned out to the last detail. That his incredible personal discipline and concentration weren't just a facade. If you sentence me to death I will kill myself. Using the guard's sidearm. He doesn't just hide from the world. He is what he is: disciplined and focused. He himself is the most impeccable, normal, and most sane—meanwhile all of it is madness.

That he would execute himself, shut the book. Even the guards are in a state of the greatest and most total confusion, without any compassion whatsoever, as if they had allowed something to break, something that had been entrusted to their care. It is mind-boggling.

As he lies there with bloodied chest, the camera drives the viewer back to where he was at the outset: good god, this man is lost!

It is irredeemable.

Gyuri, I think the recorded sound and image should be left as is. As a matter of fact this is not what needs to be worked on, because precisely this constitutes your material, just as it stands. Keep the original noise and words spoken on the soundtrack, and possibly use subtitles to convey the conversation between director, cameraman, and lighting operator. Professional commentary on the rotten equipment, about who is to do what, and with whom, and when, who should plug in what, or as the case may be, refrain from plugging in, or unplugging, and what now, who should hold the cables and where, and how, or who shouldn't, and just where exactly. The subtitles should deal exclusively with technical problems regarding the shoot.

TECHNICAL PROBLEMS.
My suggestion for a title.

Hugs,
Laci

Long weeks went by. He never sent any indication that he had received my letter, or that the project was making any progress. It must have been early June when I phoned him. Oh yes, I've received it, yes, of course, and he apologized. My mother has been after me for the past week to come over, there was a letter from you. But I haven't managed to line up the money so far, although I do believe the cause isn't altogether hopeless. I'll come to see you soon, we need to discuss issues of content. Or are you by any chance free tonight? Not tonight, I replied. Fine, no problem, he said quickly, I'll give you a call soon.

And then he died. There were many more people at the funeral than I had expected to see. At the same time I had a sensation that no one knew anyone else there, as if everybody had arrived alone. Several people placed pebbles on the grave. Then—since there was no service whatsoever—the gathering dispersed. A few of us stayed behind. Then it was only myself. I too took my leave. At the cemetery gate I noticed a young woman. She must have been watching me from behind a tree, to see when I would leave. So that she could go back. As I stepped out through the gate I looked in her direction once more and noted that she was walking back toward the grave. Then on the other side I saw another woman, an older one, who was watching the younger, evidently she too wanted to know when she would leave so that she could return to the grave by herself.

I got on a streetcar. As it slowly wound its way, I glimpsed one or two odd solitary persons on the other side of the street. Each gave the impression of waiting for something. Perhaps seeing that I was on my way, they were waiting for another streetcar going in the opposite direction that would take them back to the cemetery.

The city was full of people.
I recall the date: it was July 22.

BANKERS

Paul Werchowenski
Mürsel Ertas
Ixi Fortinbras
Any resemblance to persons living or dead is coincidental.

Your name is pretty odd you know—he turned his head toward the back seat to the man who, when they met, had only said: I am Paul's friend, Paul had said nothing in reply, and Paul didn't even help, didn't even explain what this person was doing there in the car, and even later on he didn't even find out, and when this man said: I'm Paul's friend, this man didn't even look at him, like someone who didn't consider this introduction to be important, when he came out from the doors of the terminal to the car with Paul, this man extended his hand and said something unintelligible: he held his hand, and said something in the English that they all took up immediately as their common language, but all the while he didn't even look at him, instead he cast his gaze somewhere beyond his shoulder, namely off in a completely different direction, toward the sliding doors of the tiny provincial airport, as if he were still waiting for someone else, and whoever had just arrived—that is to say, him—was not the person he was waiting for, he had been preparing for something more than this, some more significant personality: they shook hands, this clearly meant nothing to him, thought Ixi Fortinbras, clearly he must have come just now with Paul from the bank, and Paul obviously didn't know what to do with him, so you brought him out here to the airport; Ixi? Paul's friend asked with a kind of sarcasm in his voice: Ixi, with an x?—yes—you say it with an i in front and an i in back?—no, both those letters should be pronounced like the letter e in English—fine, but Fortinbras, really? like in that, um, whatchamacallit, right?—yes, that's it, he answered and as far as he was concerned the discussion was closed; he turned his head away toward the window, beyond the row of sparsely placed alternating factory buildings, tenements, and battered meadows that ran alongside the airport runways, there was nothing out of the ordinary, already in the first minutes he began to try to determine when he would recognize that he had not arrived in just any old place, but there was nothing, there were exactly the same factory buildings and tenements and fields as anywhere else, well, fine, of course it was just Kiev, he thought, but he said to Paul that he really didn't notice anything at all here that would serve to indicate that … and you won't either, answered Paul, winking conspiratorially at his friend, if this really were his friend here sitting beside him, this tense man clothed from head to toe in a discrete plum-colored Pierre Cardin-like getup and no other distinguishing features, who then added, oh, you didn't come here for that old chewed-up piece of shit, did you?—because no one is interested in that anymore, everyone is beyond that, reeeeally … well, of course, he continued, the catastrophe tourists still come, they're interested, but even if they go there to get their little dose of horror, they still find nothing, and especially not there, because there's nothing there anymore supposedly, I myself never went, but everyone says the whole thing is just so embarrassing; this man grimaced and looked at Paul, and then, because there was no reaction whatsoever, he turned his head back toward the windshield and gestured with his left hand, with an undulating movement that was hard for Fortinbras in the back seat to understand, maybe it meant: well enough about that already, in any event, he said to Paul—clearly continuing their earlier conversation that had been interrupted only due to Fortinbras' arrival and his getting into the car—originally, he said, she had been here at Deutsche Bank, then she left for a few months to go to Bucharest, and then she left again—and this is the main thing—to Tirana, and in Tirana she became the manager of Internal Audits and she spent two years there, the honest truth was that she wanted to get away from there as well, but the lady CEO, hired by the previous owner, didn't really ... didn't really like her either, older ladies never really like young women, especially if the woman, the young woman in question, Teresa, is in a position to oppose her in certain matters, and an intern ... an internal audits manager can do just that, and officially Teresa wasn't even under the CEO's supervision, but under that of the supervisory board, because the job of Internal Audits is of course to supervise the bank with the owner's interests in mind, whereas the CEO, in a managerial function, falls under the purview of Internal Audits—well, now given all this, Teresa just had to get out of there ... meaning she wanted to get out of Tirana? Paul interrupted, yes, that's right, out of Tirana, that's it exactly, the friend answered, and then whatshisnameagain, the Director of Internal Audits for Felicitas, I mean Banca Fortas in Genoa, who was responsible for the supervision and oversight of Internal Audits for all the subsidiary banks, he convinced her to go to Genoa, to work for him, this happened one and a half years ago, and they were getting on well in that situation, but then there was this distance, and there was this other position, because then Heinz was in Genoa, and sometimes he went to Tirana, well, and Teresa was really good at fulfilling her responsibilities, she did everything just as they wanted, um, the connection between Tirana and Genoa was ideal, and in Teresa's opinion this Heinz was much more professional and capable than the guy before, and after that she went to Genoa, and no doubt after a very short time, Teresa realized that she found the Italian mentality extremely difficult to bear, they are incapable of making decisions, they take their sweeeeeet time, it takes them at least two or three months to decide on something, and they always they take their sweeeeeet time, and Paul's friend made that same undulating motion again, to show just how they were taking their sweeeeeet time, Paul was quiet, he gazed ahead, his hands on the steering wheel, listening attentively to the account which—at the beginning—was not so bothersome to Fortinbras there in the back seat, because he thought: why not, obviously there was some little problem going on here and he had just dropped into the middle of things, maybe that's what Paul was thinking when he ignored him and simply let him be immediately exposed in media res to the daily life of Kiev, Fortinbras looked out the window, already they were crossing one of the concrete bridges above the Dnieper in the heavy traffic, he looked out of the window and he saw Imexbank, then he saw Pravex Bank, and then Privatbank, and Ukreximbank, Oshchadbank, UkrSibbank, Ukrsocbank, Rodovid Bank, Megabank, Bank Kiew, Brokbiznyesbank, Astrabank, Khresatikbank, Universalbank, Diamantbank, then he saw Nadra Bank, Delta Bank, Energobank, Fortunabank, Renesans Kapitol, and so on—good heavens, thought Fortinbras, what is going on here, every other building is a bank, what in the world could this be, why are there so many banks here, but there was no way for him to pose any questions, because the conversation in the front seat had remained very intense, it was impossible to interrupt or stop it, and Paul, yielding to his own forgiving character, was just letting his interlocutor speak, and he spoke and spoke, he just kept talking and talking: in my opinion, Italy is the only European country where it isn't customary for the top leadership of the bank to have university degrees; the larger part, i.e. most of them, attend vocational schools after their high-school exams, umm, and on top of that there are innumerable employees who are from completely different fields, for example humanities graduates, so in consequence she considered this Heinz to be good on a professional level, but as for the entire team working there—wait a second, Paul interrupted, what exactly was this Heinz to Teresa? Heinz?—he was the boss who lured her over there, fine, Paul asked again, but who did he lure over there, Teresa?—yes, Teresa, that's who I'm talking about, and, well, as Heinz was the lowest-level Internal Audit manager to whom people had to report, the one responsible for the subsidiary banks, so—Paul picked up the thread of conversation again: this Heinz wasn't at the highest supervisory level that the subsidiary banks had to report to?—no, no, no, the other nodded—he was the lowest-level manager, above him there were still two others, do you understand?—and these two others, who do they supervise? Paul interrupted once again with a question—they supervise the people one level below them, came the answer—so in other words, the ones who are always one level below?—yes, that's exactly right, and then there is the highest level of management, responsible for supervising the entire bank—and thus they supervise the Italian part as well, but only the subsidiary banks?—yes, only the subsidiary banks, the primary bank doesn't lie within their scope of authority, yes, only those subsidiary banks that are located in Europe, well now—Paul's friend pulled his index finger along his forehead—so what happened here was that she didn't like the Italian work ethic too much, that's one thing, the other was that—and this was something she hadn't noticed before—there was nothing to reproach Heinz with from a professional standpoint, but she just couldn't stand his style, his ways, in other words he was like, I don't know, she says that he was like—I would say this myself—a woman between fifty and sixty, with her cycles, when ooooh, she can be very sweet and everything, then she flies into a rage, and there's no way to tell when it is going to be one or the other, so they never know in the morning when he comes into the office if he will be one way or the other, it's impossible to know if his wife is the reason for this, or him, his wife sits at home all day, they're Genoese, but they live in Milan, and it could be that he was always like this, or he just got that way, but whatever, the main thing is that she couldn't stand this kind of style, or this kind of behavior that he was displaying with her, there were stomachaches, and so on and so on, and now after all this, with two years to go with this division in her contract, she sits down to chat with him and tells him that she can't stand it anymore, and so then he told her, this was last year in August, not to get so worked up, because if she could go to Moscow in the autumn for two months, mainly to clear up the conflicts and set things straight in their Moscow office, by the time she got back he wouldn't be there, of course this had to be taken on faith, and of course two months later, when Teresa came back he was still there: he was there, he is there, and with all certainty he will be there—who are you talking about now? asked Paul—Heinz, answered his friend, and she said that she certainly couldn't bear it, she sat down with Heinz more than once, and they weren't able to work things out, sometimes he's more normal and he's inclined to understand, and when he isn't more normal, then he just argues—tell me about another time when Teresa was upset, Paul interrupted—fine, I'll tell you about a very specific incident, he raised his left palm for Paul to be silent, he knew what he wanted, he already had a concrete example: here you have it, there's an internal audit, well, now you need to know that she had already been in Moscow for two months, and in Moscow the chairman was the kind of person who'd been chairman there for thirty years already, the Italian Communist Party had sent him to Moscow, I think it's clear that he had other duties, he's senile already, but supposedly on good terms with Putin, to such a degree that he visits him socially, no one dares touch him, but he isn't normal; now you have to really understand that literally he really isn't normal, well, and then this happened: Teresa was there, and after advertising several times, they hired a lady as head of Internal Audits—Ludmila, or whatever her name was—Teresa said that she had been hired from somewhere else, she was capable, this was some time . . . in October or

November, in the middle of the month, well, then it happened when Teresa came back and it turned out that this lady, as the head of Internal Audits, had the responsibility of inspecting the various divisions of the bank, they had a work plan, she was the one who created it, it had been approved in Genoa, and the work plan determined which divisions would be inspected by the employees, and it was decided that procurements had to be audited as well, and they were audited, well, now it turned out that in procurements some guy purchased something from a vendor without getting other offers, I don't know if it was hardware or software, in other words some kind of info … information technology, or some kind of service for the bank, something the bank uses for its own needs, and the main thing was that it turned out there was some scandal, in other words they had never opened tender, and in that case you're supposed to accept the most advantageous proposal, right? well, that's not what happened this time, this woman wrote a report about it, and the report first got to the CEO, and the CEO sent it on—because he had to—to the chairman, well, and now the chairman began to rage that this was absurd, and the main thing was that he wanted to kick out this woman who wrote the report, well now it was an impossible situation, it was impossible to argue with him, because it was perfectly clear that he wanted to protect the person who had arranged this purchase, well, after all this—but, Paul asked again, who arranged the purchase?—we don't know, answered the other—well, but what's his position?—maybe department head or something like that, his friend spread his hands apart, well, now after all this Teresa goes to Genoa to the department of Internal Audits, to say what happened, and discuss what to do now, and they talk, and they say that as a matter of fact this woman can't be saved, because nobody is going to confront this chairman in Moscow, because this Moscow chairman is under the protection of the first or the second most important person in Genoa who's also an old prick, who, if they call him, he hands down an order, and the result is always what they want, but Fortinbras didn't react to this, it was impossible to connect to or follow what the two people in the front seat were talking about, and they showed no sign of interest in how much their guest was able to follow their conversation—if he understood nothing at all, that was fine too, indeed maybe it was even better if he was getting nothing from this story, or account; not only was the content and meaning of this conversation unclear to Fortinbras, but the reason for it escaped him as well—why was Paul's friend putting on this performance, and why for Paul, and what did he expect from Paul—apart from listening to this account, nothing was clear, was he seeking advice, or did Paul have anything to do with anyone in this story? it was all perfectly obscure, Fortinbras determined, and in addition he could barely hope that later on he might begin to catch the drift of what they were talking about, that then it would become more clear, it was obvious that the entire story—if this was indeed a story—was just a cloud of obscurity in the best of cases and nothing else, so Fortinbras tuned out, he didn't pay attention, the words reached him from the seats in front, but he just heard them, and he no longer bothered with their meaning, they drove across a few wide intersections, then they reached a luxury residential complex surrounded by fences, with guards standing in the gates, they turned in, they parked, and they went up an elevator to the ninth floor to a large apartment—it was not at all clear to Fortinbras whose it was—and when he tried to ask, Paul smilingly choked the words in him, signaling to him that well, that's not interesting, the main thing is that you'll feel good here, you can relax, take a shower, he put his hand on his back with a friendly gesture, look, and he lifted his watch to check, in four minutes it will be twelve o'clock, let's say that we'll come back for you at two, is that enough time? of course, answered Fortinbras, I'm not tired, well, that's fantastic, fantastic and fantastic, Paul smiled at him, then they left him alone, he showered, he wrapped himself up in the towel, and he stood next to the large plate-glass window in the spacious room, comprised for some unknown reason of completely irregular angles; he stared outside, but he only saw the apartment blocks of the housing complex forming a semicircle, then through a gap between the buildings a small section of the Dnieper, he had no idea what district of the city he was in, so what are your plans, Paul asked him afterward, when he came back for him a little before three, my plans, Fortinbras looked at him confusedly, I don't have any plans in particular, but if I could choose something, then more than anything else I'd like to get to, well you know, the Zone—we won't be able to go in there, Paul explained, just maybe up to the border, if you insist on it, because sup- posedly the radiation over there is too much, I don't believe it, but I guess it changes from time to time, he concluded, and put a cigarette into his mouth, but he didn't light it, he sat leaning back against one of the windowsills, and explained to Fortinbras that he didn't think a trip to the Zone was at all worth it, and he didn't deny that it was possible to get into the Zone's inner section for one hundred fifty dollars or something like that, but he made a dismissive movement with his hand, indicating that was nothing, it wasn't a question of money, but that there was nothing to see there, and then suddenly he began talking about how Kiev was really beautiful, Fortinbras should believe him: it was much more worthwhile to look around Kiev a little bit; yes, an- swered Fortinbras, but right now as it happens I'm really interested in the Zone, because I understand, he continued more quietly, that it's not really interesting for you here in Kiev, but you know I was never here, and it's hair-raising—I know it isn't for you—how the radiation spreads out here for up to one hundred kilometers, it's just ... I under- stand, I understand, Paul nodded from the window sill, so we'll go see it tomorrow, no problem, that's fine, he said, but at least let me show you something of the city today, then we'll go have dinner tonight, all right? a wide smile, Fortinbras nodded, quickly threw on some clothes, and already they were downstairs in the car, luckily that friend or business associate was no longer sitting there so they could go just the two of them, and Fortinbras was very happy about this, he even expressed his joy, and Paul in a calm voice answered that this Mürsel wasn't a bad fellow, believe me, I've known him for a while, it's just that well, he always has something to say and it can get a little tiring, but he's a fine fellow, there's no problem with him, they cut across streets, and then they drove on through the wide boulevards, there were more unusually wide intersections, clearly they were getting closer to the city center, how much longer until the center, Fortinbras asked, that's it already, you're there, answered Paul, here's a market, and sometimes on the weekend I come here to get vegetables and things like that, vegetables?! Fortinbras looked at him, and things like that?! while his host, shaking his head, just smiled, but he didn't answer, he just nodded, yes, of course—but you eat vegetables, here?! he repeated, aha, Paul turned towards him for a moment and there was a kind of paternal forbearance in his regard, how could we not when the finest vegetables in all of Kiev are right here—well, but—there's no but, Paul swept Fortinbras's objections away, then suddenly Saint Sophia appeared before them, and the visitor was definitively struck dumb, they parked nearby, but before visiting the church they sat down in a Serbian restaurant, where they had some cold cocktails and something to eat, then they went into the silent courtyard of Saint Sophia, there were no crowds at all as Fortinbras had imagined that there would be, at least here, but there weren't any, he even asked about it: where are they, Paul, where are the tourists? at which point Paul looked at him seriously, he waited, and then finally he said: they're all in the Zone; and they stopped in the courtyard, Paul gazed fixedly into his eyes, and he looked at Paul, trying to discern if he was joking now or what, but then Paul laughed, slapped his friend on the back, and said you really are far gone, Ixi, try not to take things so seriously, but well, what was he supposed to do, Fortin-

bras thought to himself, if things were serious, it didn't make any difference if one looked away from how serious they are, they remained
just as serious, and he almost even said this immediately to Paul, but
then he didn't speak, he was a little crushed by the strange arrogance
of his friend's reply, and so a little crushed, he stepped into the interior
spaces of St. Sophia, and it wasn't only because of this arrogance, but
because generally—he had to admit to himself—his friend had really
changed quite a lot since last time they had met, it wasn't only obvious
from his external appearance—because over the past couple of years
Paul had clearly lost weight and had been working out—you could
almost see the contours of his muscles beneath the jacket shoulders—
but there were inner changes too, there in the interior part of Paul, in
his character, in his nature some great change had taken place, there
was, in Paul, a quality that he had never experienced before, a cynicism,
Fortinbras had discovered in him a kind of impudence and he was really not too happy about that, he really wasn't, because by now Paul
was his only friend, and he knew that at their age there would be no
others, but then what should he do, he kept thinking, with this cynical
impudence, what, he asked himself as he looked at the glorious church
interior, and his brain worked over this again and again, he thought
about this in front of the frescoes too, and he thought about it in front
of the mosaics, all the while realizing that what he was seeing was dazzling, but without Paul it wasn't worth anything, and in general without Paul, his true friend, nothing was worth anything, he walked back
and forth through the soft gold, from which, it seemed to him, the
entire building had been constructed, he crept here and there in the
small labyrinths of the columns and the walls, and he could hardly give
himself over to this unparalleled space, in addition to which Paul became visibly restless after just a few minutes, he—who in the old days
would have been capable of remaining in an architectural miracle like
this for hours—was impatiently waiting for when they would finish

here practically as soon as they stepped inside, yes, this was Paul now, more than anything else now he wanted to get things done, in place of the old tranquility some kind of general, restive impatience vibrated inside him, yes, this was what the world meant to Paul now, a succession of things following one after the other, in which he, Paul, had to take care of each individual thing, to take care of things on his own behalf, one after the other in succession, and then came the next one, for example him and the fact that he was here, the fact that Paul had invited him as a guest to Ukraine, and now he, Fortinbras, was the thing that had to be taken care of, and he would take care of it; just a quick telephone call to see if he was in the mood to come to Kiev, that was enough, and the plane ticket was already there in his laptop, everything happened so quickly that there was no time to prepare, my God, where am I going, he had thought about just what kind of dangerous situation was he getting himself into, and in general: anywhere, because he couldn't even bear the thought of danger, let alone a real danger, danger had been, for the last ten years of his life, a major category: it was in other words what he could not tolerate, he had excluded it from his life, freeing himself from the smallest, the very tiniest dangers, he sniffed them out and avoided them by wide margins, he never undertook anything in which even the very minutest chance of danger could be hypothesized, he wasn't paranoid, no, he was only someone who sensed the dangers that were already there, if possible, in even the most minuscule of events, so that he wasn't just imagining they were there, but he sensed—if it was at all possible to sense them—the dangers that were present already; and now it was exactly he, who had this kind of relation to dangerous events, who had come here at Paul's bidding, he, whose excessive sensitivity was well known among his friends, and first and foremost among them Paul as he knew him the best, and here he was in close proximity to the infamous Zone, not much further than one hundred kilometers, he had looked at the map on the plane,

I've gone mad, where am I going, Paul says something and I jump, fine, it was always like that, but one day I'm really going to pay for this, and maybe that one day is today, that's what he was thinking about up there in the atmosphere, but then after he had gotten off the plane these thoughts disappeared, because he was absorbed by what was around him, and if only that friend or business associate hadn't been in Paul's car, and if only he and Paul hadn't had to spend the first hours after his arrival crushed by the incoherent stories of this Pierre Cardin-suit guy, instead of both of them spending at least the first day together and having a chance to speak, because it had been almost two years since they had last seen each other, but what does that matter now, Fortinbras thought to himself among the dense curvilinear columns of the Sophia with their dark golden glimmering, here I am with him now among these dense curvilinear columns with their dark golden glimmering, and the saints gazed down on him from the mosaics and the frescoes from the opulent gold, very soulfully, they looked down on him, and for him, perhaps, because of these gazes, he had no desire to quickly be done with it, as Paul had clearly indicated with his body language, you stay here, he whispered into his ear, I'll wait for you outside, and already Paul was outside in the courtyard, but this is impossible, he thought, is this Paul? and he just looked back at the saints in the mosaics and the frescoes, as if they would know, but they didn't know anything, nothing in the whole world, they just looked at him soulfully and they just asked him: what happened to the past, they stared at him, and they asked him: where is it?—where is that place where their soulful nature would mean something, but that place wasn't anywhere anymore, what could have happened with Paul, Fortinbras asked himself worriedly, what is this whole thing with this athlete's pumped-up exterior, this frivolous cynicism, and his heart was aching, and the Sophia was so beautiful, but he couldn't put it off anymore, he had to leave these soulful saints in their golden light prematurely, because Paul's mute urging from outside made his staying there completely senseless, and once again he sat in the car, and the car glided along, and for a while Paul didn't say anything, then finally he spoke, and Paul suggested he show him the city; he thanked him, but in the meantime he had been thinking the best thing would be to sit down somewhere and discuss this matter in a tranquil setting, but of course there was no tranquil setting anywhere, and after a drive through the city, they sat down in a café, you'll like it, Paul noted as they went by foot for the last two hundred meters, and they passed in front of a house and the plaque on the house informed them that Bulgakov had lived here, and when he noticed this, he immediately wanted to take a look at the inside of the house, but Paul impatiently waved him down, saying oh, that's not interesting, leave it, there's nothing to see in there, cafés are much more interesting, let's go already, so on they went, passing among a row of repugnant street artists, you'll see, Paul kept saying, encouraging him, this place is the greatest, but it wasn't, just four walls painted in four different colors, a gussied-up stucco ceiling, Austro-Hungarian Art Deco tables and chairs, with a few better dressed figures by the tables, but he, Ixi, had absolutely no idea why Paul liked this place so much, and he understood even less what why Paul thought that he, Ixi, would like it, why would he like it, with its cheap kitsch for tourists, that's the kind of place it was, in any event he didn't want to dampen his friend's enthusiasm, so he noted in a restrained manner that it was pleasant, but immediately afterward he mentioned the Bulgakov house again, and he was asking something about Bulgakov and Kiev, but Paul just looked at him with a surprised or rather a blank gaze, he gulped down his coffee, he didn't know anything about Bulgakov, and in general Paul didn't know anything about anything, he was obviously interested only in local political and business gossip, and why—Fortinbras broke his inner silence—why don't we talk about the Sophia or about Bulgakov, he asked Paul that question, and Paul did not conceal his resentment, we already talked about Bulgakov and we were in the Sophia, Paul said harshly and a little angrily, what do you want already, but well what had come over Paul? Fortinbras asked himself ever more sorrowfully, what the hell has happened, he looked at him, he looked into his eyes, and they were Paul's old eyes, but everything else had changed, this Paul Werchowenski is not the same person who used to be my friend, Fortinbras said to himself that evening at dusk, and he was dejected, you're tired, Paul noted kindly, as they were headed toward the restaurant chosen for their evening meal, it's nothing, nothing, he brushed off the remark dispiritedly, and just sank down into the soft hum of the Audi A4, he wasn't even interested so much anymore in the Dnieper, or the city, and especially not in the restaurant that had been chosen with all the special dishes, this is the best that you can get here, said Paul loudly, and he ordered one dish after another, you're tired, he repeated again later on, but you know when you're tired you mustn't lie down, listen, and he leaned in closer towards him, I'll take you somewhere, okay? and there was a roguish look in his eyes, somewhere? Fortinbras asked, yes, Paul smiled at him, and we'll get rid of that tiredness, and they were already driving along the streets of Kiev toward the outskirts, the housing estates disappeared, and only ever larger buildings could be seen, concealed by enormous fences, inasmuch as anything could be seen in the darkness, then they stopped at one gate, Paul said something, and he showed something like a pass to the guard, they turned into a huge park, then they were inside a building that was something like a castle gone mad, there was a huge crowd, and noise, smoke, thumping canned music, but Paul just gestured for him to wait a minute, we're not there yet, Fortinbras followed him, they went upward somewhere in an elevator, and they stepped out into a corridor where there was complete silence, and it was so empty that he really thought they weren't in the same building, their steps were swallowed up by thick carpets, then Paul pressed a buzzer, and he tapped out a code onto a pad next to a door, he showed some kind of card to a camera, the door opened, they stepped in, but then there was another door, as if they had walked into an elevator, but behind their backs the first door closed with a loud bang, something had happened but it was impossible to tell what, there was a small quiver or something, that's all they could feel, then the second door opened, and then they were inside some kind of little hole and across from them was another door, then something happened again, and finally this third door opened as well, and Fortinbras took one step toward a huge open room, but he felt too much gravity in his step, yes, that was the first thing that he noticed, that movement here had become heavy, as if in this room gravity had increased, Paul gently pushed him ahead, he took another step, and he realized that they were in an aquarium, Fortinbras was rooted to the spot, he wasn't seeing an aquarium from the outside, but they were, in the most decisive sense of the word, inside an aquarium, there was no doubt, but there was not a drop of water upon them, around them there were a few naked women swimming around, their long blonde hair undulating behind them, Fortinbras just looked, then he looked at Paul, but Paul was so happy to see Fortinbras so surprised that he didn't say anything, whatever will be will be, later on he would find out what kind of trick this was, he took a few steps forward, with Paul urging him on, go on, go on, let's go, and the women floated beside them and above them with their cascading blonde hair, it was an incredible sight, around them the walls burned with gold, as did the ceiling and the floor, it seemed like it was all made of gold, the whole thing was blinding, because the light was shining so brightly from somewhere, Paul just stood half a step behind him, enjoying the effect, and the effect was huge, as even after one minute Fortinbras was incapable of speaking, then a naked woman floated over to him in the water, which could hardly be water, she stroked his chest, then her hand slid down his stomach to his sexual organs, it was very beautiful and very lovely, it was so beautiful and so pretty that in the first moment Fortinbras thought this was also some kind of trickery, just as everything here was a kind of trickery, and it might have been true, Paul gently took his arm and led him toward an almond-shaped opening leading into a kind of cave, but there he already felt the presence of water down by his legs, it splashed around his shoes, and yet nothing got wet, on the other hand real-looking women came forward, and there they were, and they greeted the two men, do you hear their English? it's flawless! Paul exclaimed enthusiastically, come on, he pulled him along, let's sit down there, and he led him over to a scarlet couch, they were served champagne and fruits, but the champagne wasn't champagne, the fruit wasn't fruit, only the women were real, they sat next to them, they wore lustrous, satiny, bluish glimmering bathing suits which emphasized their figures with unbelievable precision, so much so that Fortinbras blushed, not only because of their breasts and the nipples of their breasts, but the curve of their bottoms, and the secretive components of their vaginas were sharply and enticingly delineated; and there were only bodies here, bodies and enticement and offers and nightmares, which caused him to realize more or less where they were, yes, Paul said to him, this is what a brothel is like here, what do you think, but the women are so beautiful and pretty, Fortinbras answered faintly, there's no way they can be prostitutes, but they are, very much so, try it out, pick one, whichever one you want is yours, said Paul not bothering to lower his voice, and at his further prompting he had to choose one, all the while hearing Paul's ever more enthusiastic voice: so, what do you say, Ixi, well, what do you say to this, my old man? and the woman unbuttoned his fly, and climbed into his lap, while at the same time another woman leant over his shoulder, touching his face with a breath-light touch, caressing his mouth, prying it open with playful strength, and she pressed some kind of pill into his mouth, then he remembered that the pill was blue, the woman thrust her tongue into his mouth, and this tongue played inside his mouth spreading the pill all over his palate, but immediately after that his brain felt like it was exploding, and it was horrifically good, and then he was outside in the cosmos, for one hundred years, and, in the cosmos, there was a mild breeze blowing, and everywhere there were thousands and thousands of billions of radiant stars, and everything was ascending somewhere with insane speed, and in the meantime he ended up underneath a huge rainbow made up of a billion colors, really this rainbow was composed of a billion different colors, he was filled with unspeakable happiness, he was in an immeasurably deep space and endless darkness which nonetheless shone, and then falling, some kind of sickly giddiness, and finally just an incandescent beam of light, an unbearable thundering, every sound hurt, and a million sounds were attacking him, Paul leaned above him, then sat down beside him on the bed, please, turn it off, turn it off, he begged Paul, at which Paul, laughing, stood beside him, turned off the music, and his head was splitting with unbearable pain, close the curtains, I beg you, Paul, he begged, but I closed all the curtains already, Paul laughed, but at least he was there in the apartment that was known to him, where they had arrived before, at least Paul was there next to him, that was good, but what wasn't good was that Paul was laughing in a completely different way than the way Paul used to laugh, there was something in his laughter that was painful to Fortinbras, so he asked him: please don't laugh, fine, said Paul, then I won't laugh, and he laughed some more, but in exchange you start pulling yourself together, because it will be nine-thirty in a second, and if you really want to go we've got to set off now, he said go?! where?! Fortinbras leaned up on his elbows, well, didn't you want to go to the Zone? and it was hard taking a shower, although both of them thought that would help, it didn't help, every single drop of water coming from the shower head struck him with massive force, look, Paul opened the door from time to time, maybe instead we should just put it off if you're like this, no, no way, I'll be fine in a second, he answered, and he forced himself to let the drops of water fall on him from the shower head, and already he had dried off by himself, and he got dressed by himself, just when he went down to the elevator he needed a bit of support in case he lost his balance, because sometimes he would still lose his balance, that's the last symptom, Paul reassured him, your balance will still be looking for itself for a moment, and they were already headed off toward the nearby highway, this time on the inner side of the Dnieper, we'll pick up Mürsel here, Paul said suddenly at a traffic light, like someone who makes all the decisions in these matters, and he turned off, but at first Fortinbras had no idea what was going on: who was this Mürsel, and why did they have to turn off for him, in place of his brain there was an enormous ice-cold chunk of stone, so that he only began to realize where this was headed when he got a glimpse of Mürsel, oh, the guy from yesterday, oh no, anything but that, this flashed through the ice-cold stone, but he mumbled something to him as a way of greeting, I thought—Paul turned back to Fortinbras—it would be more pleasant to make the trip in company, no? and already in the front of the car they were launching into yesterday's theme, Paul wasn't interested in the Zone at all, Fortinbras realized, he lives one hundred kilometers from it, and it's not interesting to him, he looked at the sparse alternation of buildings next to the highway: pubs, apartment houses, farms, shops, tin-roofed churches— they had set off to the north, toward the Zone; and Mürsel, who was not wearing Pierre Cardin this time, but Cerruti, was already in the thick of things, namely that in his view, joint stock companies in shared ownership functioned exactly like those massive enterprises in the old socialist era with no supervision on the part of the owners, in which the management functions as a kind of quasi-owner, and the real owners, who are after all the distributed shareholders, have no idea of what's going on, they have zero representation at the general meetings, they tell them whatever they want, resulting in an inner structure, which, I tell you, is built upon the logic of buddies and friends, there's no role anywhere for expertise, absolutely no question of who is appropriate for a given job, and as a matter of fact this was the case with us too—don't be mad, you Pavel Morozov, Paul said to him, but the parallel wasn't completely clear—still, said Mürsel, who this time was in Cerruti, and with the strong gestures familiar from yesterday: he half turned around so he could speak to Paul, who was behind the steering wheel: but here, you see, the situation is once again personal, because this Italian, this Ficino ended up here in Kiev, because among all the countries where Banco Fortas has subsidiary banks, Kiev is the only place where they will hire someone as a chairman without a university degree, everywhere else a university degree is required, this is determined by the local authorities, so it's up to Kiev, that's the rule here, that's how it is by law for credit institutions, and that's how it should be, nothing will change in this regard, the law concerning credit institutions formulates the rules for banks, including the human rules of the game, well, what's interesting about this is—just imagine, Mürsel shook his head—Albania is the country with the strictest credit-bank regulations, and I know this because once a long time ago I was the chairman of a local supervisory board there, because over there in Albania everything is delegated from Genoa, and I was the only one with the piece of parchment qualifying me to be chair of the supervisory board, well, of course it didn't happen that way, but the joke is that I was the only one with the parchment, do you get it, the whole thing is a joke, just a joke, but that's not the interesting part, well, and so he came here to Kiev, and he lured me over here as well—who's this now? Paul interrupted—well, who am I talking about, you're not paying attention, Paul, I'm talking about that Ficino, who else would I be talking about, well, to cut a long story short, first he was in Tirana, but then he came here to Kiev, because no parchment is needed here, and then he brought me over here, I accepted the offer, I came—but this Ficino, Paul interrupted again, what is he at the bank, he's the chairman, answered Mürsel a little impatiently, because as I was telling you, even somebody without a parchment can be chairman, and he can come here ... well, now you have to know that this subsidiary had been sold half a year before we came here, previously it was in the ownership of the mayor of Kiev, it was his and only his, and for sure they paid off the Italian trade delegation and the inspectors, and they bought just one big pile of shit, because the quality of the outstanding debts was shit, how should I put it, you know what that means, and in this case the owning family had a financial interest in most of the extended credit, there's no doubt—Mürsel spread his hands apart, well, as he had gotten out of it he must have known that the whole thing was just one big pile of shit, namely that the chance that the credit would be repaid was small, if not nonexistent, the prospect, namely, of repayment, was not going to happen, or at least not any time soon, and a lot of this debt had to be appraised, on the basis of which certain provisions had to be made for liabilities which in all likelihood would not be repaid, you understand, it's clear, well, but there are regulations here, right? and the outstanding liabilities and the investments have to be classified—this is how it is all over the world—they're assessed on a quarterly basis, but here, you know, there are several degrees of assessment, and for each degree of classification there are four or five other classifications, and for each of these, with the exception of the highest one—with which accordingly there is no problem—for each degree, local legislation determines a percentage for the liability reserves, these are basic things, what can I say, but so that your friend can understand, the main thing is—Mürsel now turned around to Fortinbras—the main thing is that the provision for liabilities is taken from earnings and placed in a particular account which is not included in those earnings, well, now you should know—he turned back to Paul—that the family—that is the former owner, or mainly his son—definitely—although of course it can't be proved definitively—paid off this guy, this

177

Ficino, for a song, namely he was invited to go sailing on their personal yacht on the Dnieper, he was invited to parties at their home, to receptions and the like, and it's possible that they gave him something, the result of which was that Ficino began to prefer this family, particularly the son of this family, and this preference meant that the family had the money here in deposits, and it was earning much higher than the usual interest rates, well you understand, and now the relationship between myself and this chairman began to quickly deteriorate—he turned back again to Fortinbras—in as much as I'm kind of like a manager in this situation, but just to make things clear, in principle the CEO, and not the chairman, should be the one running the bank, because he's the one who's running the place, and the chairman shouldn't even be interfering with the functioning of the bank, but this guy Ficino interfered and he interfered because he's Italian and the bank is Italian, and the CEO is a Ukrainian who's afraid of Italians, but not of me of course; but my own position is kind of special, because normally I wouldn't be reporting to a manager but directly to the CEO, I'm responsible for the treasury, as you know, in other words resource allocation, and I always ask for—or, to put it more bluntly, order—written documentation for every verbal request, which comes to me from the Italians—well, Ficino did a whole bunch of things which chiefly favored the family members of the former owner, umm, and there were other things too, and in every instance I asked to get it as a written request, well, his tactic was that he always did what he wanted to do, and then somebody else would take the blame, and then he would scream that this idiot had screwed up, well, now, however, there was a paper trail for everything, and so he couldn't do that anymore, well, and as a matter of fact I was the one who got it in the neck when I followed this procedure every single time, which I could make light of, but he didn't, instead he was enraged continually, and he turned more and more against me, and as he turned against me, I also was compelled to react, and his position became more and more entrenched ... who's this now, Fortinbras put forth the question, but only to himself, because he was even less interested in this story, if that was possible, of which he didn't even understand half, because he only paid attention occasionally, sometimes just picking up a word here and there, so that it was difficult, he wasn't interested, the story bored him, indeed, after a while, in the heavy traffic, by the time they left Kiev, he already felt an aversion for this story, and he tried to prevent Mürsel's words from reaching his consciousness, he watched the road in front of them, which was lined with either birch trees or beech trees, he didn't know which, he didn't know trees, maybe they were birch trees, and he looked at the buildings, appearing infrequently now alongside the road, and the roadside vendors: there were many of them for a while after they left Kiev, then they too became ever more infrequent, they were selling cucumbers, lettuce, potatoes, and tomatoes on carpets spread out on the ground, my God, cucumbers, lettuce, potatoes, tomatoes?!—do you have a Geiger counter? he suddenly asked Paul in Danish, interrupting Mürsel, a what? Paul jerked his head back, a Geiger counter, repeated Fortinbras with emphasis, still in the language they shared, why would I need one, Paul frowned, and then quickly turned back to the direction they were going, because he felt that he had held Fortinbras' gaze too long, they were going to crash into something, and all the while Mürsel understood nothing, he looked at Paul, and he looked at Fortinbras, to try to see what was going on, but it didn't last too long, he couldn't bear the pause which was far too long for him, and already he launched into the story again, but Fortinbras decided that from this point on he wasn't going to listen to him at all, not even a word, he felt hurt by Paul's reaction, and by the fact that it didn't even occur to Paul that what obviously seemed to him to be a superfluous precaution, to someone else, for example to him, Fortinbras, was hardly superfluous at all, and that nothing was clearer than the fact that if somebody were headed toward some kind of dan-

179

ger—even if voluntarily, as they were now—then at the very least the most minimal of precautions should be taken, because they were headed toward danger now, on this highway with vegetable sellers sparsely scattered along its edge, more threatening than the most lethal of danger, and Fortinbras at this moment in Paul's car didn't want to explain why he insisted on approaching this menace, he didn't want to, because he knew he desired it, and while he was repulsed by his own desire in vain, he wanted to be there, because what he was feeling was something that was stronger in him than nature, or maybe it was an exaggerated fear of everything that was scary, and this was his desire, his wish: to somehow come into the proximity of that strength of which there never had been and never would be anything more formidable, because this was the one thing that man had started and had been unable to stop—so, you want a Geiger counter, Paul interrupted Mürsel, and he turned to the back seat once again, really, why didn't you say so, why are you so interested in the Zone, what the hell do you want there, Paul turned to the front again, and he seemed a little agitated, but really, tell us already, he continued, what the hell is so interesting for you that you want to go where nobody else wants to go, where nobody ever wanted to go, to wallow in catastrophe like that, it's really not how I knew you, Ixi, Paul lowered his voice, and he grimaced as if he were sorry, Fortinbras saw his eyes glancing back in the mirror, and then he realized that he was sorry, he said to himself, for certain he was sorry, and that's why he was quiet, Fortinbras was quiet, and for a while no one said anything, even Mürsel needed some time to realize that it would be best for him to start speaking and break the silence, because this silence didn't bode anything good, it had all promised to be so much fun, to take this strange character to the Zone, to take this person with a more than strange name, Mürsel noted to himself and finding his voice again, he said: he tripped me up, he simply didn't give me a bonus, claiming that there were losses in the treasury but that wasn't true because the whole bank had been having losses last year, Mürsel raised his voice, well, and then this thing happened in December—and here Mürsel held a slight pause for the sake of effect, but Paul just gazed fixedly at the road, in the back their guest was gazing at the road just as fixedly, just as people in a car usually do, everyone looks at the road, and he too was looking at the road, Mürsel thought to himself that if someone is sitting in a moving vehicle, there's nothing else to do than look at the road in front, although you could also look, for example, at the landscape on the side, if the landscape is interesting, but here it isn't, still, though, you could look at it, Mürsel continued his monologue—yes, when this thing happened in December—but actually it all began six months before that, with the liquidity problems at the bank, and that was caused, among other things, by the fact that the founding capital was too small, the parent branch was supposed to raise it, and the Italians didn't like this idea, no one liked it, and they had no intention of raising the founding capital, especially at a subsidiary, and now here comes Ficino, who—I don't know exactly what the transaction was—transferred the family's money over there through some bank, but with additional interest, it's likely that Ficino had promised the son this additional interest earlier, 10 percent on the dollar to be exact, which is pretty high, right, and now I come into the picture, because I wasn't willing to pay out this extra high interest, namely I asked Ficino to put it in writing that the interest for this transaction would be this high, and this happened six months before, and it was executed with a termination date of one year, so that the money would be with us for one year, and in the meantime in December the Italians in Genoa decided that nonetheless they would raise the founding capital, and of course Ficino was shitting bricks for something like that to happen, something critical like that, because then there could be huge problems if it emerged that here was this 10 percent extra interest on this money, so he wanted to get out of it, but still—Mr. Ertas, said Paul, what kind of sums are we talking about here, could you give me a sense of that so I can have an idea, well, Mürsel shook his head slowly, and he began to pout a little, well, imagine it to be about ten ... Paul glanced sharply at him—or rather, Mürsel pulled his index finger along his forehead—something like, umm, a sum of a hundred million dollars, well something like that, it doesn't matter now, the main thing is that in December Ficino was told to terminate the family's extra interest, but it still wasn't decided if this would be a tactical move, and they they would reinstate it on December 31, and the money would be called in once again, or was it final, nobody knew, and so Ficino and his people were maneuvering, and that was the problem, because according to the law the obligatory reserves which a given bank has to make on the basis of foreign sources, in other words for the central bank it's a question of the deposit as a guarantee for the given amount, well, now you also know very well, if you're familiar at all with macroeconomics and theory, that for every deposit the percentage will be different, and now no one could decide if it should be valid for a half-year or a whole year, and Ficino and his crew were counting on it being a transitional thing, accordingly one half year, but in the meantime it emerged that this wasn't possible, because it could only be for one year—no, I'm wrong, they were counting on one year, and it could only be for half a year, and because of that they had fewer reserves than they should have had; in cases like that usually the central bank imposes a fine, and now Ficino began to get frantic, saying that there had been a mistake, it was bungled, the calculations were wrong and so on, namely he was talking about the treasury, well, I asserted that this wasn't true: I didn't make any mistakes, and we didn't make any mistakes, because I said to him, to Ficino: you said, right here in this room what the information was, this was the conversation that I heard, and of course Ficino wasn't satisfied, they began to investigate who was responsible, the wrangling began, internal audits, and Ficino tried in every way he could to smear it on me, but I was right there with all the written orders as well as the regulation stating that this wasn't my responsibility but the responsibility of the back office, but the back office themselves could hardly be completely responsible, because if they had no information, which they didn't, then the back office couldn't decide what to do or what not to do, in any event things were looking pretty bad for Ficino, and so he decided that as the whole affair was not clean he would split the part of the bank that deals with these deposits off from Treasury, and move it to the back office so that nothing like this could happen in the future, which is absurd, because this division would have no idea what the info was, so that the problem wasn't solved, because the right solution would be for the treasury to function in two parts in coordination with each other, in other words there was a lot of tension and that's the way it is even now, and now I want to get out of there, as a matter of fact it's an open secret that I want out, but I don't know what you have to say about this, and Mürsel turned to Paul, and he was quiet, and he waited for Paul to say something, but Paul didn't say anything, and Fortinbras was convinced that it was because he also wasn't paying any attention and didn't even care that Mürsel was waiting for his reply and that this was because he was thinking about him, Fortinbras, and the situation was becoming uncomfortable, I would be so happy to jump out of this car, thought Fortinbras, I'd jump out, and I would undo the fact that I am here, he felt that Paul comprehended that something had changed between them, and that's what he was thinking about, and not about Mürsel's story, which was likely no more interesting to him that it was to his guest here in the back seat, Mürsel continued to be silent, and maybe now he just realized that his story hadn't really thrown anyone into a fever here, Mürsel cast a glance back, and this glance was clearly full of rage, and he cast a glance to the side as well, at Paul, and this glance was clearly full of hurt, the Audi A4 hummed along softly, you can't go faster than the speed limit here, said Paul in the friendliest possible voice, there are so many policemen, they're lying in wait, we can't take any risks, is that okay? and Paul turned around again, and looked at Fortinbras, and smiled at him; and that's all it took for Paul to pull himself together, Paul always needed only twenty seconds to regain his composure, and that dear smile appeared on his face again, that smile Fortinbras loved so much, and now too he was grateful for it even if it wasn't sincere, he was grateful to Paul that there hadn't been a rupture, he didn't want that, and he smiled back, and with that a very important accord was created between them, and that was exactly how their friendship had started too, when they were both still in Hungary, when they both went to pester a deputy department head at the Ministry: Fortinbras was seeking financial support for a Danish-Hungarian exhibit in his gallery, and Paul also needed funding for something at his bank from this deputy department head, and they warmed up to each other, two foreigners among the wild herdsmen, then it turned out that there was only one sum of money allocated for cultural events like this, and among the two projects only one could be awarded the sum, and then Paul came over to him, and that smile was on his face, as he allowed the money to go to the gallery project, and that's how they arranged it, and of course he, Fortinbras, returned the favor as soon as he could, so that they met up with each other ever more frequently, and they parted company as inseparable good friends, and then over the years they visited each other, and Paul said that he never would have believed that at his age he would still be able to find a true friend, and Fortinbras also admitted that the situation with him was exactly the same, he found it inconceivable that he would be able to find such a deep and true friend in anyone, and it had all started to be torn apart yesterday and today up until this moment, but now it was resolved, that is once again Paul had resolved it, he was so grateful to him there in the back seat that he didn't even know what to do, and so as not to bother Mürsel again, who had regained his presence of mind, and had expli-

cated a few of the finer points from the story—almost imperceptibly
he reached out towards the seat in front, and he gently patted Paul on
the shoulder, just so lightly, like a breath, and Paul didn't turn his head
back to him, but for a second he did a little bit, and Fortinbras felt that
he had received this reconciliation gratefully, indeed he received this
subtle indication of apology, and nothing would ever separate them
now, it was only these strange circumstances that troubled them sometimes, and maybe the only reason for the trouble was his own excessive
sensitivity, thought Fortinbras, and he gazed penitently at the road in
front of them, through the windshield in between the heads of Paul
and Mürsel, the road in front of them leading toward the Zone, the
road on which not one single vegetable seller could be seen anymore,
the road was lined by birch or beech trees—I think, thought Fortinbras, that they're birch.

A DROP OF WATER

The circle he must have drawn himself with some white powder on the sidewalk, then he must have stepped into the middle of the circle, launched himself into the air into a handstand, and then—after stabilizing himself by propping the soles of his feet against the wall—shifted his weight to one hand, the right, thereby freeing the left, and ever since then he has been standing there on one hand, only the one, while beginning to gesture with the other, he must have started like that, and he has remained like that, who knows how long he has been standing here on that one hand, while with the other one, the left, moving only this hand from the wrist, the left, he signs, he points, he communicates, for these are obviously signs, communications, words of a language no one understands except for him, bunching the fingertips together and then suddenly spreading them so they fly apart, then he starts all over and keeps it up for minutes on end, or else he revolves this left hand from the wrist to the right, and then once more to the right, or he makes a fist, then opens it, shuts, opens, shuts it again, and finally very slowly, he turns it once again from right to left but never from left to right, so that it seems he is able to turn this hand around completely in one direction; or else he extends his index and pinky with middle and ring fingers curled under, while flexing his thumb almost all the way back, a seemingly never-ending variety of finger and palm positions, all the while standing upside down, on one hand, for how many hours? how many hours now?—his legs in the air are slightly bent at the knee, the soles of his feet are leaning against the wall, though even so he may waver slightly from time to time but no one among those who surround him, not one tourist or pilgrim, can endure to watch until he collapses, until he can no longer keep it up and collapses on the sidewalk in the middle of the circle made of powdered pigment, because he can bear it longer than anyone who stops to stare, standing on one hand he can stand it longer than anyone, his greasy white beard so compact that upside down, it barely bends back toward his mouth and nose, but his long, thick, and luxuriant white hair tumbles down in dreadlocks toward the ground and from time to time these knots stir in the feeble breeze, only this greasy beard and the dreadlocks and the two hanging ends of his purple loincloth stir at times in this feeble breeze, while his eyes are open and unblinking and he stands on one hand and tirelessly keeps sending signs in the middle of the circle made of sprinkled white powder and nobody is able to wait it out until his body drops, until that one hand wearies, incredible, the tourists and pilgrims mutter, this is impossible, says a thin European woman, why doesn't someone take him down and set him on his feet, do something for god's sake, she can't look on any longer, her companion at last leads her away, and our man keeps on standing on his right hand here at Manikarnika Ghat, while carrying on with the left hand in a language no one understands, beside him, his skin is gray but this skin had once upon a time probably been black, now it is gray, as if coated by cement dust, and it is covered in many places with running sores, his feet, trunk, hands, arms have no flesh, only this skin, he sits at the feet of the giant elephants of the Annapurna temple and he does nothing else but look at the passersby with enormous burning eyes, his left thumb and index finger pinching that parchment-like skin over the bone of his right upper arm, showing that there is no flesh there, and then he spreads his arms and extends his hands forward, his palms are stretched out, in case someone will take pity and throw him a rupee, or at least a few paisas, but no one does, so he again pinches the skin on his right upper arm, pinches it and with his left thumb and index finger pulls it away while looking at the passersby with those extraordinary, flaming, enormous eyes, to show that here, take a look, he has not an ounce of flesh on his body, then he extends both palms forward, maybe someone will toss him a rupee, or at least a few paisas, but no one does, meanwhile next to his emaciated body music blares from a cassette tape recorder, a man's voice, the voice of Baba Sehgal says Memsaab oh Memsaab, and he again pinches the skin, to show that he has not an ounce of flesh on his body, extends both palms, perhaps someone will throw him a rupee or at least a few paisas, but no one does, the music by his side blares, Memsaab oh Memsaab, Baba Sehgal blares from that weatherbeaten tape recorder near the feet of the giant elephants, frightful multitudes throng the street, everyone is in a hurry, everyone has something urgent to do, for millennia they have had urgent things to do every single moment, but meanwhile men and women—a group here and a group there—stop to discuss deeply absorbing matters, one after another, suddenly finding time in this vast forest of humans, men stroll by holding hands, tuktuks dash across inconceivably congested intersections, five or six tuktuks simultaneously from different directions, at the same time that taxis and rickshaws race across, then cows, dogs, and an enormous throng of people, no one collides with another, which cannot be possible, because as a matter of fact people charge at each other in the intersections, yet all are unharmed when they reach the other side, and that's how life goes on during each and every minute of the day, because the intersections, too, run counter to every rational expectation; in the vicinity of the Bharat Mata temple, around a banyan tree's immensely broad trunk with its pale-gray smooth bark and immensely complex web of aerial roots, a very old woman in a saffron-colored sari is circling with hands held out waving them up and down and propelling herself as if in mimicry of flying, she circles round and round around the banyan tree without saying a word, her eyes are shut but she makes no mistake, her movements are as confident as if she had been circling here for millennia, and perhaps that is the case, her hands flap as if they were bird's wings, her body sways, then she opens her eyes, and now one can see that these eyes contain nothing, they are empty, dried-out sockets with functioning eyelids, dark, wrinkled pits in place of the eyes, the saffron-colored sari sways left and right, and she circles, circles tirelessly, her hands rise and descend, the banyan tree's thick aerial roots protrude from the trunk above ground and twisting and turning around their axis these awesome aerial roots reach all the way down to disappear in the ground and anchor the banyan tree which clings to the earth with a seemingly supernatural strength, but it is impossible to tell whether it is merely bracing and supporting itself here next to the Bharat Mata or whether it is the tree that holds together the earth by means of these spectral, serpentine, giant aerial roots, keeping the earth from caving in and collapsing, opening up the forty steps to the Sesa Pit, as it is called here, the approach to the lower worlds; one lazy wave of the Ganges plashes on the river bank and languidly melts away, a few hundred meters past Assi Ghat, at the fourth large bend of the horrendous putrid sewage canal bearing the same name—Assi Ghat—not far from the temple of Durga, in the courtyard of a House of Dying, ancient old men sit and lie around in the sun, someone has more or less cleared the weeds in the courtyard, crumbling cloisters surround the yard, as if sheltering them, these forty-odd old men who, judging by their looks, must have arrived here mostly from Meghalaya, West Bengal, Bihar, and Uttar Pradesh, to wait it out here until death does away with them, in the morning they are given some thin mush, but not all of them want even that, for there are some who refuse to take any food, let death arrive that much sooner, they do not talk to each other, each one is solely focused on the place he occupies sitting or lying down, focused on the

body that is still his, they are sitting or lying down, waiting from morning to night, and from night until morning, waiting for long-desired
death, their eyes do not say anything any more, they merely stare in
front of themselves but without the least bitterness, sadness, or des-
peration, least of all fear, on these wrinkled faces, instead it is peace that
reigns over every feature, peace within these men, and around them,
peace and quiet, even if it is not unbroken, since external noises from
the street and alongside the sewage canal naturally filter in, at times a
sharp cry or car horn or sounds of music, but in here nothing, no TV,
no radio, no cassette player, just peace, and waiting, weeks must have
passed, and weeks will pass like this, until one after another, seated or
lying down, these men topple over for good, topple and stretch out, to
be taken away by the staff, the untouchables responsible for burning
the corpses, they quickly wrap the body in a shroud, and are already
running with the body freed of the soul to the cremating Ghats, while
a brass band clad in the most garish colors imaginable is approaching
on Raja Sir Motichand Road heading slowly toward Maulvibagh, and
the players do not create the impression of a band since each of them
seems to be giving a private concert, at times drawing completely
apart, so that the trombone player could not possibly hear the notes
played by the trumpeter, they are that far apart, one would think that
therefore the music would likewise fall apart, but no, the band is playing in perfect unison, without the slightest hitch in rhythm or har-
mony, it is unfathomable how they do it, possibly the explanation lies
in the Sewak logos on their fancy headgear, but no one bothers to look
for an explanation, obviously there is no need to do so, there are many
locals and many pilgrims here, also many cows and dogs, street urchins
are running around, back and forth, they seem to be in near ecstasy,
and a goodly number of tourists with cameras hanging from their
necks, and about the same number of rats (in other words, hordes of
them), the street urchins follow the musicians on both sides, the fife

players, drummers, horn players, tuba players, and of course the trumpeters and trombone players, the latter are obviously the street urchins' favorites, at times a trombone player turns toward them to blow a note, even poking one with the tip of the slide, provoking flight amid great squeals of delight, they are playing British military band music, "The British Grenadiers," in one endless repeat, as they advance down the length of Raja Sir Motichand Road in the direction of Maulvibagh, but they aren't followed by a decked-out car carrying some bride or groom, nor a carnival float with an enthroned maharajah, neither wedding nor procession, neither funeral nor holiday, none of that, they simply keep marching and blasting "The British Grenadiers" relentlessly for the locals, the pilgrims, the tourists, the rats, the street urchins, the cows, the dogs, and the vendors who stand in their shop entrances taking it all in, until, by this time near Maulvibagh, this extraordinary band with its unknown purpose suddenly disbands all at once, as if they had stopped playing upon some prearranged signal, they instantly lower their instruments, however they don't depart as a band all together in the same direction but rather each musician goes his way wherever he pleases, in his expensive, colorful, fringed, and medal-spangled uniform, one going this way, another that way, indeed they scatter in all directions as if this were the normal course of events, and perhaps that is the case, for no one is amazed, everyone takes cognizance of it, the locals and the pilgrims, street urchins and vendors, the tourists as well as the rats, and they all continue where they had left off, the tune of "The British Grenadiers" doesn't die right away, but for about another half minute it fades in the air above Raja Sir Motichand Road, and only after that does the hubbub of the street resume its rule over the city, and this hubbub flares up again like a flame, and indeed it is just like a malignant conflagration that nothing can put out, nothing can abate, alongside speeding vehicles, street philosophers, handbill distributors, and humming thickets of cables crisscrossing the air, the great stars of

Bollywood pop music are blaring from radios, TVs, even from loud-speakers rigged on tuktuk cars, they blare *I burn on the pyre of eternal love for you,* and in this wildfire of noises he comes to the decision that he must leave, because he is in mortal danger here, demanding not only certain safety measures, not only an elevated attention level, but the realization that he must immediately beat it from here, perhaps the best way would be to withdraw cautiously, retreating step by step, backing out of this place, the upshot of it being that he absolutely must leave the city, he must right now take the first steps toward this end, by now he is like a bowstring drawn taut to the point of snapping, and so, tensed, he is now looking at a backpack lying among his belongings on the indescribably filthy bed, thinking that at least this backpack must be ready when the moment arrives, the backpack must be packed and ready to go, to avoid any needless delay when he would have to leave, meanwhile however the greatest question being when that moment of departure would arrive, he knows that is vitally important, the right decision made at the right time, the correct choice of the overture to either a cautious sliding away or a headlong flight at the greatest speed imaginable, for if he were to miscalculate the right moment, then he would lose his only chance of finding that opening in the midst of bil-lions of things, an opening, for him, for among the billions of things this one reality staggers the mind, indeed forces the mind to a stand-still, his mind at least, making him a minor character in a nightmare that has no meaning whatsoever in its totality or in its parts, which is why it is so difficult, almost impossible, to pick the right time, further-more the greatest problem is not knowing whether there is indeed a correct moment at all, and not simply the seemingly endless labyrinth of wrong moments in which he must wander and inevitably lose his way, an unbearable thought, so that after a while he obviously has to pick another one, which would lead to choosing yet another moment, and of course that wouldn't be the right one but he happened to choose it, meaning now he is left with a total of only sixty-six steps, for a mad cow would trample him, a tuktuk would run him over, a huge chunk of stone masonry from the window of a sacred tower would be dropped on his head, as if by mere chance, an accident, that sort of thing, but no, they could also stab him in the kidney from behind at Vishwanath temple, or trip him up in an alley on the steps leading to Kedar Ghat, or wrestle him to the ground in the vicinity of Sanskrit University, not in order to rob him but to gouge out his left eye with a giant spike, for some reason only the left eye, and then—again, for some unknown reason—they could beat his head to a pulp with a large cudgel painted red, in other words, do away with him, and then instead of throwing him into the sacred river, leave him in the vast Dumping Ground stretching northwest to northeast past the great station of Varanasi Junction, toss him on top of the largest mound of garbage, that would be that, and then the giant vultures would arrive, wild dogs, roosters, beggars, rats, and children, to devour him piecemeal until not a shred of flesh remains, as the sun is setting now over the Ganges, he can see from the light hitting the walls of the building across from the hotel—the hotel?!—the way this light gradually withdraws from the world, having turned dark orange, after which it is like blood—thick, leaden, sticky and filthy as well—as it glows above all the garbage, this is the Varanasi twilight, and it occurs twice a day, once in the morning when the light appears and once in the evening when it departs, this is the only place in the world where all this needs to be explained, because morning here is as if it were the only one ever and the evening likewise, as if there were to be no other mornings, or evenings, because that's how this city works, as if every one of its stinking moments suggested it had only one day, after which nothing would remain in place, everything would be swept away by this one and only evening, swept away by the sunset that in Varanasi can only occur just this once, for the light would never return here, this is what each and every alley radiates and in every alley every dimly outlined figure, and every minuscule star showing in the weary sunset, reflected in the dim eyes of every figure, and this is how it has been every blessed day for millennia, for tens and hundreds of thousands of years, each day it seems impossible that there would come another day, and perhaps there really is no other day, only this single one, or not even this, which amounts to the same thing now in his quivering brain, and the same holds true in this brain regarding the stories, those too had given his brain a good scare, for in vain there might be ten, a hundred, a thousand million stories day after day in this insane inferno, on that one and only day, or not even then, in vain does this or that happen and keep happening ten, a hundred, a thousand million times in the alleys and major intersections, on this one and only day, or not even then, it's as if among all those stories only a single one were true, or not even one, so that the succession of days one after another, or the stack of stories mounting up one on top of the other: neither of them holds up, neither exists, one cannot rely on them, cannot rely on anything, here everything operates under the aegis of a raving madness, albeit not at a command from above or below but because each and every element of existence is insane in its own right, raves solely in and of itself until it's done, things in Varanasi do not refer to anything else beyond themselves, positioned side by side in this insanity, but without setting ablaze some great big conflagration of madness for in fact each thing possesses its own individual madness; he stands by the window one shoulder leaning against the wall, sheltered by the imitation leather curtain decorated with giant rosette motifs, so that no one can notice him from the street, while through a chink he can observe what goes on down below, he stands there leaning against the unspeakably grimy wall, looking at the street below, then at the foul bed with the backpack on it, and finally he sees himself with the backpack on his back, taking the utmost care he first opens the door a crack to take a peek and then slips out, tiptoes down the stairs, without paying he glides past the rose-pink solid cast plastic desk resting on enormous elephant feet in imitation of a nonexistent palace or temple, constituting the reception desk of the now completely empty hotel, then he is out on the street and he is off, taking the first available turn, then once again—mind you not four times, and not always to the right, or always to the left, this is what the siren screams inside his head, not the same turn four times, because then I'm back where I started from, he thinks, terrified, and they will find me, of course they must know what I am up to, that's for sure, they knew all along what he was trying to do, allowing him to leave the hotel room, allowing him to glide past the reception desk without paying, they must obviously have a way of following him sure as death, as he turns left, then right, then left again and right, they know exactly why he is frightened, and after this insane rush disguised as a tourist's leisurely perambulation he finds himself out on the steps of Hanuman Ghat precisely where he least wanted to be, here at the ghastly scene of ritual bathing, for this—the mere proximity of the ghats—means it is utterly hopeless to think of an escape, the Ganges is death, the ghats are death, the women resplendent in their brightly colored saris at the ghats are death, the men in their loincloths at the ghats are death, but the Ganges is death supreme, this unsurpassable incarnation of sewage, this millennia-old constant of filth flowing and frothing past, his only chance would be going in exactly the opposite direction, he cannot hire a rickshaw, cannot take a cab, cannot board a train, the one and only direction (if any such exists) may offer a promise of hope only if he proceeds mindlessly, only if he doesn't premeditate the where and the how, his only chance is trying not to think about what the sole possible mode of escape could be, consigning himself solely to his panic, that should do, and there is plenty of it, ever since he set foot here, ever since he arrived in Varanasi, and set eyes on his first ghat, set eyes on the Ganges, he knew that he should not have traveled here, in fact the whole plan to visit India had been ill-conceived from the word go, as a matter of fact, he hadn't wanted to come here, I never wanted to, not I, but I simply couldn't say no when I could and should have, and written to the man from Bombay whom I'd met in Sarajevo that it wasn't a good idea, after their meeting and his own rash and courtesy-prompted show of interest he should have replied to the letter of invitation from Bombay that no, after all this was not the right time for a trip to India, always say no, always, without exception, that is what he should have done, he had so many chances to do so, he could have at the time of buying the airplane tickets, he could have done so afterwards, when he already had the tickets, he could have still changed his mind right before the departure, or even after arriving in Delhi, seeing that things were happening too fast, when you act without thinking, when you simply take things as they come, however he had not only been rash but downright reckless, irresponsible and dumb, a man out of control, it wasn't the first time this had happened, with him this was a chronic condition, and since he knew himself well, why had he not noticed that there was a problem, there would be trouble, that he shouldn't think of going to India, he should not allow things to just happen to him, because then one fine day you find yourself in India ... but he allowed things to happen and so he found himself in India, what is more in Varanasi, the last place he should have allowed himself to visit, where he fell and kept falling and was unable to stop falling, he was caught in a trap, he knew right away that he was trapped when, having arrived at the main station after a brutal train ride he managed, in spite of every stratagem of the skin-and-bones tuktuk man, to have himself transported to Assi Ghat, where he immediately became aware that this should not be happening, as he caught sight of the Ganges, and regarded the winding river, the rows of tumbledown buildings with their crumbling forms and fading colors—they were heaped upon each other on the hills curving all along these bends in the Ganges, this was already enough, this first hour, this miasmic air shimmering in the filthy, muggy heat was in itself enough, the timeless bathers in the septic water, who had been there ever since the time of Vishnu, dipping into and drinking the disgusting water of the Ganges, it was enough to see the appallingly oafish, clueless, and shameless herds of fat and not-so-fat tourists with their prohibitively expensive photographic equipment attempting to make something of the fact that this city was a sacred place for hundreds of millions, it was enough for him in the horrendous smog to catch a glimpse of temple buildings, palaces, towers, shrines, and terraces heaped one atop the other along the hilly banks of the winding river in order to see that each one was useless and senseless; these first impressions should already have sufficed to make him realize what he had gotten himself into, but actually it took the stench of Varanasi to make him truly panicked, the omnipresent putrefaction, the overpowering, stifling, cloyingly sweet, acrid, gluey smell of decomposition, because even if he didn't right away attribute a fundamental importance to it, he did so upon waking after the first night, when he could feel it in his mouth, lungs, stomach, and brain, and then on his first outing after a few steps he stumbled upon the first open sewer drain and the endless succession of dungheaps with cows browsing around them along with stray dogs, rats and children, and the odor hit him—from which one couldn't free oneself, this was, such was, the smell of Varanasi, and after that he kept smelling it, sleeping and waking, it permeated the roof of his mouth, his throat, lungs, stomach and even his brain, it was stifling, yes, and cloyingly sweet and acrid, gluey and murderous, which latter, this murderous potential, contained an especially cruel element, namely that according to locals and pilgrims Varanasi is at least as much the city of peace as of death, there is no crime here, announced the smiling young men walking hand in hand, oh no, there is no robbery here, laughed the women on the banks of the Ganges, believe me, no one comes here intending to do harm, insisted everyone from the street barber to the skinny craftsman of fancy leather goods who also repaired remote controls, because beside peace, this was the city of Kashi, as they called it, the city of longed-for oblivion, but don't let that put you off, explained the policeman wielding his long, crooked staff at the intersection, don't be astonished by that, growled a lanky meditator at a Shiva temple, in response to which, like everyone else, he at first kept nodding, yes, he understood, naturally, of course—but afterward, and most certainly by this day, he stopped doing that, and he was no longer willing to take part in what for him was a devastating game: how can he do so now when he no longer understands anything, understanding is impossible here—he plunges into the first alley after the first turn from the hotel—because how can one be reconciled to the fact that at least three million people live here who mistake the abnormal for the normal, maybe this has been so for millennia; for now, hoping he is at last making his escape, he reflects that in this city pervaded by the very smell of death, children and grown men will find a suitable spot of even a few square meters and instantly start up a game of cricket, no, this cannot be normal, he thinks, that wherever there is a small open space between two dung-heaps which five or six kids or adults consider qualified to be a play-ground satisfying the minimal requirements of the game, why, the bowler is already throwing the ball, the fact that such multitudes of infinitely pitiable humans (at least three million every day) not only know that there is such a thing as cricket but actually play it, well, this cannot be called normal, there are batsmen and bowlers, in place of cricket balls they use tennis balls, or anything vaguely similar that can be thrown and batted, and this game is played by horrendous masses of people who thrash about in the world's most destitute inferno: they play the game, as if it were the most natural thing to do in the midst of this smell of death, that is insane, he thought after his first few hours here, and he still thinks this now, as slowing down his steps, slowing down to keep from breaking into a run, he roams through the alleyways as he had resolved to do: mindlessly, not even relying on his instincts, relying on nothing, simply tramping on, turning right, then left, something is bound to happen, something other than what he can count on happening with high likelihood, but nothing happens other than what has already alarmed him more than once, for as he walks along every few meters at least one person wants to sell him something, it hardly matters what, something, anything ranging from a delicious glass of chai with milk to the unexplored mysteries of Varanasi, and they are all very thin, with delicate bones, enormous brown eyes, white shirts, light gray pants made of synthetic fabric and ironed to a sharp crease, shod in flimsy Chinese flipflops or not even that, but the essential fact is their touch, for as he advances, he keeps feeling their touch, and he has never encountered this kind of touch: not aggressive, not invasive, not impertinent, not rough, on the contrary, they are the tenderest of touches, absolutely singular, gentle, warm touches, taking hold of his arm or hand, or rather they only graze his arm or hand, his waist, back, or shoulder, quite tenderly, he should have gotten used to this but he could not, on the contrary, he had a horror of these tender touches, and he has a horror of them now as he walks on and can feel another one, and yet another, and once again, and again, it will never end, he refrains from looking at them, because then he would be lost, because then he must stop and hear out why he should drink a delicious glass of chai with milk right now, why he should go ahead and hire a tuktuk now, why he should purchase a carpet, a transistor radio, an authentic Sony mini-TV made in Japan, a necklace talisman for good luck, or possibly a large quantity of quicklime, or a lot of garden lanterns or ten wagonloads of bamboo sprouts, please come with us, these touches entreat, come to a much finer hotel than where you are staying, please come with us, here are Bengali music and dance the like of which you have never experienced before, please do come, you will learn where the

Sesa Pit leads into a realm in the bowels of the Earth, come, do come, it matters not where the Pit leads, because something will await you there; and he doesn't wave them off, because then he would be lost, he gives no sign of acknowledging these offers, although it takes the greatest effort to ignore the accompanying touches, to not pull away his arm, his hand, to keep his shoulder from shuddering, because that would already be taken for a sign of compliance, a response to the offer, and then once again he would be lost, because they would distract him from proceeding where he wanted to go, which is anywhere away from Varanasi; even as he is about to run away, he mustn't lose his self-possession here where these touches take place, because that would get him swept away, and detoured back toward Varanasi instead of out and away from it, back down into the depths, ending up inevitably at the ghats of the Ganges, where death awaits, where—as he was told at the very beginning—death is more than a joyful liberation, and that is precisely what he refuses to accept, he wants liberation not from death but from Varanasi, for him the Ganges is not sacred, he doesn't know what it is, nor does he want to know, the Ganges is a river carrying dead dogs and dead humans, moldy shreds of linen and Coca-Cola cans, lemon-yellow flower petals and planks from a flat-bottomed boat, anything, everything and forever, he would love to rave now as he forges ahead, going somewhere, anywhere, but he cannot afford to rave because his raving would immediately fit into the reality of Varanasi, as a raving madman he would be instantly accepted and absorbed by Varanasi, and of course it is still possible that would be his fate, that suddenly he would break down and go stark raving mad, overwhelmed by a desperate seizure, and then it would be all over for him, because Varanasi would swallow him up, it would take him in, that is from then on he would belong to Varanasi, but for now he is still hanging on, he has unplugged his brain, his instincts, he has completely shut down everything inside him, for he is certain that otherwise he would not have the ghost of a chance: away, get away, not even this is throbbing inside him any more, nothing is throbbing inside him, he keeps walking, from the alleys toward the wider streets, then back to the alleys, pretending to be a tourist, his movements mimic distracted rubbernecking, to lessen the likelihood of being accosted, to make those touches go away, but of course they do not, he shudders at the thought of these touches, but is nonetheless able to master his trembling, as another dull wave of the Ganges thuds against the shore, unseen but heard by him, as he hears it dying away on the lowest stone step of the nearby embankment, that means he has once again found his way to the riverbank, therefore he turns quickly around and sets out in the opposite direction, keeping on for a while, in order to get as far away from the deathly tranquil sites of ritual bathing, trying unsuccessfully to walk around the enormous, flattened yellow-green cow pats, as he steps into one he stops to scrape the shit off his shoe against the edge of a curbstone, and he is already surrounded by them, they say please by all means buy a hair dryer, or for a thousand rupees they'll take him to Sarnath, or else for a very reasonable price they know of original Dancing Krishna paintings from the period of the Bundi School, strictly speaking it makes no difference if some of it remains on his shoe, the important thing is to get rid of the bulk of it so he won't slip and fall, the stink is all around him anyway, for this type of shit smell plays a dominant role in Varanasi, as it does during the cooler winter months when the city is heated, for the ones that more or less solidify in the dust of the street are harvested, it is the sole livelihood of one class of untouchables who have been collecting it assiduously for millennia in small push carts to heap them up in towering stacks, ripening or drying, depending on what they are destined for, although actually in some instances their purpose doesn't matter, for it can happen that the heated ammonia explodes, demolishing one of these towers of shit and then it is a total loss, so that passing one of these shit towers—and the inner city is full of them, one better be careful—after the first few weeks the visitor's attention is called to these, he is very cautious by now, as he passes one of these shit towers, the stench is thicker than usual, he gags, he can smell the ammonia but there is no explosion, he has squeaked past; a sizeable covey of small schoolchildren darts past him wearing sailor blouses, book bags on their backs, one in the center of the group holds an iPhone and all the kids want to see it, there is something very interesting happening on it, this is how they pass him, swirling like a whirlpool around the hand holding the iPhone, he can feel he is getting tired, on the go all morning, and still dawdling here in the inner city; this is getting impossible, it is endless, he must try to think straight now, so he decides to plug back in, to reconnect his brain, but he needs a place for that, a secure zone, which presents itself as he passes behind the Ashok Nagar post office where he comes upon a bit of green—lawn and shrubs and trees—of course the place is also full of people, perhaps because of the shade, at any rate after a lengthy search he encounters an ancient old man, bare bones, with coal-black skin and a thick crop of white hair, wearing a loincloth, sitting in a yogic pose with his eyes closed, this will do fine, he settles down by the man's side and turns his brain back on, what to do now, he thinks, and this is precisely what he'd believed he must avoid at all costs, that in fact there is nothing else he can rely on, nothing but the Ganges, for at least the river has a direction which he can follow to get out of Varanasi, there's no other way, he thinks by the side of the ancient old man with coal-black skin and luxuriant crop of white hair, who, his eyes closed in deep meditation, has also chosen total immobility on this forenoon, and he too closes his eyes, he needs rest; his shoe stinks of shit, his feet are burning with fatigue, his waist and back hurt, his neck hurts, his shoulder hurts, his head is about to fall off, something is stinging his eyes awfully and his tears well up, and now maybe on account of these tears—for his eyes are full of them as if he were weeping, perhaps as a result of the murky, insidious power

of the sunlight filtering through smog—here comes one offering picture postcards of London, Paris, Rome, and won't you buy some cast-
iron frying pans, come, I'll take you there, to see what no tourist has
ever seen before, I'll take you to Baba Ka Ghar, Baba Ka Ghar, you can
see it for two-fifty, three boys are sitting around him now, probably he
had fallen asleep and they didn't want to miss this opportunity, here,
look at this compact manicure set with a mini Taj Mahal in the middle,
buy this complete Placidomingo, the best buy in CDs, believe me, so
that he cannot remain here any longer, somehow he manages to leave
those three behind, although evidently they still have plenty of other
offers for him, where were they going to take him? never mind, he must
reach the Ganges, which is not difficult to do, he knows from past experience, no matter which direction you set out in—and this is precisely the problem—you always end up by the Ganges sooner or later,
and so he too arrives there not much later, it takes barely an hour, and
he is there already, stopping at the top of the flight of steps leading to
Dasashwamedh Ghat, down below through the thick crowd of men
and boys a single possible path opens up, only to immediately close
behind him as he makes his way in their midst, the men are seated
tightly packed side by side on the steps, staring at their navels as the
saying goes, chatting, contemplating the scene, there really is no other
way down to the water's edge besides what they, sensing him, open up
expressly for him, as if they were guiding me, he thinks, but immediately decides it is better if he again shuts down all thinking and intuitions, so that reaching the lowermost step of Dasashwamedh Ghat,
toward where he is now descending through the throng, he may set out
downhill, facing the Ganges, downward, that's how it should be, but
when there remain only a few steps between him and the riverbank, he
bumps into an unexpected obstacle in his passage through the tempo-
rary path that continuously opens up and then closes behind him, although this is not the way to describe it, every word is inaccurate: unexpected and also obstacle are inaccurate terms, and so is "bumps into,"

since throughout his downward progress he has had a feeling something was about to happen, so that it was not unexpected, and how could he call it an obstacle when it is that well-known Varanasi hand, that familiar soft touch that stops him with gossamer delicacy, something you can't bump into, since it is the merest caress grazing his leg, a signal that won't let him pass on; naturally on account of the downward momentum he wishes to move his leg away from this touch, but the touch is determined, determined to stop him, so what else can he do but stop, he sees a man of uncertain age, an obese figure that is unusual, in fact extraordinary among Hindus, he could possibly belong to the highest caste, on the other hand he is practically naked so it is hard to tell, he has only a dirty loincloth and great big ears with elongated lobes and thick snow-white hair held together by a rubber band in the back and outsized, bulky, black-rimmed glasses on the bridge of his nose, as leaning on his elbows he contemplates the water in front of him, then he turns his head left and looks up at him, his three enormous jowl-creases echoing the movement in an amusing way, as that head seeks him out, even as he is still in the process of withdrawing his leg from that touch, but for that to succeed, the ankle should be released, but it isn't, the man is still holding on, although most delicately, to that ankle, and keeps looking at him, although not in the manner of one accosting another, but rather as one chatting with someone in the middle of a conversation, about to point out a new aspect of the subject under discussion, and the man casually remarks, did you know that according to local tradition a single drop of the Ganges is in itself a temple? his voice is soft and gentle, deep and friendly, and instead of the peculiar local English, the man speaks the most immaculate Queen's English, which makes him drop his guard for the first time in many a day, and he makes a mistake ... an error, because he says something in turn so that the man should release him, he flings out something without thinking, it is only a HELLO, but this, this oversight, this mistake, this error, this HELLO is to have serious consequences, that is to say, it already has, because within seconds he finds himself on the receiving end of a vast monologue, which he should not in the least have allowed to happen, meanwhile there is no way back, because it is all over for anyone who utters a single HELLO, and this is what indeed happens, the man with the eyeglasses, partly recumbent and partly twisting and turning his enormously obese body toward him in the midst of the throng, now makes it definitely obvious that he is not moving aside, but maintains the same gaze as before, faintly mocking and faintly commiserating but not in the least bit unfriendly, while holding on to the ankle and saying again that a single drop of the Ganges is a temple, what do you think of that? asks the man, addressing him, and he just stands there waiting for the downward path to open up, he stands there and looks down at the man who is still looking up at him, and far from releasing him, is either actually holding, or seems to be still holding, the ankle of the one addressed, somehow this exerts the same power on him, the thick arms and thighs like four elephant trunks, the entire body like a giant globe of fat, but up above, at the level of the head that is melting down into pathological obesity—and the onlooker is confused by this—the original features can be distinctly made out and the face thus discernible from the vague outlines of eyes, nose and chin is beautiful, and the mouth in this beautiful face now resumes, repeating for the third time, just think, a temple in a single drop of water, did you know about this—however before he has a chance to reply by not replying but giving unmistakable evidence of his desire to move on, the fat man once again employs that special Varanasi soft touch—and now he briefly recounts, again as if they were in the middle of a long ongoing dialogue, that he has been cooling his heels here for a while, and, imagine, he has been musing about why on earth do the locals believe and say that, he has been giving it some thought, and has made some headway which he would be glad to share now, so he suggests that, if you don't disdain my company, why not sit down here, and hear me out, it will be worth your while, for he has reached some fascinating conclusions, whereupon you try to express by means of a gesture that no, it is out of the question, except that this gesture doesn't turn out to be too convincing, moreover a hand, the man's, even assists and transforms this gesture into an overture leading to the movement of plopping down by his side, thus the refusal is nullified and you find yourself sitting on the step by the man's side, and he crowns his momentary triumph, that is, having you sit down instead of going on your way, by pushing up his eyeglasses on the bridge of his nose and turning his enormous head back toward the Ganges, rearranging the triple folds of his vast jowls under his chin, and he's off, saying that first of all he merely posed himself the question, since he happens to be somewhat familiar with the physical aspects of the problem, for he works as a production engineer at the Sankat Mochan Foundation, did he himself actually know the structure of water, and he concluded that indeed he knew it, indeed the whole thing was tied in with the geometry of the surface—he looks on at the Ganges—and not only does he not appear to be overbearing, but the beauty of that hidden face is becoming more and more obvious, that beautiful face enfolded within the mass of blubber is anything but aggressive, just like his voice, it too contains something heartening, so that it seems unlikely that these introductory words would turn out to be a preamble to some business proposal, therefore he commits the further mistake of staying put and making no attempt to stand up, even though at this point it is still within his power to do so, he remains sitting where the man with that horribly tender gesture of the hand had seated him, and he keeps sitting there, perplexed by a certain innocence, something ethereal, some element of a higher order in this outlandishly fat man's voice and bearing, all this enhanced by the impression that the man is speaking mostly to himself, as it were, while at the same time he seems to be grateful, bordering on the fraternal, and this conclusively dispels his suspicions, making him vulnerable, so that he must pay attention, that is he must hear out attentively how the man with the eyeglasses had always been fascinated by spheres in general, and specifically by the surface geometry of spheres, for example what holds a drop of water together, and here after all, the man says pointing at the waters of the Ganges, if you sit around here for a while, the question obviously surfaces again, whereupon one with his training first of all had him thinking that it has to do with intermolecular hydrogen bonds, no doubt, and the man smiles at him, no doubt you too know what intermolecular hydrogen bonds are, anyone who has studied physics knows that, well then, if you picture this hydrogen bond as well as the covalent bond and keep in mind the simple fact that water in a liquid state is an alternating system of covalent and intermolecular hydrogen bonds, well then at this point matters start to become interesting, the man winks at him merrily over the top of his glasses, since as matters actually stand water in a liquid state is a pseudo-macromolecule with only a *partially* regular structure that is held together by flexible hydrogen bonds, as it is taught at school, and if now one considers that it is because of surface tension that liquids, and therefore a drop of water, assume forms with the least possible surface area (which is none other than the sphere), then you will no doubt agree that it's worthwhile to pursue this one step further, which I—and the man pointed at himself—have indeed done, actually he went back a bit to the problematics of surface tension, that is to say, in his imagination he has bisected a water molecule, whereupon fascinating things came to mind as he listened to the splashing waves and watched the light playing on the surface of the water, because what came to mind was that there are, you see, these oxygen atoms and these hydrogen atoms that form these tetrahedral structures, this much is obvious if you follow me, and equally obviously we may next recall that oxygen carries a slight negative charge, and hydrogen a strong positive one, resulting in a connection between adjacent molecules, these are what we call hydrogen bonds; it wouldn't hurt, the man thought, and here he chuckled as he turned toward his listener, it wouldn't hurt at all to collate all this, for curious notions will arise in one's head, as one sits watching the river flow, for instance he seemed to remember that hydrogen bonds are much weaker than the internal bonds holding a molecule together, meaning the resulting arrangement favors the formation of the most stable system possible, so what do you think happens? asks the man raising his eyebrows, well, the most stable arrangement will be if every hydrogen bond aligns with an adjacent molecule, so that each molecule of water is surrounded by four neighbors, thereby forming a pyramid, a tetrahedron, and we know what that is, the tetrahedron, right? this brings Plato to mind and the Platonic solid, leading directly to a likewise well-known fact, namely that two hundred eighty molecules constitute a regular icosahedral agglomeration, and while formerly it had been thought that water in a liquid state is composed of such regular agglomerations, the world has changed since then and nowadays we think otherwise, namely that water *fluctuates* between regular and irregular structures, since the hydrogen bonds are constantly breaking up and giving rise to new bonds, and at this point, you see, he says pensively, eyeing the Ganges again for a while, at this point, you see, he continues, pushing his eyeglasses back up, one may ponder what's going on between the tetrahedral water molecule aggregates, or between the solitary random water molecules, for we may as well put it that way, he adds as if speaking to himself, and then the answer offers itself naturally from the foregoing, that the tetrahedral water molecule clusters are located *among* the solitary, random water molecules, and there you have water—and here the man's eyes seek his companion's for a moment but not finding them he asks is he following all this, whereupon the listener, confused, admits that no, he hasn't been able to follow a single word of this, well then, pay attention to me now, the man points at himself with one of his enormous sausage fingers, according to what we know about surface tension all liquids, and thus drops of water as well, obey the laws of surface tension and assume forms with the least possible surface area, and what do you think that would be? he asks, what form would that be? and receiving only silence in answer, well, it would be the sphere, that's obvious, isn't it? the man spreads his ele-phant trunk arms and keeps looking at him, inducing him to nod in agreement, which the man acknowledges with a sigh of satisfaction, and continues, well then, so this much is self-evident, fine, let's move on, and let us suppose that it is not quite as self-evident that hydrogen bonds are far weaker than the bonds holding a molecule together, this is not quite so obvious but conceivable, and you too can see it is so, he says, and you can also see that the resulting arrangement manifests the necessity for the formation of the stablest possible system, that is to say—and here the speaker turns back toward the Ganges again, speak-ing again as if to himself—*in other words,* this whole thing will have the strongest, stablest structure, you see, when every hydrogen bond finds that neighboring molecule, for then each water molecule will be sur-rounded by four others, creating a pyramid, which is the tetrahedron mentioned earlier, in fact we have covered all of this, but it needs to be mentioned again so that you too will understand it perfectly, in fact for your benefit I'll also repeat—and he repeats again—that there is this fluctuation whereby the regular and irregular systems *fluctuate,* be-cause the hydrogen bonds constantly keep breaking up, and new bonds are coming into existence, so that, what do you think, may we now pose the real question?—again the man turns in his direction, and he gazes back into the man's eyes, above the thick rim of the huge spec-tacles, he is looking straight into those wonderfully lit-up eyes embed-ded in fat, and a cold shiver runs down his back, because in these eyes he glimpses something very strange, mysterious, and inexplicable, he cannot say exactly what, some unknown depth, not of knowledge but rather a depth of time, as if he glimpsed a vista of several thousand years, and this completely befuddles him, after all who is talking here, who is this exceedingly fat man who stopped him in this insane city, to deliver this totally insane talk about water here on the banks of the Ganges, this is what he wants to ask, but doesn't get very far because the other man's voice constantly eclipses his own, constantly overrides the questions forming inside him, and gains the upper hand, saying that the surface area of a liquid always strives to be the smallest possible, and that this intention, following from the nature of the previously mentioned bonds and attractions, this intention is most perfectly expressed in the form of a sphere, that is, *the intention manifests in the sphere,* he repeats this a few times, as if savoring the words, still looking at the water's surface and not at him, indeed as if he were speaking only to himself, but not really, because as soon as a question presents itself in his head, or even a thought, the other man is able to immediately direct his listener's attention back to himself, the man's words constantly overcome the words he is weighing in his head, because he would like to be on his way, because he ardently longs to be freed from the captivation of this man, but he doesn't leave, his brain has turned on by itself and he cannot unplug it, and the other man, regardless whether he is staring at the water or looking in his direction, seems always to know precisely when his listener's flagging attention must be directed back to himself, and always manages to pull him back just in time, and he now says that the force of attraction between identical molecules is in every case far greater than that between differing molecules, in other words each molecule strives inward, toward the interior depths of the system, intending to fill it up, and in this intention those molecules that remain up above, meaning—and the man slowly turns his ponderous body toward him, but only for a slow instant—up on the surface of the water, well then, these molecules desire the least possible surface, simultaneously, and this would be the sphere, isn't this obvious? the man asks, and his listener replies for the first time since the moment of their strange encounter, he replies that yes it is obvious, whereupon the other man smiles and gives him a questioning glance, shouldn't we put it in even more unequivocal terms? whereupon he again says, yes, let's do that, and he nods, whereupon the man smiles again and says, well and good, then let's say that only those molecules remain on the surface that exhibit a smaller force of attraction, while these too are tugged down and inward by the internal forces of attraction, so that they draw together as close as possible on the surface, we may facetiously say that they *demand* the least possible surface area, or that the surface itself demands the least possible surface area, isn't that so? indeed it is, he asks and answers his own question almost triumphantly, it demands the ideal surface which is the smallest, in sum: it seeks the ideal, and seen this way I believe the matter seems to be perfectly clear, the man says and his listener replies that yes it is, perfectly, but now the man turns quite grave, as if a shadow flitted across that handsome face in that massive head, and in an altered voice, somehow softer, he gently asks himself, is it all right this way, and he replies, no, it is not all right, and he casts a glance in his listener's direction before going on, no it is not all right because all that we have said may be sayable but is not really of any use, because water itself somehow escapes approximations of this sort, because after all of the foregoing it still possesses a tremendous number of other properties that should not exist, yet they do exist, properties that powerfully differentiate it from all other liquids, as if water were something other than a liquid, or not a liquid at all but rather ... well, yes, pure water, an extraordinary substance, a primal element that guards its inner secrets, so that we may hold forth here, as I have just done, up to a certain point about what we know regarding water from our vantage but in the end I must confess that actually these attempts I have made just now will not bring us any closer to the essence of its structure, these attempts get us nowhere when we consider water having such properties as memory, for example, which must exist for sure, since after we melt ice back into liquid water, this ice returns to the identical liquid crystal system it had possessed previously, in other words water, even in the form of ice, preserves its structure, nor is it comforting to know that on top of all its numerous anomalies water is able to store information, endless amounts of information, *that is,* water knows about everything that has happened on Earth, and is currently happening, so that our knowledge is insufficient for understanding even a single drop of water, can you see that, he asks in a husky voice, and now can you see why I sit here pondering why the locals keep saying that a single drop of water from the Ganges is a temple? he asks, but he knows he will not receive an answer, so a profound silence sets in, as if indeed a distance of several thousand years separated the two of them now, he knows he should be moving on, but he doesn't dare to do so yet, or he simply cannot, he looks at the man's enormous triple chin with those three folds reposing against the chest, he looks at the giant black-rimmed eyeglasses barely balanced on the tip of the nose in the sweltering heat, he looks on at this other man contemplating the water, and he can see the outlines of the beauteous face buried in that mass of fat that is the head, that beauteous face which he could not possibly have encountered before but that is nonetheless so startlingly familiar, and presently he feels that now, right now he has the energy to make his move, and he makes his move, slowly getting up from the step, and he tries to find suitable words to say before he leaves, but the other anticipates him, looks at him again, and his glance is slightly mocking as he asks, do you happen to have a hundred rupees on you to help me out, hearing which the words instantly freeze inside him and he takes the step down, the fat man moves aside a bit, apparently allowing him to pass, so it is over, he is relieved, and hopeful, and indeed a narrow passage toward the lowermost step is already opening up for him through the throng, he still intends to say something in farewell, but again the other beats him to the punch, and shouts after him, just think! we have considered only a single drop of water from the Ganges, and do you know how many drops there are in the Ganges? to which naturally he doesn't know what to reply, except nod by way of a goodbye, after which he does not turn around, for there is still a chance that the man could summon him back, after all, if the man were capable of stopping and engaging him to exchange words—something that no one has been able to do since his arrival in the city—if the man were able to do that then indeed the danger exists that he would not be able to free himself from him and he'd have to learn even more about the inner mysteries of a drop of water, perhaps even get to understand the *actual essence* of a drop of water, right here, next to the scandalous frothing scum of the Ganges, but no, when he looks back after walking about a hundred meters, the man shows not the least sign of any further interest in him, all he can see is that the man is still sitting in the same place as before, that is, more or less reclining on the lowermost steps, that enormous melting body, practically naked, except for the filthy loin cloth and the huge eyeglasses, and that triple chin, and so he is free to move on, he has probably had more than enough of that man, good god, he thinks now, speeding up his steps, how could I be so careless, how could I plunge headlong into this madness, and anyway, what on earth was this absurd conversation, these covalent bonds, these Platonic solids, and surface tension, just what I needed, truly, a conversation such as this, get it out of your head, give it no further thought, don't try to figure out what it meant, because that was exactly what Varanasi has been doing to him ever since he had arrived here, constantly tantalizing with the possibility that the things happening here, the things he has experienced, seen, and heard possess some sort of portentous connectedness, whereas there is no interconnection whatsoever, only an immense unfathomable chaos, or as this elephantine man would have put it, a powerful disorder, that's what we are talking about, a universal, all-consuming, infectious chaos, this is what he must find his way out of, if there is a way out, and now he recalls that a few hours earlier he had still been at the hotel, standing by the window, peeking out at the street through the chinks in the synthetic leather lace curtain decorated with giant rosettes, pondering about a suitable moment to make his escape, good lord, how long ago was that, how long has he been walking, he is so weary that even if given the chance, he would not sit down because he certainly wouldn't be able to get up again, and that was obviously what the Ganges wanted, what Varanasi obviously wanted, to inundate him with madness, so that he would feel at home in it, but no, he still has enough strength to keep going with his mind unplugged, as he had decided, and he trudges on along the bank of the Ganges, mindlessly and desperately, it is difficult to tell which is scarier, the fact that the city occupies only one side of the river, or the reason for the emptiness of the other side, for that is the situation here, Varanasi lies exclusively on the left bank of the Ganges, while the right bank is completely, or nearly completely empty, who can tell what the meaning of this is, no one can tell, and he would not listen anyway, he marches on along the bank of the Ganges against the flow of the current, back, if all goes well, in a westerly direction, but nothing goes well, and once again he sees himself back there in the hotel room, as hours earlier he stood there behind the curtain, looking down at the whirling commotion on the street and for the first time, truly panicking, trying to decide the right moment to depart, he stood there leaning one shoulder against the wall, casting an occasional glance at the filthy bed, at his backpack; and he could clearly recall now on the bank of the Ganges, heading west, what back then, hours earlier up in the hotel room had gone through his unplugged mind, that he must think of his backpack, it had to be packed and ready to go, and so he started doing that, first he went out to the bathroom—the bathroom?!—and brought in his toilet articles, and without bothering to organize them he simply tossed them in the backpack, same with the t-shirts, the shorts, the two white summer shirts, the change of underwear, the guidebook, the camera, the phone, the compass, the raincoat, the medicine box, the wallet, and the map, one after another, and when everything was in the backpack, and he pulled the last zipper closed, suddenly he looked up at the ceiling, at the plaster peeling in layers, revealing a long-ago painted torso of Vishnu peeking out from underneath as if in farewell, and he thought, get away? away from Varanasi?! but goddamn, shit, fuck! Varanasi was the world; using the utmost caution, first he looked, then he slipped out of the door, tiptoed downstairs, sneaked past the reception desk of the empty hotel, stepped out into the street and turned at the first corner, and then turned at the very next again—making sure that it was not four times, and not always to the left, or to the right, this is what screamed like a siren in his head, this thought, not four times, not in the same direction, because then there is no escape, then I will be back where I started.

DOWNHILL ON A FOREST ROAD

For the first time ever he had some difficulty in getting the key into the ignition and eventually forced it, if only because there was no way but force, then he turned the engine which sprang to life and reversed onto the hill road, forgetting all about the key problem, though he did wonder while still maneuvering whether everything was all right, for after all there shouldn't have been a problem getting the key into the ignition of a car as new as this, but the thought vanished as soon as he started downhill, not a shred of it remaining, and he concentrated on driving in second gear before switching to third then climbing again to reach the highway above the village, the highway that would still be deserted because half past eight was too early for tourists and too late for locals, not that he knew the exact time because when he looked at the car's clock it showed eight minutes to nine and he thought, oh, better get a move on, and he stepped lightly on the gas while on either side of him the branches formed a tent over the winding lane, the whole scene was so beautiful with sunbeams penetrating the boughs, the light sprinkling the road, everything trembling, and the highway ahead; quite marvelous, he thought, and he could almost smell the scent of the greenery still wet with dew, he now being at the straight part of the road, some three hundred meters leading straight down where the car naturally picked up speed, and he thought it would be nice to have some music, and was just reaching for the car radio when suddenly he saw, some hundred or hundred and fifty meters ahead of him—that is to say about half way or two-thirds of the way down the straightaway—a patch on the road that made him frown and peer trying to guess what it might be, a discarded piece of clothing, a machine part, or what?—and it flashed through his mind that it looked exactly like an animal, though it had to be a rag of some sort, something thrown from, or dropped from a truck, a rag that had remained curiously tangled, but when he saw that there was something at the side of the road as well as in the middle, he leaned forward on the steering wheel and tried to get a better look at it but couldn't quite see where one form stopped and the other started, so he slowed down just in case, because if there were two of them he didn't want to drive over either, and it was only once he was very close that he could make them out and was so surprised he could hardly believe his eyes and put his foot down on the brake, since the thing didn't just look like an animal, it *was one*, a young dog, a puppy, sitting perfectly still on the white line in the middle of the road, a rather thin creature with a patchy coat and an innocent look there in the middle of the road watching him in the car, quite calmly sitting on its butt, keeping a straight back and what was even more frightening than the fact of its presence was the look in its eyes, the way it didn't move, the quite incomprehensible way it just sat there despite the big car, what the hell was it doing there with the car practically on top of it so you could see the dog wasn't going to move even if he or his big car did, because this dog wasn't interested in the car or its proximity though he was almost touching it; and it was only then he noticed that to the left of the dog sitting on the white line there was another dog at the side of the road, its flattened corpse apparently hit by a car that had sliced it open, its stomach visible, and though his own car had reached them, the companion of the dead dog—what was the relationship between them? were they companions?—hadn't moved an inch so he was forced to drive around it very slowly on its right side, his right wheel off the road so he could get by, only just avoiding it by a few centimeters if that, the dog was still sitting there straight-backed, and now he could look directly into its face though it would have been better if he hadn't, because, having carefully passed it, the dog was slowly following him with its eyes, with its sad eyes that showed no trace of panic or wild fury or of being traumatized by shock, the eyes simply uncomprehending and sad, sadly gazing at the driver of the car moving around and away from him, still not moving from the white line in the middle of the forest road, and it didn't matter whether it was fifteen miles from Los Angeles, eighteen miles from Kyoto, or twenty miles to the north of Budapest, it simply sat there, looking sad, watching over its companion, waiting for someone to come along to whom it might explain what had happened or just sitting and waiting for the other to get up at last and make some movement so that the pair of them might vanish from this incomprehensible place.

He was just a few meters past them and immediately wanted to stop, thinking I can't leave them here, it was just that his legs refused to move for some reason, to do what he would have them do, and as the car rolled on he watched them through the mirror, the dead one lying half on its side, its internal organs spilled onto the pavement, its four legs stretched stiffly out all parallel, but he could only see the back of the puppy, fragile but ramrod straight, still sitting in the middle of the road as if it could afford to wait for hours, and he worried it too might be struck by a car, and I should stop, he said to himself, but kept rolling on, it being two minutes past nine as he found when he glanced at his watch, what to do, I'll be late, he fretted, his foot already pressing on the gas, in two minutes I shall be in town, then one bend followed another and he was already past the winding part of the road and it had been two minutes past nine when he checked his watch, he pressed his foot harder down on the gas when for a moment he remembered the dog again, the way it was watching over its companion, but the image quickly passed and for the next minute he concentrated entirely on driving, picking up speed to just under sixty since there was no one else on the road except a slower vehicle ahead of him, a Skoda he decided as he approached, fretting because he had to slow down instead of overtaking it, the possibility of overtaking diminishing as he approached, but I won't wait, he thought crossly, not behind this ancient Skoda, not for the bend, and because he knew the road well having driven it a thousand times and realizing there wouldn't be a chance of overtaking the Skoda until they reached the sign for the town, he put his foot right down so as to pass it before the bend when suddenly the Skoda began to swing slowly towards the left just in front of him and everything happened almost at once, he glancing in his mirror and signaling that he was about to pass, pulling left on the steering wheel, entering the other lane and starting to overtake, when the other man, having failed to look in his mirror, also swung out left because he wanted to turn off or to turn right around, who knows what, and maybe his left indicator had just started blinking, but only at that moment, as he swung left, by which time it was too late of course and it was no use slamming on the brakes because the Skoda, being so slow, was now practically straddling the road, as if the image of it had frozen and he could neither avoid it nor brake, and in other words, there being no means of stopping it, he crashed into him.

The onset of catastrophe is not signaled by the sense of falling through the dark to an accidental death: everything, including a catastrophe, has a moment-by-moment structure—a structure that is beyond measurement or comprehension, one that is maddeningly complex or must be conceived in quite another manner, in which the degree of complexity can be articulated only in terms of images that seem impossible to conjure—visible only if time has slowed down to the point that we see the world as indifferent owing to the available circumstances and having doomed preconditions that arrive at a perfect universal conclusion, if only because they are composed of individual intentions—because the moment is the result of unconscious choices, because a key doesn't immediately fit into the ignition, because we do not start in third gear and move down to second but we start in second and move into third, rolling down the hill then turning onto a highway above the village, because the distance before us is like looking down a tunnel, because the greenery on the boughs still smells of morning dew, because of the death of a dog and someone's badly executed maneuver when turning left, that is to say because of one choice or another, of more choices and still more choices *ad infinitum,* those maddening had-we-but-known choices impossible to conceptualize because the situation we find ourselves in is complicated, determined by something that is in the nature of neither God nor the devil, something whose ways are impenetrable to us and are doomed to remain so because chance is not simply a matter of choosing, but the result of that which might have happened anyway.

THE BILL

For Palma Vecchio, at Venice

You sent for us and we knew what you wanted so we sent Lucretia and Flora, sent Leonora and Elena, followed by Cornelia, then Diana, and so it went on from January through to June, then from October through to December we sent Ophelia, sent Veronica, sent Adriana, sent Danaë, then Venus, and, little by little, every plump, sweet whore and courtesan on our books turned up at your place, the important thing, as for every male Venetian, being that their brows should be clear and high, that the shoulders be broad and round, the chest wide and deep, that the body should open out, the way it opens out under a deep-cut chemise, and that your eyes should be able to dive, as from a cliff, from the tempting face down to the fresh, sweet, desirable bosom, just as you described to Federico who brought us your order and who then described it to us in turn, saying yes, just as before, just as wide and deep as the valley, the valley of Val Seriana, where you yourself come from, Federico grinned, because, according to him, that was what you were really after, that valley in Bergamo where you were born, and he went on to tell us, and the others confirmed this, that nothing else concerned you, that you were not in the least interested in the dark secrets of the flesh, only in waves of blonde hair, sparkling eyes, and the slow opening of the lips, in other words in the head, and then in the prospect opening from the chin down and spreading below the broad round shoulders to the landscape of the scented body, not the rest, and that you were always asking them to slip the straps to below the shoulder because, you told them, you had, as you put it, to see the shoulder utterly bare but at the same time to see the lacy white edge of the chemise on its concave arc from shoulder to shoulder, that arc just above the painted nipples of the breasts, which reminded you of the horizon above your village in that deep valley, the valley of Seriana, though you didn't make that perfectly clear to anybody at the time, that idea being something that occurred to Federico, and only after a while, though he didn't articulate it either, and, in the end, it proved impossible to discover why it was that you painted so many not exactly fat but extraordinarily large women in your pictures, because you would not answer a single question about that, you were, in any case, known for your lack of patience, and when impatient, you would often expose their breasts entirely so they said, only to cover them up again most of the time, so they never really knew what you wanted, and some were scared of you because they'd heard all kinds of rumors and were ready for anything, their chief fear being that you, in your *bottega*, might demand something of them that they weren't able to do; but, as they went on to say, you didn't really want anything anyway, and, what is more, it often happened that you paid in advance, and, once you stopped painting for the day, you sent them away immediately without even a bunch of grapes, never allowing those enormous women to take you to bed, and they just had to stand there, or sit on a sofa, they had to stand or sit for hours on end without moving, it being just a matter of the hourly rate and the fear of what might happen, because you pretty soon got a reputation that the Bergamo man, as they called you, wasn't in the least interested in fucking, and wouldn't even touch, merely instructing the model in his quiet polite way how she should sit or stand, and then he'd just look, watching how she looked at him, and then, after an age of waiting, he would ask her to lower the left shoulder of her chemise a touch, or to ruffle up the folds of her dress a little more, or that she should uncover one breast, though he was always standing a good distance away, beyond touching distance, and, so the ladies would tell us, you'd be sitting in an armchair as the two servants led them outside back to the landing stage so they might return by the waiting *mascareta* and that you never actually came anywhere near them nor would allow them to touch you, unlike those, they giggled, who just wanted to stare while they themselves mounted some man; because you weren't like that, the girls told us, that wasn't why you hired them ... you just looked at them and they had to stand there for hours (which was impossible), or sit, and of course, they were fully prepared, there being painters enough in Venice who paid for the visit of a whore or a *cortegiana onesta,* they'd stood or sat for every kind of artist, some having served you before, and some, from time to time, having even posed for the great Bellini, only to face the universal ridicule of seeing themselves depicted as the Mater Dolorosa, or Mary Magdalene or St. Catherine in S. Giovanni e Paolo or the Scuola di S. Marco, which provided everyone with a laugh and, boy, did they laugh! though in your case, Signor Bergamo or Seriana, whichever you prefer, when you'd finished with them people didn't, for some reason, feel like laughing, and when one or the other of them told the others what it had been like with you after a couple of visits, they kept saying they had no idea what you were about, and, above all, they couldn't understand why you turned them into such vast mountains of flesh, since, said Danaë, my shoulder is nowhere near as enormous as that, nor am I anywhere near as fat as that, said Flora pointing to her waist, and, to tell the truth, there was, after all, something incomprehensible about these disproportionate figures, because, despite the exaggerations, they remained lovely and attractive, and no one could understand how you did it, nor, more importantly, why, but then your whole art was so peculiar, everyone said, that it seemed it wasn't exactly art you were aiming for but for something about the women or in them, which led to ever greater confusion because the filthy way you looked at them was quite intolerable, they said, so even the most experienced whore felt nervous and looked away, but then you'd snap at them and tell them to look you straight in the eye, though otherwise you treated them well enough, it was just that you never laid a finger on them, that being something they could never understand, the reason they were scared of you, never looking forward to visiting you, although you paid them well enough, giving even the lowest of them a few miserable escudo, and as for the freshest youngest whore or *cortigiana onesta,* you paid well over the usual for her, despite the fact that for all your fame, you're far from the wealthiest of them and, they say, all those pictures you painted of Lucretia and Danaë and Flora and Elena are still stacked in your store, the religious paintings being the ones that sell, the ones in which Danaë becomes Mary, and Flora becomes St. Catherine, one under some tree with the baby in her arms in a pretty country scene, these all having been bought as we know, while those where you painted for some lecher wanting a picture of his whore, well, you couldn't always convince the customer that what you gave him was exactly what he wanted because all your lovers remained stubbornly just Lucretia, or Danaë or Flora or Elena, so most of the paintings were still in the bottega, all stacked up on top of each other, because, despite having sold a few, you sometimes couldn't hide your own dissatisfaction with them and went back to them time and again, which was why you occasionally sent word with Federico for the same woman, albeit in a different shape, and we could see why you'd want to do that because we've had a thousand, ten thousand, indeed a hundred thousand such requests in the *carampane,* and ever since you first moved to Venice it was obvious to us that it was always the same woman you wanted, and so we supplied you with Lucretia and Flora and Leonora and Elena and Cornelia and Diana from January through to June, and Ophelia and Veronica and Adriana and Danaë and finally Venus from October through to December, though all you wanted from January to June, and from October to December, was the same woman, and only after giving considerable thought to the question of why you painted our ladies as fat as you did did we at last cotton on to the secret of why these enormous women looked so devilishly beautiful on your canvases, or at least one of us cottoned on, meaning me, to the fact that what you wanted, beyond any doubt, was precisely the same thing each time: that's to say, that valley in Seriana, you filthy reprobate, that is to say the valley between a whore's shoulders and her breasts, that is, the valley where you were born which might perhaps remind you of your mother's breasts, which is not to deny you are a handsome man with a fine figure, though the most attractive part of you is your face as everyone who has met you knows, because all the whores notice that and they would have done it for you for nothing but you didn't want them, no, all you wanted was to stare at their chins, their necks and their chests, and they quickly got to hate you because they didn't have the least idea what you wanted and we had to tell them to calm down and just go along if you asked for them, because they'd never make an easier escudo and, what is more, you'd dress them up in fine clothes as you dress everyone, which, by the way, makes us all the more suspicious that you really are searching for something, and, as the years passed, there came ever new Floras and Lucretias and Veronicas and Ophelias, and they were all different, but all the same to you, and they had to take their high-heeled shoes off as soon as they got to the door, in fact had to take off all the clothes they'd come in, because, you had them strip down to their knickers and you had your two servants give them a lacy chemise and anything else necessary, inevitably some gorgeous robe embroidered with gold thread, or a dress or, sometimes, just a blue or green velvet jacket, then you softly asked them to expose one breast, to pull the chemise down a little, and then gazed for hours at those soft, wide, round shoulders, the innocent-corrupt smiles on their faces, and it was as if you hadn't even noticed the hot perspiration on the fresh skin of those naked breasts, took no notice at all of what they had to offer you, because you had no use for narrow waists, the milk-white belly, those ample hips and the delicate hair of the groin, you were uninterested in the way the lips, the knees, and thighs opened, the warm lap and those clouds of perfume that could drive men wild, and however one or the other tried words and looks and sighs, everything she knew of the thousand ways of seduction, it all left you cold, you just waved her away, told her to stop all that and that all you wanted her to do was to stay absolutely still, to sit quietly on the sofa and look at you, to keep her eyes on you and not look away, not even for a moment, and you insisted on this to the point that all of them—every single one from Lucretia through to Venus— was astonished at this idiotic and pointless game of you-look-at-me-I-look-at-you, because what after all are we, they complained, raising their voices, looking really angry, child-virgins from the lace factory? though we, of course, knew that what you needed wasn't them, not as people, but what you could get at through them, and I, personally, always thought we should stop talking in terms of any specific model and concentrate on what lay behind her, some idea like the female figure being the *serenissima,* and the male, the *carampane,* though from all I have said so far it will have been clear to you for some time where I'm coming from, I mean this person is telling you what an unusual man you are, a man uninterested in women as such, more in what might be found by way of a woman, someone who is looking to perfect the most scandalously refined, devilish sensation, to whom, from that point of view, a woman is just a body, an idea one can understand and agree with because one may think we are nothing but body, end of story, though what you can tell from this body—if you catch it in the moment of desire, at the moment when the body is most alive and burning with desire—is just how deep and mysterious and irresistible the desire is that drives you to want—to demand—possession of the object for which you are willing to sacrifice everything, even though it's nothing more than a small patch of skin, or a faint flush on that skin, or just a sad little smile, maybe the way she drops a shoulder, or bows her head, or slowly raises it, when a tiny blonde curl, a maddening strand of hair, accidentally falls across her temple and this strand promises something, you have no idea what, but whatever it is you are willing to give, to give your whole life for it, and maybe it is precisely because of this I feel convinced—and you too will become aware of this—that it isn't the fact that they drive men crazy the way they peel off their clothes; oh no, quite the opposite, nor is it the way the breast pops out, or how the belly or the lap or the rump and the thighs appear, for any such appearance means the end of unfettered illusion, no, it's the moment when the faint flickering candlelight reveals the animal in their eyes, because it is this look that drives all men crazy, crazy for that beautiful animal, that animal that is nothing but body, which is what people die for, for the moment—that splinter of time—when that animal appears, beautiful beyond comprehension—and that's the light you sometimes catch in the eyes of Cornelia and Flora and Elena and Venus, while all the time being fully aware, since you've lived long enough, of the fact that it is just how Cornelia, Flora, Elena, and Venus happen to look today, that they are already old and wrinkly inside and out and that nothing interests them except filling their bellies and their purses, though most of the time both are empty, and so you call them again and again, and we keep sending them in ever new shapes, so off they go: Cornelia and Flora and Elena and Venus, and their eyes might do the trick and hit the perfect spot, because clearly that is what you yourself want and that's why you forbid them to do anything that otherwise they would normally do, so you don't let them take off their clothes and completely reveal their breasts and everything else they've got because you know that animal essence is a matter of deferred pleasure that exists only in the act of deferral, that the promise of the eyes is just a promise that something will happen later, maybe soon, or indeed at the very next moment, just as we are unbuckling a belt, when all our clothes drop away at once, the way their eyes promise, which is the look you are searching for and which you clearly want to immortalize in your picture, and, on a good day, you find that look straightaway, and it promises satisfaction now, yes, right now, but only *perhaps* ... for deferred pleasure is the very essence of this essentially infernal arrangement, the cage in which you too are imprisoned, as is every man in Venice—in the world at large—and though you might always be wanting to paint the pending moment, that moment the promise is made good with all that that entails, the whole process recorded in color and line on your canvas, that process being inherent in the look you buy for one escudo (that's if you get what you paid for), this painting you so desire to paint is, in fact, about something else that no one could ever paint, because that would be a picture of stillness, of stasis, an Eden of Fulfilled Promises where nothing moves and nothing happens and— what is more difficult to explain—where there's nothing to say about this immobility, permanence, and absence of change, because, in fulfilling the promise, you have lost the thing promised, the thing that vanishes in the fulfilment of that promise, and the light in the desired object goes out, its flame quenched—and so desire limits itself, for however you may desire, there's nothing more to be done, because there is nothing at all real about the desire, desire consists entirely of anticipation, that is to say the future, because, strange as it is, you can't go back in time, there's no returning from the future, from the thing that happens next, no way of getting back to it from the other side, the side of memory, that being absolutely impossible, because the road back from the present inevitably takes you to the wrong place, and perhaps memory's whole purpose is to make you believe that there once was a real event, something that actually happened, where the thing previously desired existed, and all the while the memory is shepherding you away from its object and offering you its counterfeit instead, because it never could give you the real object, the fact being that the object doesn't exist, though that's not exactly your way of perceiving it, for you are a painter, meaning someone who inhabits desire but can reject it in advance, consoling yourself with the thought that there will come a moment when the chemise drops away, though believing the promise of that thought makes you a guilty man, a miserable sinner, a man condemned to sinning miserably until the day of judgment arrives, albeit that day is still far off for you; so, for now, you can carry on believing and desiring, and you need not think; you can go crazy, you can rage and thirst so you can hardly breathe—and then you can remember Federico and send him over to us, and we can send you Danaë, Veronica, Adriana, and Venus, the lot of them, and we can carry on sending them as long as Federico arrives to tell us what you need...but there will come the day when we draw a line under it all, when we call it a day, add up everything you ordered, and then, there will be no more Palma Vecchio, no more Iacopo Negretti, then it will be over and we'll send you the bill, you can be sure of that.

THAT GAGARIN

don't want to die, but just to leave the Earth: this desire, however ridiculous, is so strong that it's the only thing in me, like a deadly infection, it's rotting my soul, and it cuts into me, namely that in the midst of a general yesterday it seized upon my soul, and well, this soul could no longer free itself, so that well, yes: it would be so good to leave the earth, but I mean really leave it, to lift off, and go up and up and go ever higher into those dreadful heights, to see what he saw for the first time, he who was the first person able to lift off and attain this dreadful height, it's not just since this general yesterday I've been the victim of this infection, but that with this infection I've already been rendered somewhat idiotic by the thought that I will do it somehow—I know I shouldn't talk about it, and I know that I can't show this notebook to anyone because I would immediately be accused of sensitivity or something even worse—in any event, to one side they would be holding up the dose of Rivotril, on the other gesturing that I'm an idiot, and all the while looking suspiciously directly into my eyes, because they know full well I'm not an idiot; in any event nobody would even consider taking me seriously, no one would understand what exactly brought me to this place, and I hardly know myself; in any event, all I know is that there's no way out now: I close my eyes, and I see myself rising, and now I'm getting dizzy, I open my eyes ... but then I already know that I'm not going to lift off from anywhere here, not even by as much as a centimeter, I will stay here in this cursed place, like a tree rooted to this ground; I can't move, I can only think; at the very most I can only try to conceive what he was like—he who did this for the first time: and that's how it all began; there I was already on that downward slope, at first I'm just ambling along the road, and then I'm not even sure where it's sloping down to—I begin in the library, and I'm asking auntie Marika, who's always there on Wednesday afternoons from three till five, I ask her if there's something about Gagarin—who? auntie Marika stares at me, I pronounce the syllables slowly: Ga-ga-rin; auntie Marika purses her mouth, I don't know who that is, she says, but I can take a look—of course you know who he is, I say, Gagarin, he was the first person in space, you know, oh yes, *that* Gagarin, she smiles, as if now acknowledging that she too is essentially a person of that era, and for any person of that era—just as in my own case—it is perfectly obvious who that Gagarin is: she looks at a box full of index cards, she flips through the cards, she stops in one place, flips the cards forward, flips the cards backwards, well, there's nothing, she says, I'm very sorry; but this is only the beginning, after all this is only a small institutional library, then I take the morning bus to the district town, and there, and even there, somebody just flips through the index cards, standing in one place, he flips the cards forward, he flips them backwards, shaking his head, nothing, he says, and I go on further with the morning bus: I go to the county library, and someone flips the cards forward, and flips them backwards, of course now on a computer, and now I'm sitting on the train on the way to Budapest, it's dreadfully hot, the windows are wide open in vain, the scorching air rushes in from outside, striking whomever it reaches, it doesn't reach me though because I'm not interested in this train, there's only one thought in my mind, and I'm already standing in front of the counter at the Ervin Szabó Library, Gagarin?! the librarian asks, and he just looks at me, and it's possible that in front of the counter at the Gagarin Library they would look at me that way if I were to pronounce the name of Ervin Szabó, no matter, from this point onward everyone begins to look at me like that, that is to say strangely, that is to say distrustfully, or because they think that maybe I'm just putting them on or because they're trying to make out if I'm really an idiot and really, no matter where I inquire to try to get some information—it's futile to try to come up with some sort of acceptable explanation instead of the actual one—their faces immediately grow suspicious, no matter how this matter concerns them, they don't understand what I want, and somehow they sense that the explanation I've given them is unconvincing: they can see in my eyes that something else is going on, they don't believe me, don't believe that I'm planning a lecture—what else though could any of this be good for, though, as my original occupation was that of a science historian, so they could actually take my word—but they don't believe me, because who the hell today would be interested in Gagarin, well, stop kidding me already, I see that in everyone's eyes, although nobody says it aloud, that's what their eyes say, as they look at my personal information card, or, when I am registering with the library, and they ask about my profession, and they wonder: how did he became a science historian, and there are even worse cases that that, because still one out of ten thousand will recognize me, because they saw me once or twice before, years ago on a popular science program on TV, and then it gets even worse, because then, when I tell them about the Institute and everything, they wink at me conspiratorially, indicating that fine, they understand: they know full well that the end result of this will be something serious and scientific, and then there arises this horrific familiarity as if with a customary glutinous substance and customary persistent odor, of course at times like that I flee, meaning that I move on, but I can't really go too far, because well, I'm interested in this, I ask, well, nothing about Gagarin? well, as far as Gagarin is concerned, there's nothing, they say, so then what have you got, I ask, what about Kamanyin for example? and they just shake their heads, they don't even understand the name, Ka-ma-nyin, I pronounce the syllables yet again and I could even mention that's there's a kind of memoir about him in Hungarian—obviously edited to death by the KGB—but then I let it go, what's the point of sharing this with anyone, driving yourself mad with explanations, God preserve me, this whole thing is enough to make one ashamed, maybe I am ashamed too because I can't really imagine that I would truly say to somebody why I'm researching Gagarin with such persistence, such obsessiveness, when I don't even know myself why I'm doing it, in other words it keeps changing as the days and the weeks go by, in the beginning I knew, or at least I was convinced that I knew, but then it all became ever more obscure, and as for today, as I stand here with Kamanyin and of course Gagarin, and of course hundreds and hundreds of books, documents, films, and photographs, if I were to ask myself why, everything would grow completely dark at once: so I don't even ask, and then it emerges all by itself, and everything is so sharp and clear, like a splashing mountain brook in the dark, but of course nobody asks, I don't even ask myself, others don't ask me, it's completely clear that I myself have no idea what I want with this whole thing, just as that original desire works within me uninterruptedly: yes, that's it, to leave the Earth, but as for how Gagarin and the others will help me with this, I really don't know, of course at one point I had some kind of idea about it, but that was still at the beginning, and I'm not at the beginning anymore, no longer with auntie Marika, so I try to concentrate only on Gagarin, however there's a problem with that; because my brain can't do it, fifty-seven years and on Rivotril, it's over, that's more than enough for one brain, and it's not just a question of concentration but it's about the entire being, meaning my own, and the ability to pull oneself together, namely I'm not able to pull myself together anymore, the only thing I can do is focus now and then on only one aspect of a question that I'm preoccupied with, always on just one such aspect, I concentrate on the

detail of one aspect, and that's fine, and actually it goes well, I can shut
out the world, shut out what's going on around me at a given moment—because the world of course is there, it goes on working in its
own rational way, namely in a particular moment of time and in its
particular details, namely today, at this particular moment, as I'm writing this, namely on the date of Friday, July 16, 2010, the world is still
functioning rationally—it's just in relation to the entire thing there's
no meaning to how and why it works—because it has already emerged
about this concept is that it's senseless, and I mean that there never was
any sense to it, never, in any kind of historical past; people believed
only from necessity that there was some point to it, whereas today we
know precisely that it's irrational, that words like "world" and "whole"
and "fate destined from afar," and all such things are simply empty and
meaningless generalities, about which it would be simplest to say that's
it's so much humbug, because that's what the whole thing is: just one
big humbug—and not because these are inconceivable abstractions
and things like that, but because there are errors in the formulation,
that's what's going on here, a misunderstanding, when a person gets a
short-term contract for one human life, and he starts to believe in these
abstractions, in part directly, in part as a confirmation, he spreads them
all around like carpets, and look at this, he says, life goes on, I even
explained this to Dr. Heym, but of course he just listens and doesn't
say anything, although he understands what I'm talking about perfectly and "due to my outstanding logical faculties" he doesn't deprive
me of the right to come and go freely between the Institute and the
outer world, as he expresses it: he KEEPS me at large, and then we just
smile at each other as if we were both thinking about the same thing,
I'm not though, I'm thinking that one day I will definitely be done with
him, and there will be no other cause at all other than how he smiles at
me, I am complicit with him in nothing, one day I'll wring his neck, I
stand behind him, he doesn't notice, he never notices what's going on

behind his back, well, one day I'll pick myself up, and I'll steal over there, and I will grab this head smiling in complicity, and crack it, that'll be it, there can't be any other end but this, but until then I've got enough to do, for example here is the question of Gagarin, this Gagarin and the others, and I really have to get to the end of it if I really want to leave the Earth, I do really want to leave, once and for all, this is my desire, no matter how ridiculous it may seem, so strong that this is the only thing within me, like a fatal infection, it's been rotting away my soul for months now already, I really don't know anymore, the beginning is lost in obscurity, and only Gagarin is becoming ever more clear, I see him right here in front of me, they're taking him somewhere on the bus, and behind him is Tyitov, both of them in their spacesuits, both of them pretty serious, there's no joking here, although we know about Gagarin that he was inclined to things like that, his nerves were made of steel, that's what Kamanyin said about him, or maybe Korolev said it, I don't remember anymore, right before takeoff his pulse was measured at 64, the doctors couldn't believe their eyes, 64, well, but that's what it was, a pulse of 64 in Tyuratam in the Kazakh desert, where the alarm clock went off at 5:30 Moscow time—and not UTC, that is Universal Coordinated Time—and it was about 7:03 when the First Person took his place in the spacecraft, and then this First Person, this Lieutenant by the name of Gagarin from the tiny village of Klushino, the son of Alexei Ivanovitch and Anna Timofeyevna, this peasant boy hailing from Smolensk Oblast and measuring 157 centimeters tall, on April 12, 1961, entered the tiny cabin of Korolev's shockingly dangerous spacecraft, and was obliged to wait for a long time, and then the time came, and once again, thumbing their noses at the clock hands of Universal Coordinated Time, at 9:07 Moscow time the engines of the Vostok 1 started up, and within minutes Gagarin had lifted off with terrifying bravery into the stratosphere, so that under the overwhelming pressure of the acceleration, as well as subsequently entering escape velocity, he could go into orbit, in other words: leave the earth to take off from here and rise up and up, and he says, from these heights, from a height of 327 kilometers above the Siberian desert, that it is AMAZING, he says Внимание, вижу горизонт Земли. Очень такой красивый ореол ... Очень красивое, that's what Gagarin said, when as the very First Person, he glimpsed the Earth from one of the windows of the Vostok 1, and he didn't try to explain just how much it was *ochen'*, and how much it was *krasivoye*, because he saw something—the Earth—as no one had ever seen it before, but let's not dwell on this, let's go back to before the takeoff, to Korolev in the takeoff center after he had spent the whole night awake, or to put it more correctly, in deathly fear, because particularly when in the yoke of the so-called evening darkness, when everything tends to show its most threatening side, he felt that in placing Gagarin in this time bomb he was sending him to an almost unpredictably fatal journey, this sober and reserved man was like someone who could immediately, from the sleeplessness and his considerably rational anxiety, bite the head off anyone who might happen to approach him now, so that nobody really approached him, not a single colleague, they merely followed his orders from a respectable distance, and they sent Gagarin up the stairs next to the portable scaffolding into the capsule, they let him make—as was his right to utter these last words—a kind of proclamation to the Soviet people and to the Party, then they sat him down in the seat in the capsule, they closed the door, and then everyone, including Gagarin himself, began to work vehemently on the preparations, checking and checking and checking everything possible again and again and again, so that Korolev would be able to address Gagarin by radio, so he could shout out that famous sentence—among others—into the microphone during the next one hundred and eight minutes, a sentence that still can be heard today, namely that Zarya was calling Kedr. The spaceship is about to lift off, Kedr—upon which Gagarin announced with all the decisiveness that was expected of him, but at the same time with childish enthusiasm:

Wonderful. Fantastic mood. Ready for takeoff.

At which point Korolev yelled into the microphone: first stage, middle stage, final stage! Lift off! Go! to which the mischievous Gagarin only said:

Поехали

in other words, to put it loosely, but aiming for the essence: "Well, we're off," and this time too there was in that sentence the same, that usual, dear impudence on Gagarin's part, but there was also the fact that he was preparing, with the others, to strike it big; accordingly he was impudent, but impudent in an uplifting way, and the others felt it too, they felt it in his voice across the crackling loudspeaker that something big was in the air, and the big thing in the air was Gagarin and the others—although all of them were aware that today Soviet Science was taking a dizzying step forward in the history of Mankind, all of them were thinking about that, it fired them up, although something else could have been firing them up as well, because this was about something much, much larger: namely that Man had entered into an unparalleled, dizzying adventure, stupefying in its consequences, in the context of the History of Mankind; or at the very least upon the first stage of this adventure, namely the rocket carrying him roared, and with a continuous blast manifesting itself in sounds never heard before, the Vostok 1 lifted off from the Kazakh desert, from the Earth, and beneath him the spacecraft roared, and the Vostok lifted off ever faster and ever faster, and everything beneath him, beside him, above him, and in him too, was shaking, and within a couple of minutes Gagarin reached the speed of Delta-v—ten kilometers per second—and in contrast to what Kamanyin noted in his diary, he was quickly on the verge of unconsciousness from the insane acceleration, so that the conversation between Earth and Vostok, namely between Zarya and Kedr, which until then could be described as undisturbed, was halted for a few seconds: his face contorted, Gagarin tried to survive until the thrust lessened, until the pressure on his body—more than five-g—abated, and the Vostok 1 reached the desired speed, so that he could overcome the gravitational pressure and the drag; and for that he needed to reach, in the Vostok 1, a certain number of km. per sec., and then finally at 6:17 Universal Coordinated Time, that is 9:17 Moscow time, he reached the point where he could reassure Korolev that

The spaceship is functioning normally. I see the Earth through the Vzor. All is according to plan;

but of course, at that moment he could not have seen the Earth directly through the Vzor: he only could have seen it later on through one of the three windows placed around the height of his head, but right now, and generally speaking, above the clear hemisphere of the Earth, this Vzor—an optical device in the shape of a half sphere placed at his feet—aided him, as it always showed, in symbolizing the Earth, where the Vostok was at that particular moment, that is as a kind of clever little navigational mechanism, using the rays of the sun by means of eight mirrors, it always clearly conveyed to Gagarin where he was at that moment in relation to the Earth, but let's not dwell on this, because now we're going to dwell on how it all began among the most horrifying circumstances possible, because it began with various kinds of animals being launched into space, hence conveying the following information about space: if anyone at all would be able to remain alive in it, thus obliging the being in question to penetrate into space (the

whole thing beginning in parallel to the development of rocket technology, in the course of which sometime in 1947 someone had the idea
that maybe living beings could be sent up there too, and not just space-
ships), in all likelihood these first living beings were fruit flies, launched
into space by the Americans on a V2 rocket, and the primary goal of
this launch was to examine how the so-called living being could endure
so-called space, but of course these attempts in the '40s and the '50s
were uncertain, entailing certain sacrifice, because it was not really possible to regard these living creatures launched into space as anything
else but sacrifices, as in the beginning the poor wretches hardly survived, this is also demonstrated, for example, by the Americans' "Albert
operations," where five monkeys named Albert were sent into space
five times, one after the other, but all five perished in the end, killed,
for the most part, by the impact: and then on September 20, 1951, a
monkey named Yorick survived the trip, and only a few hours after his
return, he died from the removal of an infected electrode—people began to speak of success, but to put it delicately, success was still a long
way off, because until that point untold animals still had to perish, we
don't even know exactly how many died, it's only certain that there
were very many; in the first place, concerning the Soviets, it was customary for them not to speak of the death of animals launched into
space if they could avoid it, which they couldn't always manage, of
course—namely, not to speak about it—and so there they are: Ryzhik,
Lisa, Albina, Pchyolka, Mushka, and who even knows how many stray
dogs from Moscow died before the famous Laika came along, Laika,
hailed by the Soviets as a great hero, and that wasn't the problem, of
course Laika was a great hero, but she didn't become that in the way
that the official version told it—because while Laika wasn't expected
to survive anyway, there wasn't even a landing unit in the spaceship,
according to the official version, she survived seven days up there until
they put her to sleep with a quickly acting poison—actually the reality

was much more ruthless, namely: due to the presumed failure of a heat shield the dog was already suffering in the moments following the launch, maybe in the fifth or the seventh minute, as she couldn't withstand the trauma, more than 41 degrees instead of the normative value of 20° C, simply put: she died a torturous death from overheating, or according to others she was just burned alive, and so this poor little carrion circled around in space one hundred and sixty some-odd days, after the almost instantaneous death by torture occurring on November 3, 1957, until the entire spaceship burned up upon returning to the earth—but one thing is certain: Korolev and his crew would have swallowed the fictitious poison meant for Laika themselves in order for people to be able to withstand existence in space, and that came about too, and now there was just this one big jump in 1961, when, after so much suffering and sacrifice in the Kremlin, it seemed that the time had come in Tyuratam to shoot off a human being—namely one of us—into space, and they did fire one of us off, less than four years after Laika: Gagarin in his spacesuit climbed the steps of the silo, got into the Vostok, positioned himself in the spaceship cabin, then they strapped him in, equipped him, checked him, and in the end shut the cabin door on him, and that had to be the most frightening moment— when for the first time in history the door of a spaceship was closed on a man—and there he was alone face-to-face with what I want too, but of course don't really need, and I won't rush ahead too much, because the situation is such that there were antecedents, indeed how should I put it, there was a horrific quantity of antecedents, and I would really have to write all these down if it were possible: every, but every single antecedent—because nothing ever happens without antecedents, actually everything is just an antecedent, that's how it is: as if everything were just always preparing for something else that came before, as if it were preparing for something, but at the same time, and in an appalling manner, as if preparing without any final cumulative goal, so that everything is just a continually dying spark, and I don't mean to say that everything is just the past, but rather I am saying that everything is always striving toward a future which can never occur, what no longer exists strives toward what does not yet exist, and if we wanted to put it humorously, we could think that there really is something like a future or a past in reality too, but I don't want to put it humorously, in no way do I think that would be the case, as in my opinion this whole thing with the past and the future is just a kind of characteristic misunderstanding, a misunderstanding of everything that we call the world and about which—speaking in all seriousness—nothing can even be said beyond the fact that in addition to antecedents there are merely consequences, but not occurring in time; I've spoken about this innumerable times to Dr. Heym, but to no avail, because Dr. Heym is not the type of person to prick up his ears on hearing such things, he doesn't prick up his ears for anything, a person can say anything to him, and he just hangs his particularly enormous head, he is used to people around him saying idiotic things, and all the while that huge head of his just droops down, because for him every conversation is just a symptom of something, he would never believe that, at least in my case, there is an immediate relevance to what I'm saying, no, not Dr. Heym, he just sits there and he pretends to be listening attentively, but he neither approves nor refutes, he just lets people speak, this is the natural order of things, for sure this is what he's thinking: just let them speak, let them go on talking, they can do whatever they want, the injections will be jabbed into them, the pills will be shoved down their throats: with me it's just Rivotril, and that's it, as far as he's concerned it's all taken care of, I talk to him every Wednesday starting at nine a.m., but nothing, he doesn't even budge—I'm not just talking about anything, though, I just think many times he's really not there, but it's not that he's not paying attention, because if I were to say to him what's going on with you, Shitbrain—I tried it once—he immediately says:

May I ask to whom or what you are referring? so you can't just pump him full of lead because he notices, even when he's not really there, once he hears Shitbrain he immediately wakes up, but if, for example, somebody talks to him about antecedents, or about the past and the future, then nothing, not a single wrinkle quivers on his forehead, but then exactly who am I supposed to tell this to apart from him—there's no point trying with anyone else, because everyone else here is sick, really, although I really don't speak of this willingly, because then it would be as if I were sick too, accordingly I just talk to him, I talk to him and I talk, of course I don't tell him everything, but again why not, as something should always start from the beginning, I tell him, for example—when the name of Korolev or Kamanyin or Keldysh comes up—that this was the great trio in this affair, and it's because of them that you have to know everything about this a person could possibly know: how the impossible became possible, and yet at the same time it's pretty difficult because with the Soviets the whole thing was so classified that anyone who is involved with this can only recognize certain fragments, and even with these fragments he can't be too certain of what he's come across because the secretiveness in space travel was really insane during the Cold War, so that it's even difficult to imagine, as the facts concerning the chief protagonists, let's say, reached the public only in completely falsified form, and by that I mean that we only know with certainty what the protagonists' names were, but to really pick out what they were doing, and how it all came together so that a human being could be hoisted into space is horrendously difficult, because any information that was public was false, and what wasn't public was secret, and what was secret was obscure, that's where the matter stands, and that's where it will remain, but standing nonetheless—as the nurse István always says, only when he's capable of speaking, he's the most idiotic one here, that's for sure, I say that to Dr. Heym, and Dr. Heym says aren't you putting that a little sharply, so I take my words back immediately and I continue, saying that what is really strange is that it's not as if there was any lack of material, as, for example, almost all of them wrote their autobiographies, Gagarin was the first one, of course, but Korolev and Kamanyin followed with theirs, and then the academician Keldysh tried to insert himself into world history, then a younger second cousin of Gagarin's showed up with a book that was pure conspiracy theory, and I could go on, I tell him—of course, these are all just fairy tales, how could it be otherwise: scribbled lies, mawkishly composed, then written and rewritten thousands and thousands of times, revised, copied out, then rewritten again, revised and then copied out, but if we want to know at least something about the antecedents, and about the Great Journey itself, we don't have anything else, so we have to read these accounts over and over, almost as many times as they did—the nameless secret police officers, the dear officers and the dear little officers who were standing right BEHIND the Gagarins, the Korolevs, the Kamanyins, the Keldyshes, the nephews, and the second nephews—how should I put it, they did what they had to do so that these writings would never be a documentation of space travel in any real sense of the word but mere forgeries of history, forgeries of events, and it's not enough to say that "this is the most squalid aspect of the whole thing," because immediately it must be stated that this squalor was NECESSARY, well, let's not exaggerate here, Dr. Heym interrupts me, and then I don't even feel like telling him anymore about where I stand with this matter, and now I only write this here into my own notebook: that without this squalor, without this falsification of history and events, the gigantic fact of history coming to pass would have never emerged, and it brought this forth, just as it brought forth my own life, this Hollywood, as we are called in the village, indicating that—and it's true—that the only people who end up here in the Exceptional Old People's Home are those whose nests are well feathered, and well, why deny it, everyone here has or, more precisely, had a pretty well-feathered nest, because when you move here, every single resident leaves the whole of his significant property to the Institute, as did I, just like the others, there was a big pile of this and that, and now there's nothing, I used to have a lot, but now I don't even have a cursed penny, I gave it all to Dr. Heym so that every Wednesday starting at nine a.m. he can droop that horrifically enormous head while he listens to me, and I let my brain hang down while I listen to nurse István, this isn't a lunatic asylum as the villagers claim, officially speaking it's nothing like that, and even if there is something to that rumor, it's because besides me almost everyone here is an idiot; Hollywood, well, yes, and the fact that we're shut in here, and that you can only step out of the door if you have an official Pass to Leave signed by Dr. Heym, as I do, I don't care about anything else, but going out is of vital necessity for me, and that's why I insist upon it, and there have been no particular obstacles, and even despite the regular doses of Rivotril I haven't become an idiot like everyone else here, along with that accursed István, who hounds me so he can talk to me, but he has no idea what he wants, he comes after me, I can feel him already, I don't even have to look around, he's watching sneakily to see when he can pounce on me so he can say something, but for a while he just whimpers and doesn't say anything, he stands in front of me, not looking into my eyes, but he looks off to the side flatly beside me, then just hemming and hawing he starts muttering: there's something I want to tell you because you are an educated person, but he just hems and haws all kinds of gobbledygook, and then: you are an educated person, and already when I hear things like that, how should I put it, I DE-FINITIVELY shudder, and there is no liberation from this shudder-ing, I am one single shuddering if I think about this István, I feel dread as dark as the depths of a police boot: he comes after me, clearing his throat, and says, I'm telling you, I want to talk to you because you are an educated person, and you will understand, and then comes all this gobbledygook about the moon, I am not joking, this István is always trying to say something about the moon, that he has discovered the secret of its halo, this is no joke, he's been trying to tell me this for years, but he always gets confused, or more precisely it's not just that he gets confused, but that he starts off from this confusion, because this confusion is right there at the beginning of his words, he can't even speak properly; it's possible that Dr. Heym hired him because he's even more idiotic than the patients he takes care of, well, whatever, Hollywood, István, Dr. Heym, I've been living here maybe six years already, I don't keep count, I don't care how long it's been or how long is left, nothing remains now, that's my present situation, it is very clear to me, what's the point of lying to myself, I don't even have a single day left: my life is over, The End, no more, but by this I don't mean to say it's as if it had any meaning before, because it didn't, just as it's never possible for life to have any meaning, and so for me there was none before, and there will be none later, and if I say now there's not too much sense to it, and it doesn't mean anything, I mean the days go by one after the other, I do my research, I read, I examine archives, I listen to recordings, I watch recordings, and actually not too long ago when the first snow fell, I even succeeded in personally questioning one of the participants who was pretty close to the key to all this, and if I say pretty close, I mean that I'm talking about someone who—even if in the most diaphanous sense—was affected by this while not noticing anything at all, like when a swallow takes a nosedive behind a person's back, and shoo! by the time person has turned around it's gone already, well something like that could have happened with a certain General Tihamér Jászi, because he was the one whom I was able to get to a few weeks ago, it was so easy, like child's play, I was prepared for it to take months, but one telephone call was enough, because to my great surprise he said: fine, come on over, and I said to myself, fine, so I'm going, and already I was sitting in his apartment, I'm a retired general, he corrected me jokingly, when I addressed him as General, and we began to address each other informally right away, he was good-hearted, decidedly friendly, so that I wondered how this Jászi became a soldier, and I hoped that my surprise didn't show on my face, because the general was decidedly friendly, direct, good-natured and ready to help, a kindly old UNCLE, or rather UNCLE TIHI, and it was he who was the closest in understanding everything that happened with Gagarin, and so I said to him: Mr. General, does it ever strike you that we know almost nothing about that period of Gagarin's life following his one single trip in space, and then his world tour, we know nothing about what happened to him after his great triumphal tour—but of course we do, he became the director of the training center in Star City, he snapped back with some visible confusion—but the answer came too quickly, too mechanically, and it was almost that that made me notice that there was something not right with his answer, the left eyelid of the general was trembling a little, and from that left eyelid I immediately perceived: there's a problem here, indeed, when I put the question to him, I largely already knew what the answer would have to be, I am often like that, I picked up this habit from my earlier activities, let's call them that, activities, I got used to explaining a certain phenomenon in such a way that I would be posing a question, to which I myself would provide the answer with razor-edge precision, actually at such times I don't even ask, I'm just helping out with the question, so that the audience, in my former popular science lectures—which used to weigh heavily upon my soul, although in general they don't anymore—would understand what I'm talking about, and so it was as I sat next to this good-natured soldier, whose wife was almost immediately extending a platter through the softly opening door, and on this platter everything was arranged in exactly two nice parallel lines, with two shots of Unicum, two glasses of water, two small bowls of salty hazelnuts, and finally on two little plates, a few pieces—no doubt equal in number—of so-called ROPI, or breadsticks, so there in front of us were the glasses, the bowls, the platter, and the Unicum: I think, the general said very good-naturedly, I think I'm the oldest, so hello, let's not be formal, and he already had raised his shot glass, and we were already using the informal address, well, as you know, this is what is known about Gagarin: we know he was in Star City, then there at the end there was that horrific accident, well, I said at this point, and I tried to bring him back to an analysis of the beginnings, and this was successful too, but while I was listening to the information about the beginnings, I was occupied in my thoughts trying to figure out if my new-found friend, this dear UNCLE TIHI, actually knew something about what had happened, after all, I thought, he was the highest-level commissioner for so-called Hungarian space travel; warmed up by the Unicum, I looked at his dear face, and after a while I said to myself, no, UNCLE TIHI doesn't know anything about what I'm interested in, he knows nothing about what happened with Gagarin AFTER—and at this point I cannot write with my pen in big enough letters this AFTER, because when I began this whole thing, there came a time when I realized something wasn't right here, for days on end I shook my head, I turned over the materials in my possession again and again, and it began to seem that we know not only very little, but in essence nothing at all, about Gagarin AFTER, there's the training base directorship, then at the end there's the official version of the accident and innumerable unofficial versions, in other words rubbish, guesswork, fairy tales, as to why he came crashing down, as to what was really going on with the test flight on March 27, 1968, with the—as they called it—piece-of-cake practice assignment, at 10:31 he's still there, but by 10:32 he's gone, in one split second Gagarin had disappeared from the picture, there were huge problems with these MiG-15s, because although, in the early '60s, they were already out of use as supersonic military fighter jets, they were still considered to be serviceable for practice flights, in part for pilots in training wishing to fly real military aircraft to practice maneuvers in them, and in part for cosmonauts to "maintain their flying practice"—and this is already in and of itself strange enough: on the one hand, the heroes of the nation, and on the other these scrapped supersonic pieces of junk, because these MiG-15s were pieces of junk: if a person takes a closer look at them, the fuselages were too short, and it was this original weakness that made them unreliable, so that after a while, accordingly from the beginning of the '60s, they were as a matter of fact not good for anything, but it was precisely the cosmonauts that had to fly in them—who ever saw anything like this? well, whatever, it doesn't exactly pertain to the subject, in any event, Gagarin was sitting in the first seat, ready for maneuvers, and his companion, Seryogin, was in the other seat, and at 10:31 Gagarin informed the control tower in a calm voice that they had finished the maneuvers and they were returning to the base, at 10:32, however, they were already out of the picture, and of course, due to the reticent Brezhnevian report, and Brezhnevian reticence in general, no human being could ever believe this, and so the rumors containing every possible explanation spread like wildfire: they were shot down by the KGB, they weren't even in the plane, and every kind of muddle, some hyena of a journalist pressured a poor second cousin into revealing something sensational, saying it had all been arranged by the KGB, and now what I'm about to write may seem surprising, but it could have been anything at all, that's what I say, that IT DOESN'T MATTER what happened, IT DOESN'T MATTER what happened with those MiG-15s, and IT DOESN'T MATTER what happened to Gagarin, because the main thing is that Gagarin had to die BY ANY MEANS POSSIBLE, and the miracle is that he was able to delay the event for seven years, that event which of course shook the entire world, but most profoundly it shook the Soviet Union, people wept openly everywhere in the homeland upon hearing the news of his death, Gagarin was the kind of hero the loss of whom nobody was prepared to withstand, because while I have to say here that the people hadn't even the slightest idea of what had really happened, they had no idea of what had led to this point, it was, however, unavoidable, Gagarin had to disappear for good, and of course the way in which he had died—one of the nation's, indeed one of the world's greatest heroes perishing in the course of such a simple test flight—was inconceivable, I understood this, but then I began to preoccupy myself with what happened to Gagarin after the Great Event, and I found almost nothing, it began to look suspicious to me, and I researched some more and I came upon some documents showing Gagarin's life after 1961 or 1962 in a completely different light, namely these documents began to show me a person who was hardly scornful of vodka before his journey around the world, but this was nothing in comparison to what he did afterward, following his Great Triumphal Tour: from that point on he began to drink VERY MUCH, and DIFFERENTLY than before, during his amusements, after the Great Journey, it was no longer drinking for fun—in vain did they try to eliminate from every single document the slightest sign that Gagarin was drinking like a dog—they couldn't hide it from me, I immediately seized upon this when between two facts something was missing, that was exactly what made me suspicious, something wasn't there that should have been there, it's difficult to pull the wool over my eyes, I would've made a good spy or a cryptologist, but the main thing is, well, that I found traces, mainly I found them because it was obvious at one point that certain things were missing, although I have to say that later on I was even amazed at myself—or I would be at anyone else following Gagarin's path even a little bit—that it didn't leap out at me immediately that these documents were silent, to put it very simply there isn't one stinking word about what happened with Gagarin after the Great Flight and the Triumphal Tour that followed, and why—I put the question to myself—well, why aren't we allowed to know what he did, there were still seven years left to go in his life, seven years is a long time, and essentially we know nothing; Uncle Tihi said, well, he was the director of the training base, then he attended the Flight Science Academy, is there so much to chew over in that, he says, why wouldn't it just be—now that it's all finished—that in those times any information associated with space travel was completely classified well, that's why, said Uncle Tihi to me—and these Uncle Tihis always said this to everyone, to anyone, to the world, if they were asked about it— he says, well, what else is there to know about this Yuri Alekseyevitch Gagarin, while it is also true that in reality when he smiled at the world, the story of this Yuri Alekseyevitch came to a halt in people's heads, and he said yes, people, believe your eyes, because I am the First Person, and that was it, that was what the world wanted to know, finished, that was enough, no more, this world didn't care about anything else, all over the world they knew the story of this Yuri Alekseyevitch, they placed that smiling face beneath the soldier's cap into their brains, they packed it away into the vitrine, if I may put it that way, with the sliding glass closed shut and a lace doily on top—but as for Yuri Alekseyevitch himself there was just one small problem, because although the Great Journey really was the high point of his life—what else could it have been?—in a strange way, his Great Story didn't come to an end with this Great Journey, it BEGAN, but I don't know what's going on with me, sometimes I rush ahead too much, sometimes, like now, I double back too quickly, it's always like this with stories, I've noticed they're already ended, and I don't even know for how long it's been like this, in other words in this modern age, or this more-than-modern age there is always a problem with these stories, I'm always being shown some story, well, it isn't one, or it never was one, or it only has a beginning, or what comes after the beginning, and moreover, even if at one time or another it could have been a story, every one is the same anyway, there's nothing new under the sun, as they said in the olden days, well, I don't agree with the idea that there are no stories, there are only stories, there are billions of stories, a thousand billion, a gazillion trillion stories, I won't go on, but to say that there are no stories, well we are only made of stories, but another question altogether is that we simply cannot find the MIDDLE of the stories, we always talk about how, well, here are the antecedents, and all these antecedents are going to lead to a story, and then we say here are the consequences of the story, and they enumerate, they enumerate the innumerable everything that comes after, but the middle part—namely the story itself—isn't there, the kernel, the essence, namely, we lose the story itself while it is clearer than day that we live among ten billion trillion stories, it is however indisputable that when we try to pronounce this essence, when we try to present, conceive, to bring the kernel of our story to the conscious-ness of anyone by whatever method, in general our endeavors don't meet with success, either because we remain detailing the antecedents at length, or we lose ourselves in a detailed explanation of the conse-quences, and I've even noticed with respect to myself that there is a problem in this regard, so that I need to constrain myself as well, I know—fine, enough of this haste to present the antecedents, and enough of what came after them, so there's no need for this damned confusion, so let's stick with those MiG-15s, let's have a look—that's what I did, at least, as I sank even deeper into the documents—I was, by that time, well known in many places: in the Ervin Szabó Library, in the Széchenyi Library, in the Military History Library, in the Space Travel Office, indeed even in the Flight Science Library, I no longer had to say who I was or what I wanted, they already piled up for me what was mine, while noting: this might be of interest to you, they car-ried various materials to me, as no one else was interested in these materials anymore, and they were happy to bring them out; although usually librarians aren't like that, librarians hate libraries, and when we ask for something from them we in fact cause them horrific pain, be-cause these people, confined to their own misery, spend their entire life just carrying things out of the storeroom, and that is something that could really make a person sad, I can't even imagine it myself, somebody is always coming along, there they are standing in front of you, they hand you something written on the library call card, then you have to go into the storeroom, you have to find what this person wants—this in and of itself must be detestable: a librarian is forced to confront the fact that somebody is interested in something, here almost everyone burrowing over to their counters is unworthy of having something brought to them, so that no matter where librarians may cast their gaze in the storeroom, nearly every book solicits hatred, because they begin to suspect that at one point yet another unworthy individual will walk into the library and without further ado say to them: bring me this, please, and they will have to bring it, well, that's clearly enough to drive a person insane, and it's clear that librarians would go insane if there didn't occur every once in a while one of those rare cases when a great mind WORTHY of a library and the librarian in question asks for something, this is what librarians like, because then they experience the library, the work being requested on the reader's card, the stumbling around in the storeroom, and finally the bringing of the desired work into the light of day in order to give it to someone who is WORTHY, they see it all in a completely different light; cases as these, however—and this can be seen in the eyes of a librarian—occur maybe, maybe, maybe three times in a lifetime, a visit to the counter by a so-called worthy reader, so that in general the atmosphere in one of these big libraries is like that of a morgue, with only repressed hatred and repressed insubordination—but in my case and this whole Gagarin affair, at least until now I have only encountered the fullest of good intentions, the librarians and the archivists and the museum workers and other such experts gladly bring me everything I need, clearly they believe that I am an imbecile, but that rare kind of imbecile who somehow solicits a sympathetic response from his surroundings, well, maybe because of this, or maybe because of something else—who can understand the soul of librarians and that mournful existence of theirs—they brought the materials to me, and it was as if these materials had been previously filtered somehow, because they all began to point in one direction, so that I began to sink further and further down, and this happened even last week, while I was in the depths of these materials, actually having reached the lowest point there so as to begin my journey upward again like some deep-sea diver, because, yes, something had taken me there, something that I had to examine yet again, in other words: what do we know about these MiG pilots ... because I didn't understand how it was possible that in a military environment such as this, where everything is supervised a thousand times over, that this supervisory structure could allow a drunk or hungover Gagarin to take off without any further ado—in other words, for a long time I thought that the essence of the secret resided in the fact that Yuri Alexeyevitch had become an incurable alcoholic, and well, with someone like that it's no big surprise if after he lifted off it ended in tragedy, I realized this just one week ago when I understood that this is the part of the whole Gagarin story that doesn't make sense, when all the same I felt that this Gagarin disappeared from the picture precisely because they couldn't manage him anymore, in vain they pleaded with him: don't drink, little brother, the eyes of the entire Soviet Union and the world are on you now, they're watching you drink yourself into the ground, but he just drank and drank, and they couldn't control him, what else could they have done, I thought to myself just a week ago, other than make the hero of the Soviet Union and the world disappear from the Soviet Union and the world—and for a long time I didn't even find as much as one photograph from his last years, and when I did there was just that one photograph, the so-called last photograph which merely strengthened my suspicion that my train of thought was going in the right direction, because there can be no doubt that what was going on here was complete senility, I looked at Gagarin, and I saw in this photograph a completely distorted, bloated-looking

figure smiling crazily, with a rough cross-shaped lesion on his left eye-lid—the only problem was that it was right beneath a pilot's helmet, and another problem was that this helmet formed part of a pilot's uni-form with parachute straps, and a further problem was that the person wearing all of this was visibly sitting I N S I D E an airplane with the para-chute and straps attached to his body, this was impossible, I stared at the photograph, chilled to the bone: this could not be Gagarin, it was, however Gagarin who was just then doing up the strap to his pilot's helmet beneath his chin, and with this senile grin!—I was stupefied, and I even told Dr. Heym about it this past Wednesday, not as if I would've hoped this would be interesting to him, but I told him—be-cause I couldn't really keep it just to myself, and because I believed that I had come upon something, of course I'd come upon something, and this was one of the cleverest tricks of the whole thing, contrived exactly so that you would never realize the truth—somehow this picture turns up, and for a while you're satisfied with it, but only because it seems certain that people would be satisfied with this so-called open secret, leaving aside, of course, any further investigations, and suspicion would die out—well, suspicion died out in me too, but not forever, only for a few days (and well, how could it not have?) but I felt during those few days like anyone else, I think, anyone else attempting to solve something, I too had "solved" what happened, I "came upon it," here, in the Unhappy Nursing Home, Where Everyone Awaits Only Death, I came upon the fact that Gagarin, as a hopeless alcoholic, was ever more isolated or even directly shut away from the world, and this last possibility is the more likely one, he lived for almost seven years more, and then they let him take off, and of course he plunged to earth immediately, because something happened while he was descending— now of course it doesn't matter if he had been confused by some roaming fighter pilot, or if he pointed the nose of the plane upward suddenly to avoid a flock of birds, it doesn't matter because the speed with which the plane was flying (it was already close to the ground) in that last fraction of a second in his last report was so great that any sudden movement would send him plunging to the ground—as happened in all likelihood, according to hearsay the nose of the plane crashed into the ground at a depth of three meters, supposedly they found more of Seryogi than of Gagarin but never mind, this is insignificant, in fact the entire matter of the immediate cause and circumstances of his death loses its significance if one thinks about what led up to this point, Dr. Heym asked me about this on Wednesday: what on Earth was I up to now, because it seemed even to him that I had stopped my researches, because earlier he had seen me feverishly investigating for months on end, spending ever more time in Budapest, continually traveling, coming and going, completely galvanized, and that's how it was because until the beginning of last week, I was completely galvanized, because I sensed a trace and I immediately started after it, and it seemed that finally I had reached that trace and suddenly everything changed, and then at the beginning of last week I suddenly stopped, I quit my researches, because something new had come up in this entire Gagarin affair, so that on Wednesday Dr. Heym asked me: what's going on with you, before you were always fidgeting, and coming and going, you were completely galvanized, and yet now, once again there you are sitting as in the old days, well, yes, I answered, for a few days I really had been sitting there in the same place, just like the old days, sitting once again in the far right-hand window of the sitting room by "my window," as nurse István confidentially calls it, and from where—as I did before this whole Gagarin affair began—I can look, at the farthest possible distance from nurse István and these other idiots, I look down from the heights here on the sixth floor, and it's good like this, I look down, just like the old days, sometimes not even coming down for meals; and of course I just avoided answering Dr. Heym, who repeated: but you were always going somewhere, you came and went, you were completely galvanized, what happened to you, what the hell is going on, of course I didn't tell him what was going on, I changed the subject, and I did well to do so because it's none of his business, nothing of this whole story is any of that big-headed Dr. Heym's business, it was Wednesday, and somehow I talked to him, then came Thursday, and now today it's Friday, I'm sitting in the window, and I'm thinking, as I look down, about how I should describe this precisely: it wasn't as if I picked up a new trace last weekend, but suddenly there it was in front of me just as now, here before me, is the complete face of the truth, I didn't seek it out, but the solution presented itself to me, and here it is, and now I have nothing more to do, I'm not going to say a word about this to Dr. Heym or to anyone else, there aren't going to be any lectures—because Dr. Heym is sure of it, he's urging me to give a lecture about this "matter," namely about Hungarian space travel, because I told him that's why I'm interested in this, that's why I come and go, why I fidget, and why I'm completely galvanized, so as to uncover the real story of Hungarian space travel; Dr. Heym, to be completely precise, wants me to present a lecture for him—FOR HIM!!!—as part of his weekly program for the Institute: a nice little talk, that's how he put it, and clearly he was satisfied, he just drooped, as always, that enormously large head of his, and he just kept on saying very good, very good, so at last you'll give a nice little talk based on all this material, a nice little talk, he used these words more than once, I just looked at him, wondering why he wasn't thinking that I was going to break his neck now, I saved it for later though, namely to break his neck just for that, but really how could this shrink with this enormous head begin to think that I was really going to give a talk for him—although to a certain extent it was reassuring to realize that he really didn't know anything about me, if he considered my participation in his cultural program to be a possibility, me in his cultural program!—until that point I had never stepped up, and I'm not going to, either, but he takes it as a given; well, of course I'm not interested in what he's imagining or what he wants, because nothing like that figures in my plans, as for appearances onstage, Dr. Heym, they are finished once and for all, I will only sit by "my window" as in the days of old and scribble some more into this notebook, and sometimes, as I turn over all the pages in this notebook, it comes to me that everything that I jotted down here isn't so bad, not so lacking in interest, maybe it's better if something has to remain after me . . . if it isn't going to be a fountain pen, a wristwatch, slippers, a dressing gown and such items, then let it be THIS, I will give it, for example, to nurse István—oh no, chills are running down my spine, anyone but nurse István—but then who should I give it to, this is no easy question, the best thing would be to destroy it after all, because there's still nurse István, well, I turned back to the first pages and I thought—I'm thinking about it now too—about how far away already that moment is when for the first time, in that general yesterday, the notion began to form within me that I want to leave the Earth; I've never even spoken about this before, because in the end I wish to betray my plans to no one, although to confess the truth I'm not planning anything, there is no plan, beyond scribbling a few more sentences here, maybe I'll write down what I came upon, maybe not, I don't know yet, in any event I'll just sit here and look out from the sixth-floor window a bit, I'll still exercise my memory a bit, recalling that turn of events a few days ago, because it was a turn of events, that is indisputable, for I felt that there was something in this alcoholic version that wasn't right, and so I kept on researching, actually I was researching in my head, I researched and I reflected intensely, and I was convinced that now everything was virtually in my hands, everything was in my possession, I thought—which in general is all that a person can really wish for—it's all up to me now, on my ability to think, on my brain, if it can hold out long enough, if it can focus on the essence long enough, so that I knew—this is what I mean to say—I needed thought in order to realize where a new suspicion could lead me, because I came upon it suddenly, and that day was in fact yesterday, and not that symbolic general yesterday of which I spoke earlier, it was, factually, yesterday, or well, who the hell knows—does it matter?—if it wasn't yesterday then it was the day before yesterday, it doesn't matter, the main thing is that as soon as I came upon this, I immediately wrote it down here in this notebook, for which, otherwise, I expend much energy trying to devise newer and newer hiding places, mainly from nurse István, because according to my own personal hypotheses, if something happened to me, he is the one who would comb through the entire Institution looking for it, because he has already betrayed countless times with his stares how interested he is in this notebook—well, no, but still, him?! I don't know—and yet I did find a very good hiding place, although I'm not sure that it's the best, perhaps the best is if I just keep it with myself at all times as I've done up till now; until now it's been well hidden in the lining of my long coat, respectively, in the evenings, in the inner pocket of my dressing gown, which I always keep beneath my head, originally I sewed in the pockets to keep money, but since that time I also keep my notebook there, so why should I change anything now? yes, it will stay there, in one of the pockets, but I'll see, because I really don't think that if something happened to me anyone apart from nurse István would be interested in this notebook, nobody is thinking about it, I think, although of course I should really destroy it, yes, this is an excellent option, later on, if the day comes, I will destroy it, and the day will come, it's not far off, it's almost here, I think, because as I say, there came a point and I understood what had happened, but for this, of course, it is necessary to know the antecedents and the consequences, and of course I knew those as well, there's no doubt of that, because it was on the basis of these that I realized what was going on here, namely that there had been a tiny error in my methodology, an error which we all make frequently when we want to get at the essence, the kernel, the central point of a story, and we do not attend adequately to these well-known antecedents and consequences in our possession, we just want to get at this essence, this kernel, this central point in haste, fine, I said, it's abundantly clear, I want to get at the essence, and let's say I made a mistake, on the other hand nothing is lost, because I am still in possession of those certain antecedents and consequences, so let's try this again—and I began to think, I began to run it all through my brain, so that, well, those antecedents and those consequences could run properly through this brain again and again and again—and then suddenly like lightning, it cleaved through my brain, really, like that swallow taking a nosedive behind your back, only that in this case it wasn't behind my back, it's as if something were swooping across my brain, because this brain, or this swooping, indicated that earlier on, something had happened on high, up there in orbit, during those one hundred and eight minutes, that's what this lightning flash of a swallow plunging down said to my brain: that the essence of the story, the kernel, the central point is that up there in those one hundred and eight minutes, when Gagarin, as the First Man, ended up there with the Vostok—up there in space (said the plunging swallow to the brain), there and then something must have happened to him, and at that point I got stuck, and so I just began to browse through the American materials mechanically, I had a special folder for this, indeed, to be precise I had several, but I just rooted around in the sentences written by a certain astronaut named Michael Massimino when he gave one of his renowned lectures at MIT on October 28, 2009, and then from these printed sentences one of them jumped out at me, and it was the one where this Massimino, who moreover is a sheer giant, looked out through the window of the International Space Station, and he saw the Earth, and he said: *I felt like I was almost looking at a secret ... That humans weren't supposed to see this. This is not anything you're supposed to see. It's too beautiful*, well, and then what? I recall that I was thinking about this, or something like that, and I dug around some more in these sentences, then I began to comb through a thrown-together pile of pictures of the Earth, in a different folder, taken by another American, a certain Ed Lu, photos of the Earth taken in the same way from on board the ISS, I rifled through these photographs, but these sentences of Massimino just kept ringing in my head, they wouldn't leave my brain, especially the part about how *humans weren't supposed to see this*, and maybe there are some people who recognize the feeling when a person's body is flooded with heat because they just realized something all of a sudden, or because something unexpectedly happened to them, well, then this plunging with the swallow, or vice versa, came over me again, and I felt that my body flooded with heat, and already I knew what had happened, I understood everything, I realized why Gagarin had disappeared, because I realized what had happened to him up there when for the first time he saw the Earth from one of the windows of the Vostok, and he said: *ochen' krasivoye*, I understood that he, the First Person among us, not only saw the Earth from space, but as I realized, he too had understood something, a millennial secret, and when he returned, he was clearly silent about it for a while, he didn't know how to begin, and as usually happens, a little time went by, so that it wasn't immediately following his return, but maybe about a year later, and then he began with only his most inner circle of friends, but they most likely thought it was the expression of some kind of poetic enthusiasm, and in the general euphoria they didn't really notice, and the next time Gagarin mentioned it, they had to react somehow, so they all just waved it away, the devoted wife, Valya, and his parents all just waved it away, because what else could they have done hearing such strange things, they just looked at each other, then they told him what beautiful thoughts he was expressing, and they truly hoped that they were capable of understanding them, but they also thought that he, Gagarin, would be far better off packing all of this off to hell, and so it could have gone on like this, as well as in the next two or three conversations following, in his most intimate circles, only that Gagarin could not be calmed down and he might have thought, oh, my dear wife, my dear father and mother, they are simple people, and I am only disturbing them with thoughts of such far-reaching import, and so he took the next step, and he went on and unburdened himself to Korolev, of course, taking all precautions to ensure that no one could hear them, he said what he had to say to the great man: first, that up there he had not only seen the Earth, but he had seen that Paradise of which every book of old speaks, and the first time it happened Korolev could have thought that Gagarin was still under the influence of the experience, or that he was Under the Influence in general, and that a poet was now speaking through him, fine, he stopped him, fine, Yuri Alekseyevitch, you need to take a little rest now, and he said things like that, and I think that for the first time Gagarin started to be a little afraid, because it was at that point that he suspected that what he knew now about the Earth would be very difficult to convey, and maybe it enraged him a little bit as well, and he might have repeated in his most military manner, saying: listen here, Comrade Korolev, you don't understand, I really saw Paradise, and Paradise is the Earth, and clearly Korolev first just smiled, and nodded, fine, fine,

Yurka, that's enough already, you have a nice rest, we have more than enough work, I'd like to send you up there again so you could see your paradise again, you go have a nice little rest now and then we'll pick up where we left off, but nothing came of it, because all around Gagarin things began to turn serious, mainly because Gagarin's Triumphal Tour through the various nations of the Earth had ended, and he had returned to the routine of a cosmonaut's daily life; and after Korolev he started going to Kamanyin, and after Kamanyin he went to Keldysh, and after Keldysh he went to Petrov, and after Petrov he went to the Party leadership, and if neither Korolev nor Kamanyin nor Keldysh nor Petrov had taken him seriously, it is completely clear that the Party leadership did not take him seriously, the sole difference being that those people, being farther away from Gagarin, had even less sympathy for his "analysis," and they conveyed to him in one way or another that he should leave the production of theory for the academicians and the great scholars of Moscow; he should continue his studies diligently at the Cosmonaut Academy and occupy himself only and exclusively with practical questions, for that was his field, and that is what Korolev and the Party had entrusted to him, so that after a while it had to become clear even to Gagarin that everyone considered what he was saying to be mere idiocy, or in the very best of cases: nobody believed a single word he was saying, nobody, but nobody believed him, and this clearly filled him with immeasurable bitterness, and in this state of nerves he had to pour his heart out, more specifically he had to pour his heart out ever more frequently, namely to pour out one's heart and not drink vodka at the same time, well, that is inconceivable for a Russian soul, so it could've happened that Gagarin began to drink regularly for this reason, or for reasons of heredity, and he began to slide down this slope with horrific speed—in the first years, though, it still wasn't possible to completely write him off, for he still was the First Person in Space, the Hero of the Cosmos, the Symbol of Human Knowledge, and so on, so they let him continue his so-called research at the Academy, and then he also had his own assignment in Star City, but it became farcical and, speaking among themselves, along with his ever more obstinate insistence on his own decidedly anti-Leninist theories, it became ever more evident that they were never going to let him get anywhere near space travel, and they didn't let him get anywhere near it, so that after a few years he would have had to comprehend something that he would never be able to resign himself to, namely: that they would never let him fly again, especially after the Komarov tragedy, in other words, he who desired ever more hysterically to see, from up there that . . . that Paradise would never see anything from up there ever again, and clearly he lived his days in wretched drunkenness, and clearly a great shadow was now cast over him, and in this great shadow his family life could have fallen into ruin, there was Valentina Ivanovna, there were Galya and Lenoshka, but he just drank and drank until he passed out, and all the while he spoke and spoke and he said and he said what he had to say to whomever happened to turn up in his path, from Tyitov to the cleaning staff of Star City, so that finally they would understand that what he was saying was nothing bad, so that they would understand already that what he was talking about only meant the greatest possible good for all of humanity, because what he had to say was that there really is a Paradise, and all of the sacred books— which until now had not been meaningful to him—all over the world they speak of something like this, and this doesn't even have any kind of mystical content, because the millennial belief that there was a Paradise, that there is a Paradise, and that there will be a Paradise *completely corresponds to reality*, and the pages of the sacred books should be turned over differently now, because all of them, just imagine, that every single sacred book IS LIKE THIS, and because of this, religions should be treated differently, because in reality they mean something else than what we, the Soviet Communists, thought about them, and what he had to say—he leaned in closer to the people backing away from the stench of vodka—could make every single person on this Earth happy, and make them happy he must—if they would only finally let him speak, and if they would only finally understand how vitally important it was for him to finally announce on the radio to all the people of the Earth that the end has come, the end of the old world, and a new era greets them with the simple truth, altogether comprised of three words, that actually ALL IS TRUE, the message of the Bible is true, the message of Buddha is true, the message of the Koran is true, the message of all of the temples is true, and even the smallest sect, in its own idiotic way, is true, it's just that UNTIL NOW we haven't understood these messages, that's how I imagine him saying it, even if not word-for-word, I imagine it like this, and in the same way one can imagine the Soviet comrades with the Hero reeking of vodka in front of them, the Hero demanding ever more insistently to finally be allowed to speak to the public, because he wants to say to the world, to all of humanity, he wants to tell them what he saw up there, and then finally peace shall be upon the world, because if every single person can understand this, then every opposition, every hatred, every war will lose all of its meaning, and the era of general peace will dawn, well, this was pretty much enough, during the Cold War, among the fossilized Soviets, for them not to let Gagarin address even a small audience, so that even if he had to give some kind of address very infrequently, or if he had to pronounce some speech, then they made him vow on the book of Party members—this is how I imagine it, but it must have been so—not to mention THAT THING, and after a while not only did they not let him speak—because they couldn't trust him to keep his word—but of course they withdrew him from space travel, and of course the time had to come quickly when he was just a marionette, both in Star City and in Soviet space research, a vodka-reeking marionette, with his bloated head, his face disfigured by this or that wound, who, in accordance with the customs of the time, had to be hidden away in one or another lunatic asylum in order to get his nerves or his organism into order, and of course neither his nerves nor his organism were put into order, but they didn't keep him in there for too long all the same, they let him out again and again, back to Star City or to some other training position, but he no longer was in the first row, nor even the second row, and not even in the third row, but in the very last row, from where his voice could no longer even be heard; Korolev and his crew and all of his comrades-in-arms and his friends, who all knew so well this formerly sweet peasant boy, this brave hero, this inimitable, charming person, whom they had once loved so much, simply could no longer allow Gagarin anywhere near the public, and he himself clearly was becoming ever more enraged by this repudiation, fully incomprehensible to him, he felt himself to be impotent, he was simply unable to conceive what was wrong in what he was saying; that impenetrable environment, whether hostile or lenient, was incomprehensible to him, and it began to separate him from everything and everyone once and for all, so that at the very end he couldn't think of anything else, only of Paradise, and he could have repeated this to his older brother Valentin, who visited him in his last year, 1968, in order to talk some sense into him, but to no avail, because he, Gagarin, just kept repeating that even if they were to tear him apart he still wouldn't be able to say anything else: that's why they put him aside, that's why he couldn't fly, that's why he was withdrawn from space travel, that's why they put him out to pasture, and you know why, Gagarin said to Valentin, because wherever I look, I see only this: Paradise—wherever I am, it's not just in my mind, but I SEE IT continually while I'm talking, God knows what they think of me, that I'm naïve, that I'm a simpleton, that I'm a child, anything rather than understanding that Paradise REALLY exists, and that it is nothing other than our own Earth, you understand, my dear brother, this Earth, our own Mother Earth ... and he began to weep like a child, he flung himself onto the table, and he wept, and this is obviously how it went with his drinking pals, with his wife, indeed—if they let him anywhere near them—with Galya and Lenoshka, so that they would not look upon human life as before, no, because humanity would come to know something through him, and because of this every evil upon the Earth would become completely meaningless; there sat a man enveloped in the stench of vodka, the hero of the Soviet Union and of the world for all time to come, a man who was being driven mad by the fact that nobody believed what he was saying, he was completely alone, the world had split into two: there was Paradise, of which he was the only resident, while in the world, with humanity suspecting nothing, knowing nothing of this great situation, simply continuing on with life as normal, as if nothing in this heaven-sent world had happened with the Great Journey and the Great Discovery, the world just kept going on like before, and this is what Gagarin's nervous system couldn't bear, and this nervous system destroyed his organism too, in the last days he could no longer bear being alive, this became completely clear to me, he could bear it only with vodka, only in complete drunkenness, and he became so alone: and if anyone was undeserving of this, it was this man—what a bitter consolation that here I am now and I can write everything down into this notebook, because on the one hand, I am most likely going to destroy it, so that no one will ever be able to read it, on the other hand it's useless for me to be here, it was useless for me to come, and it was useless for me to understand the great secret, it can no longer be of help to little brother Yuri Alexeyevitch, because in any event the best thing for him to do was to die, so that this could come to pass—it doesn't matter why—that *humans weren't supposed to see this*: in any event it's because of this, and the deeper meaning of this sentence that I will finish with the thought that IT IS SO, BUT IT IS NOT FATED: I understood that, and I understand it in this moment too, and in every

269

single moment to follow, so that it is time to finish this affair, I have no desire to wait and see what will occur of its own accord, it cannot be otherwise, as my researches and my discovery have deprived me of that which I thought would give me strength, although if I'd known I wouldn't have begun—the whole thing started off so nicely, it was still summer, with scorching heat, was it July? August? it no longer matters, I sat by "my window," and I thought about how I wanted to leave the Earth, and now this day has come, this day of December 29, 2010, it's damned cold outside, and I can't conclude this notebook in the same way that I began, saying that I want to leave the Earth, only that I wanted out—so that I've taken care of everything with Dr. Heym and his cervical vertebrae, and I've taken care of everything with István, and this notebook too (if it's necessary for something to remain after me, let it be this rather than anything else), then, as I don't want to spend a single day here, and since I already know that leaving the Earth won't work from "my usual window"—that is, for me to open the window, step outside, push myself off, and there you have it, up I go—instead, after I've finished with everything (and I'll still give my notebook to nurse István), then I'll open up the window here on the sixth floor, I'll stand on the windowsill and push myself off, because whatever doesn't go up with all certainty goes down. Because from the sixth floor to Paradise: the time has come.

OBSTACLE THEORY

You can take the Earth, and you can take the sky, he says, you can go wherever, go deep into the earth, or up into the sky, it's the same everywhere, you can study the innermost atomic structures through IBM microscopes, or imagine giant computerized rulers in the humongously huge galaxies for measuring the diameters of the universe, you can study the most enormous things and you can investigate the tiniest particles, it makes no difference whether you study entire societies or a single family, the fate of one man from the beginning, or living creatures one by one, or rocks one by one, or ideas, sources, theories, cognition, sensation, intention, volition, or what the Venus of Milo is looking at, or who loves who and why, or who doesn't like what and why, it's all the same, take for instance him and this two-liter plastic jug, which by the way he'll be finishing soon, here's this jug, and you may be sure that if anyone took the trouble to study him then they'd be looking at how he lifts the plastic jug and takes a good swig, *how* he drinks and then lowers the plastic jug down on the filthy, slimy pavement here, but not the *why*, not why he lowers the jug, well, they would never ask that, not why he doesn't drink more, meaning right now naturally, why his mouthful of swig is what it is and no more, in other words why doesn't he keep the jug to his lips longer, and why does he put it down right here—and now he mashes the jug's bottom against the slushy faux marble pavement in a corner of the underpass at Nyugati Station—and I'll tell you something else, he says, first of all everything that is now in the world, in this whole wide world, everything that is in place, is there because it cannot fall any farther toward the earth, the force of gravity is pulling it down, but something doesn't let it go, *something more powerful,* or let's take a river, he says, it happens to be important which way it meanders, he for one surely knows how important, which way it meanders, exactly what kinds of turns it makes on the way to the sea, but these bends in the river, every last one of them, are determined by how water runs to a certain point on the ground, so it goes around it, in other words the river runs up against something that is on higher ground and this deflects it, well then, these countless deflections create the river's how shall I put it—the line of the riverbed's course, the so-called riverbed lacework, why it bends this way and that, where it has to bend, and then here come the cartographers and navigators and dam builders and god knows who else, but they aren't interested in what's really happening here, they just flock like flies to shit, and nobody considers the essentials, because they only see that for me this much and no more constitutes a mouthful of swig, they only see that the river bends here and over there, and they even add that the ground level is higher there, but they see none of the essentials, absolutely none; or take another example, you look around you and because of gravitation everything in the world is in place, but has anyone asked himself, what makes this the particular place of one object and not another? what causes things to have their place, what causes the world to be the way it is?!—well, you see, it is because everything, on account of gravitation, gets stuck somewhere, and does not fall any lower, *and that's how the world is,* but take another case, take for instance snowfall, like right now; looking outside upstairs, the way those snowflakes fall, well now, it's the same story, why do they happen to be falling at that low speed, what do they usually say about it: weight and mass and air resistance and wind and gravitation, that's what they come up with, tops, but no one, nobody, says that there is an invisible gigasystem at work here, *and that's how the world is,* this, just this, is simply of no interest, they point to resistance, gravitation, forces, so there, it's all so obvious, no need to ruminate over it, whereas this is exactly what shows that everyone here is absolutely, truly ignorant; or take another example, because there it is, let's look at the Earth, then you'll see there are things that stand still and things that will sooner or later come to a standstill, that is, at the moment they happen to be moving from one place to another, there is stoppage and delayed stoppage, there are these two if we consider only the Earth and the way we see it, but if we take the realm of the invisible where, let's say, he says, neutrons and protons and electrons and hadrons and leptons and quarks and bosons and superpartners bicker and so on and so forth where the series is endlessly continuable as time passes—because they too are only assembled out of something—well, no matter, the point is that here we see motion, the interruption or stoppage of which, how shall I say it, is deferred forever, so that we have stoppage and motion, but behind both, and pay attention now, he says, there is that elusive, unfathomable gigasystem that determines what is it going to be, stoppage or motion, and beyond the worlds there are other worlds, every world perfectly conceals another world, of course, although the whole thing can also be expressed by saying that any one world is only a gateway, a secret door to billions of worlds, which are reachable only through this one and only world, and there are worlds upon worlds, but really, a huge topsy-turvydom, a gigachaos, one might say, and that doesn't express what we're talking about any better than if we were to recognize the whole as hierarchical parts of a single vast system, of course these are only words, and words never reveal anything, no, it's absolutely certain that they exist precisely *to hide* the way out, playing the role of the hidden, no, the bricked-up door that will never open, and of course things aren't much better with thought either, thought too always gets stuck at some threshold, exactly where this thought should cross over into the beyond, in short, no matter if it is words or thoughts, this is just like a border closing in the old days—no way in, no way out—while the enclosed area in its tense causality quivers there like a jelly-like mass, worthless and misleading, but we could go one step further, because if earlier we have agreed, he says, on there being either stoppage or delayed stoppage, behind that entity that decides whether we stop or move, behind that too there is an unfathomable but still conceivable gigasystem, and *this is the same identical one*, in every example of his the same gigasystem is at work, all this giga-ing isn't very helpful but he can't think of a better term right now, and anyway it's of no interest which word is unable to express what he wants to say, this isn't the first time he's run up against this problem, for alas he can only repeat that this is the situation with words, that words are helpless, it's always a merry-go-round, around the thing itself, never a bull's-eye, that's words for you, so that he for his part doesn't get too excited that he too is unable to find the right word, for today let's go with the giga-system, it doesn't express anything anyway either, that is to say, compared to what it should be expressing, that as a matter of fact the reason this system is there immediately behind each and every piece of the visible and invisible realms, that in fact this system is there in the realms of tremendously vast universal units and of tremendously mi-nuscule universal units, and this is not the world any longer, it is the essence, as he takes another swig from the plastic jug here in a corner of the underpass at Nyugati Station where he sought refuge from the winter's cold, for there is the world and there is this essence of the world, and presumably there are these various worlds, each with its own essence, but simultaneously, all together, because that's how we must think of it, all of it is simultaneously together, these worlds and their essence don't separate from each other, they are made of the same cloth, this essence is woven into, so to say, into its own particular world, speaking of which—and here with a look of deep significance he low-ers the plastic jug down into the filthy slush of the faux marble pavement—we are not wrong to speak separately about the world and separately about its essence, insofar as it is possible, that is, the essence about which he himself, here at the Nyugati Station, in the thick of Christmas rush, before he empties his plastic jug, he will say this much, so you will be able to imagine it for yourself in a simpler form—although he can understand that our attention is flagging—if you take time to do so, you can see it in the form of a jumble of obstacles, a horrendous, monstrously vast, funny obstacle course, nothing but invisible obstacles and nothing but concealed resistance everywhere, for imagine the world in front of you, or to be more precise, imagine an enormously vast world, as enormously vast as you can think of, and then you'll be able to see that each and every event in it hinges upon an obstacle, it depends more significantly upon that obstacle than on the impulse, so to say, that propels it forward, or would put it into motion if it could, this is not so complicated, he says, it can be imagined, let your mind run through the entire world from the inexhaustible realm of subatomic particles to the inexhaustible realm of universes, and you will be able to see the facts, that are either events, or things, or absences of events, or absences of things, but if they are the latter, even then, they are absences, possessing the diametrically real fact of the non-occurrence of things or events, well then, and now he attempts to struggle to his feet but falls back on the layers of overcoats spread under him, we can clearly recognize this essence of the world, of the various worlds, for it is clearly visible now, no? that it is obstacles that hold it together, obstacles that give it structure, insofar as it is possible to speak of structure, obstacles determine what will be and what will not be, *obstacles,* whether it will be this or that, the Big Bad Wolf or Little Red Riding Hood, which one it will be, and which one it won't, where it will go or where it will stop, or when it will start or will it start at all, there is nothing, he says with his back flung against the wall, to the crowds surging past in the earsplitting racket of the underpass, nothing that is not brought about by Him, or done away by Him, lord of life and death, the mightiest world order behind the world, the most tremendously monumental structure in existence, that is all too extant, while—and this is really not very funny—while … he repeats, raising his free hand in warning to the crowd that takes not the slightest notice of him, this essence is not at all present in existence, for in existence it is present only through its consequences, *and this is the world;* or, to put it more plainly, take a look at him for instance, he is no less uninteresting than anyone else in this mad Christmas rush, so he will do as an example, he had a life, in his life he went here and there, there was stopping and there was going, meanwhile he could not go this way, then that, one thing is sure now he is standing, now it is nothing but obstacles everywhere, a gigacheckmate, you could say, when the only thing that remains is those last swigs in the plastic jug, he can still drink that, another swig and mouthful, before he stops for good, before he disappears for good, before that great stinking blur swallows him, completely, so that no one will bring him back—here by the subway entrance of Nyugati Station—you can come back and see for yourself, here by the side of the ticket office, in the recessed corner; the draft is pretty bad here, tomorrow is Christmas, just one forint please, it's snowing upstairs, and tonight, here is this empty plastic jug, in his lap grown cold.

JOURNEY IN A PLACE
WITHOUT BLESSINGS

I.

A church is that place where the Holy Scriptures are read and understood.

II.

The diocesan bishop sits sadly among the congregation and he says: this is the end of the reading of the Scriptures, for there has been no understanding.

III.

Then—because in a sacred place only that is permitted which will serve the practice of the adoration of God, and all which does not accord with the holiness of the place is prohibited; and as the sacred places have been degraded by means of the deep injustices, scandalous to believers, which have taken place within them: henceforth no divine service may be held as long as this injury has not been corrected by means of a penitential ceremony. The diocesan bishop says to the congregation: "The Lord was with you!" and then after the morning it shall be evening, then the end of evening, and it shall be eventide and midnight, but the congregation doesn't keep vigil all night, but falls asleep, and when twilight descends the diocesan bishop takes the Holy Sacrament from the tabernacle; he extinguishes the sanctuary lamp, and he pronounces these words:

"We do not supplicate! Because our comprehension has not been filled with the truth, we do not stand in glory before the Lord. Our Lord, receive not the gifts offered by Your bitter congregation, for Your people have not gained eternal salvation in this sacred building through the mysteries. And it is worthy, just, fitting, and beneficial for us to confess this, and now we withdraw in sadness from this temple of prayer built with human labor, and so may this temple here be the house of salvation unfulfilled, the hall of the sanctities of heaven forever unattainable."

IV.

My Dear Brethren, says the diocesan bishop.

V.

Then he blows out the candles placed upon the altar, gives them to one of the attendants, and addresses the congregation. "Light of Christ! Almighty Eternal God! Withdraw Your mercy from this place, for Your divine help to those who prayed to You was all in vain."

VI.

The diocesan bishop gives the tabernacle to the other attendant, then he takes away the flowers and the altar cloth as well. "Withdraw Your blessing from these objects," he says, "and receive no more the prayers, the thanksgivings, the appeasement, and the requests of all those who formerly fell to their knees before Your Holy Son."

VII.

"Your Holy Son, who lives and reigns with You forever and ever."

VIII.

The diocesan bishop takes the frankincense from the censer, he extinguishes the embers, and in the meantime he says: "Our Lord, our prayers did ascend here before Your Presence like frankincense. Never shall they ascend again. I rescind the censing of the altar, the walls, and of this congregation."

IX.

The congregation is silent.

X.

The diocesan bishop turns to the walls, and he washes from them the signs of the twelve crosses once rendered in chrism. Then he steps to the altar, and from the four corners he wipes away the memory of the sacred oil.

XI.

And this he says: "Our Lord, who has sanctified and guided Your Church, we have praised Your sacred name with festal songs; and yet we shall do so no more. Because on this day, Your withered people ceremoniously return this temple to Prayer itself; this temple, where, although You were honored, but from Your Word nothing was learnt, and by Your sanctities no soul was nourished. And so it was that this church symbolized the Church, sanctified by Christ with His own blood, so that He might choose it as His glorious betrothed, to be kept in the purity of belief as a resplendent virgin, becoming a happy mother through the power of the Holy Spirit. And so it was that the vineyard of the sacred Church, chosen by the Lord, the twigs of which replenished the entire world—and its shoots were made to grow upon the crucifix—was raised to the country of heaven. This was the shelter of God among people, a church built from living stone, which, like a foundation of stone, is built upon the apostles; and within it Jesus Christ Himself was the cornerstone."

XII.

"And the Church was majestic," says the diocesan bishop, "the city built upon the top of the mountain, which shone in pure radiant light before everyone. And within it, the glory of the Lamb was radiant, and the song of the happy ones echoed. And now, Our Lord, we yearningly implore You to withdraw every blessing of the heavens, to make this place sacred no more, because the currents of God's grace can no longer wash away the sins of the people, because Your sons did not become as dead to sin, and they were not reborn to eternal life."

XIII.

"And around the table of the altar," says the diocesan bishop, "no longer shall there gather Your believers dispersed, no longer shall they celebrate the holy secret of Easter, no longer shall they be nurtured by receiving the Word and Body of Christ. Here, in the heartless voice of farewell, resounds the arrogance of forfeiture, because no human word shall unite with the songs of the Angels. No longer shall prayers ascend towards You for the salvation of the world, because those suffering in need shall no longer find the path to assistance, and the downtrodden shall never again come upon freedom: between every person and the dignity of the Son of God shall extend a chasm vast."

XIV.

"No one shall attain," says the diocesan bishop, "no one shall attain heavenly Jerusalem, and the distance which leads to Your Son is unutterable."

XV.

"Your Son, who lives and reigns with you in the unity of the Heavenly Spirit, one God for ever and ever."

XVI.

The diocesan bishop takes down the altar with the two attendants, then they remove it, and he speaks: "Withdraw Your blessing from this place, our God, because there is no longer any sign of the love of Jesus, who sacrificed, for us. The ardor of the congregation was not worthy of this beautiful altar. In vain did sound the call, they did not gather round, and they did not take part here in the Holy Sacrament."

XVII.

The diocesan bishop takes down the pulpit with the two attendants, the place of proclamation of the Word, he has them take it out, and he says: "Withdraw Your blessing from this place, our God, because Your word resounded here in vain, it was not fruitful."

XVIII.

And the diocesan bishop, with the two attendants, takes down the images that were hanging there, and they move the statues, and the images and the statues are all taken away, and so he speaks: "Almighty God! No longer shall it be permitted for us to see Your Holy Son ..."

XIX.

"Your Holy Son, who lives and reigns with You forever and ever."

XX.

" ... Or the likenesses of Your saints, because if we gaze upon them here, they only make us think of our sins and the path that leads to baseness, and not of sacred life. So withdraw Your blessing from us, our Lord, because as we look at them we are not strengthened in our faith, and thus those who sought intercession from Your Saints, praying before these icons and these statues, shall never gain shelter upon this earth, and eternal glory in Heaven never shall they gain."

XXI.

The diocesan bishop gathers up the relics from beneath the altar, and then he says:

XXII.

"My Beloved Brethren!"

XXIII.

"Nevermore shall our pleading ascend to Almighty God in the name of Christ our Lord! Nevermore shall the Saints hear our pleas, the Saints who took part in the suffering of Jesus, and who were guests at His table. My Lord, have mercy on us! Christ, have pity on us! Sacred Virgin Mary, Holy Mother of God, Archangel Michael, have mercy on us!"

XXIV.

"St. Michael Archangel, All Holy Angels, St. John the Baptist, St. Joseph, the Apostles Saint Peter and St. Paul, St. Andrew the Apostle, St. John the Apostle, St. Maria Magdalena, the martyr St. Stephen, the martyrs

St. Perpetua and St. Felicitas, the martyr St. Agnes of Rome, St. Gregory the Pope, St. Augustine of Hippo, St. Athanasius of Alexandria, St. Basil of Ceasarea, St. Martin of Tours, St. Benedict of Nursia, St. Francis of Assisi and St. Dominic of Osma, St. Francis Xavier, St. John Vianney, St. Catherine of Siena, St. Therese of Ávila, St. Stephen of Hungary, St. Gerard of Csanád, All the Saints of Our Lord, deliver us!"

XXV.

After the Liturgy of the Word is abandoned, the diocesan bishop draws out from the walls and from the entire congregation all traces of the water that once had been consecrated; then he stands in front of a vessel filled with water, and he speaks:

XXVI.

"My Dear Brethren!"

XXVII.

"When we ceremoniously consecrated this building, we begged Our Lord and our God to bless this water, which reminded us of our own baptism. Now we beg Our Lord to withdraw this blessing, because we did not follow the promptings of the Soul. Our God! We could have attained the clarity of life through You, but in vain did You decide that, cleansed, we would arise to a new life: we did not arise to a new life, and we have not become the inheritors of Eternal Happiness. So withdraw Your former blessing from this water, so that we shall never remember Your heavenly mercy, a mercy which we shall never ever attain."

XXVIII.

And then the diocesan bishop, with the silent congregation following after him, withdraws from the church, closes the door, and hands
over the key to the emissary of the former master builder, then—after
the diocesan bishop withdraws all the former requests concerning the
blessing of the grounds of the building, and forbids processions to take
place there—with the help of the master builder he digs out the cornerstone, shoves it into a ditch and says:

XXIX.

"And so it was, that I, John, saw the new heavens and the new earth.
And the first heavens and the first earth passed, and the oceans were no
more. And I, John, saw the holy city, I saw the new Jerusalem descend
from heaven, from God, like a bride adorned in ornament, descending
toward her husband. And then I heard that strong resounding voice
speak from the throne: 'Behold the shelter of God among the people!
He shall live with them, and they shall be His people, and God Himself
shall be among them. And God shall wipe every tear from their eyes,
and there shall no longer be death, nor mourning, nor lamentation,
nor pain, because all that had been before has passed.' And He who
sat upon the throne spoke: 'Behold, I shall create everything anew.'"

XXX.

The congregation dispersed, and the bishop vanished from sight.

THE SWAN OF ISTANBUL

(seventy-nine paragraphs on blank pages)

in memoriam Konstantinos Kavafis

NOTES

Page 287. *suddenly forgot*: after the kind personal communication of At-
tila Golyo Gulyas-Kovacs (Rockefeller Institute, New York) 9.30.2011.

Page 287. *the rapid forgetting of details*: after the kind personal communication of Balint Lasztoczi (Columbia University, New York)
9.30.2011.

Page 287. *he was aware that he was forgetting, that some kind of confusion
had developed between himself and the world, in this case between him
and the ...*: David S. Martin: "Man's Rare Ability May Unlock Secret
of Memory." CNN, May 2008.

Page 287. *and then he roamed all over the place, without any memories; he
entered the bar where there was no indication to remind him of what he was
doing there*: Parker, E. S., Cahill, L., McGaugh, J. L., "A Case of Unusual
Autobiographical Remembering," *Neurocase* (February 2006).

Page 287. *the intent to remember something stayed with him throughout*:
David S. Martin: "Man's Rare Ability May Unlock Secret of Memory."
CNN, May 2008.

Page 287. *this too would pass, and he would no longer be aware of having forgotten something, of having a sense that the situation is confusing,
and this state had indeed set in, a state of happiness, everywhere he went
or found himself he felt happy, in part; however part of his mind was increasingly burdened by an overall problem, for example Istanbul, this had
turned into an overall problem, he felt completely that ...*: Porter, S., Birt,
A. R., Yuille, J. C., Herve, H. F., "Memory for Murder: A Psychological

Perspective on Dissociative Amnesia in Legal Contexts," *International Journal of Law Psychiatry* (January–February, 2001).

Page 287. *one cannot say that he had seen Istanbul, only that he knew what Istanbul was like*: Kritchevsky, M., Chang, J., Squire, L. R., "Functional Amnesia: Clinical Description and Neuropsychological Profile of 10 Cases," *Learning & Memory* (March, 2004).

Page 288. *He rapidly began to forget the details and simultaneously a similarly dangerous alteration occurred in his thinking regarding overall problems, that is to say he perceived these problems in an increasingly "overall" manner, as the outlines of these problems began to broaden more and more ... until in the end he perceived the extent of each overall problem as so enormous that although he was able to grasp it the operation began to split his head apart, so that finally there he stood in Istanbul with a split head, and it was as if the plane could only transport him home in two pieces, his head and the rest of his body, that is, no longer the entirety of his overall person*: cf., short-term memory/long-term memory: Roediger, H. L., Dudai, Y., Fitzpatrick, S. M., *Science of Memory: Concepts*. Oxford University Press. New York. Danziger, Kurt. *Marking the Mind: A History of Memory*. Cambridge University Press, 2008. Fivush, Robyn, Neisser, Ulric. *The Remembering Self: Construction and Accuracy in the Self-Narrative*. Cambridge University Press, 1994.

Page 289. *at an undefined point of the outskirts of town, at The White Dervishes ...*: Rumi. *Spiritual Verses*. First book translated from the latest Persian edition of M. Este'lami. Penguin Classics. London and New York, 2006.

Page 289. *The White Dervishes not quite like that...*: *The Masnavi*. Book Two, translated by Jawid Mojaddedi. Oxford World's Classics Series. Oxford University Press, 2007.

Page 289. *The White Dervishes the whirling...*: *The Essential Rumi*. Translated by Coleman Barks with John Moyne, A. J. Arberry, Reynold Nicholson. Harper Collins. San Francisco, 1996.

Page 289. *The White Dervishes are no longer persons in the...*: *The Illuminated Rumi*. Translated by Coleman Barks, Michael Green contributor. Broadway Books. New York, 1997.

Page 289. *As the garment maker for The White Dervishes...*: *The Mesnevi of Mevlana Jelalu'd-din er-Rumi*. Translated by James W. Redhouse. London, 1881.

Page 289. *On the other hand the White Dervishes instantly disbanded*: *Masnavi-i Ma'navi: The Spiritual Couplets of Maulana Jalalu'd din Muhammad Rumi*. Translated and abridged by E. H. Whinfield. London, 1887.

Page 290. *caydanlik*: Tula's verbal communication, Istanbul.

Page 293. *Sultanahmet Camii*: cf, Cesar de Saussure, *Travels in Turkey*.

Page 293. *Samahane*: Letter from the Galata Mevlevihanesi, 9.10.2011.

Page 297. *Qanun*: Recording of a qanun on the terrace of the Derwish Café, Cankurtaran Mh., Kabasakal Caddesi 1, Istanbul.

Page 298. *in the direction of the Kariye Muzesi*: *Chora: The Scroll of Heaven*. Text by Cyril Mango. Ed. by Ahmed Ertug. Istanbul, 2000.

Page 298. *In this city of events He is the Lord,*
In this realm He is the King who plans all events.
If He crushes his own instruments,
He makes those crushed ones fair in His sight.
Know the great mystery of whatever verses we cancel,
Or cause you to forget, we substitute better for them.
In: *The Spiritual Couplets of Maulana Jalalu-'D-Din Muhammad Rumi.*
Story XVI.

Page 299. *The Kariye Muzesi was not the ...*: "Mimar Sinan," in Goodwin,
G. A., *History of Ottoman Architecture*. Thames & Hudson, Ltd. London,
1971. Underwood, P. A. *Third Preliminary Report on the Restoration of the
Frescoes in the Kariye Camii at Istanbul*. Harvard University Press, 1958.

Page 299. *qanun, heaven's dome over their heads*: Verbal communication
from Kudsi Erguner and Omar Faruk Tekbilek.

Page 299. *and from here on another sky, qanun heaven*: Yarman, Ozan.
*79-tone Tuning and Theory for Turkish Maqam Music as a Solution to the
Non-Conformance Between Current Model and Practice*. Istanbul Technical University. Institute of Social Sciences, 2007.

Page 299. *under the firmament of the qanun the musicians lose their personal ...*: Pohlit, Stefan, Weiss, Julien Jalal. *A Novel Tuning System for
the Middle-Eastern Qanun*. Ph.D. Thesis. Istanbul Technical University.
Institute of Social Sciences, 2011.

Page 299. *it has no meaning under the firmament of the qanun*: verbal
communication from Julien Jalal Weiss.

Page 300. *with the masters of qanun*: verbal communication from Master Mohamad Parkan.

Page 300. *The swan of Istanbul*: Kelemen Mikes. *Letters from Turkey.* 1794.

Page 300. *according to the famous story*: Cristóbal de Villalón. *Travels in Turkey.* Europa. Budapest, 1984.

Page 300. *the dream of the Quraysh*: Ignac Goldziher. *The Culture of Islam, I–II.* Gondolat. Budapest, 1981.

Page 303. *To forget the swan*: Alan Baddeley. *Az emberi emlekezet.* [Human Memory]. Osiris. Budapest, 2005.

III. BIDS FAREWELL

I DON'T NEED ANYTHING
FROM HERE

I would leave everything here: the valleys, the hills, the paths, and the jaybirds from the gardens, I would leave here the peacocks and the priests, heaven and earth, spring and fall, I would leave here the exit routes, the evenings in the kitchen, the last amorous gaze, and all of the city-bound directions that make you shudder: I would leave here the thick twilight falling upon the land, gravity, hope, enchantment, and tranquility, I would leave here those beloved and those close to me, everything that touched me, everything that shocked me, everything that fascinated and uplifted me, I would leave here the noble, the benevolent, the pleasant, and the demonically beautiful, I would leave here the budding sprout, every birth and existence, I would leave here incantation, enigma, distances, the intoxication of inexhaustible eternities; for here I would leave this earth and these stars, because I would take nothing with me, because I've looked into what's coming, and I don't need anything from here.